'A dark an⬚⬚⬚⬚⬚⬚ ⬚⬚⬚ ⬚⬚⬚⬚ ⬚⬚⬚ ⬚⬚⬚⬚ ⬚ystopian eye
⬚⬚ ⬚⬚⬚ p⬚⬚⬚ in an u⬚⬚⬚⬚⬚⬚ ⬚⬚⬚⬚⬚ ⬚ry way.
All hail Megan Campisi'
Emma Donoghue, author of *Room* and *The Pull of the Stars*

'Rich with imaginative and historical details, *The Sin Eater*
is ultimately a timeless story of one woman regaining her
power. I loved it from beginning to end'
Christina Dalcher, author of *Vox*

'A riveting description of hard-won female empowerment
that weaves together meticulous research, unsolved murder
– and an unforgettable heroine. Exhilarating . . . great
storytelling . . . reminiscent of *The Handmaid's Tale*'
Washington Post

'Magnificent . . . Hilary Mantel's *Wolf Hall* and *Bring Up
the Bodies* brought new vividness and insight to the court
of Henry VIII; in *The Sin Eater*, Megan Campisi brings as
much or more energy to the court of Elizabeth I . . .
The only disappointment it offers is the absence of a
massive body of work waiting for the reader to
devour when this first book ends'
New York Journal of Books

'The atmospheric, historical fantasy setting combined with
May's jarringly eccentric personality creates a novel as
strange as it is captivating'
BuzzFeed

THE SIN EATER

Megan Campisi is a playwright and novelist. She has previously received the French Alfa and ADAMI prizes for her plays, which have been performed in France, China and the United States. In 2019 she received a Fulbright Specialist Award to give masterclasses at Tatbikat Sahnesi in Turkey. She holds a BA from Yale and a Diplôme (MFA) from L'Ecole Internationale de Théâtre Jacques Lecoq in Paris. She lives in Brooklyn with her family. *The Sin Eater* is her first novel.

THE
SIN
EATER

MEGAN CAMPISI

PAN

First published 2020 by Atria Books,
an imprint of Simon & Schuster, Inc.

First published in the UK 2020 by Mantle

This paperback edition first published 2021 by Pan Books
an imprint of Pan Macmillan
The Smithson, 6 Briset Street, London EC1M 5NR
EU representative: Macmillan Publishers Ireland Ltd,
Mallard Lodge, Lansdowne Village, Dublin 4
Associated companies throughout the world
www.panmacmillan.com

ISBN 978-1-5290-1907-0

1 3 5 7 9 8 6 4 2

A CIP catalogue record for this book is available from the British Library.

Typeset by Palimpsest Book Production Ltd, Falkirk, Stirlingshire
Printed and bound by CPI Group (UK) Ltd, Croydon, CR0 4YY

Visit **www.panmacmillan.com** to read more about all our books
and to buy them. You will also find features, author interviews and
news of any author events, and you can sign up for e-newsletters
so that you're always first to hear about our new releases.

To my sisters

AUTHOR'S NOTE

Sin eaters existed in parts of Britain until roughly a century ago. How many and who they were, apart from being social pariahs, is almost entirely lost. What we know is that they ate a piece of bread beside people's coffins to absolve their sins in a folk ritual with Christian resonances.

The story I've written starts with this sliver but is spun out of fantasy. Some of the characters resemble historical figures, but this is not history; it's fiction.

🕷 A SELECTION FROM 🕷
A Compendium of Diverse Sins Both Large and Small and Their According Foods

Adultery ———————— Dried Raisins

Bearing a Bastard ————————— Grapes

Betrayal ———————— Mutton Chop

Blinding ———————— Pork Pie

Blood Sacrifice ———————— Hippocras

Burning ———————— Kidney Pie

Conspiracy ———————— Brandy Posset

Deception ————————Whipped Syllabub

Desecration ——————— Shortbread

Dissembling ————— Sack Posset

Drunkenness ————— Hippocras

Envy ————————— Cream

Fault finding ————— Eel Pie

Heresy ——————Honey Cake

Idleness —————Pickled Cucumber

Incest——————— Dried Plum

Inhospitableness ————— Garlic

Lies ————— Mustard Seed

Lust —————Rose Hips

Miserliness ————— Garlic

Murder (in Defence) —— Rabbit's Heart

Murder (Wrathful) ———— Pig's Heart

Oath Breaking ————— Cake Bread

Original Sin ——————— Bread

Poisoning ————— Pigeon Pie

Quarrelling ——————— Humble Pie

Rape (Child) —Lamb's Head in Ewe's Milk

Rape (Woman) ——————— Capon's Head

Recreancy ——————— Neat's Tongue

Revenge ——————— Black Pudding

Sacrilege——————— Gingerbread

Slander ———————Crow's Meat with Plum

Spying ——————— Cock Brain Tart

Tale Bearing——————— Stewed Gurnards

Thieving ——————— Roast Pigeon

Treason ——————— Beefsteak

Vagrancy ——————— Frumenty

Witchcraft——————— Pomegranate

Wrath ——————— Gristle

❧ ROYAL FAMILY TREE ☙

KING HAROLD II —— *m.* Constanza of Castile
  —daughter Maris

  —— *m.* Alys Bollings
  —daughter Bethany

  —— *m.* Jenette Cheney

  —— *m.* Clelia of Berg

  —— *m.* Helen Culpeper

  —— *m.* Katryna Parr

  (*m.* Titus Seymaur
  —daughter Miranda)

BEFORE

OAT PORRIDGE

SALT FOR PRIDE. Mustard seed for lies. Barley for curses. There are grapes too, laid red and bursting across the pinewood coffin – one grape split with a ruby seed poking through the skin like a splinter through flesh. There's crow's meat stewed with plums and a homemade loaf, small and shaped like a bobbin. *Why a loaf in such a shape?* I think. *And why so small?* There are other foods too, but not many. My mother had few sins. She was a fox, running from the scent of trouble with wary eyes and soft feet. Tussling only when she was sure she'd win. The salt, mustard seeds, and barley grains are the only foods I know the sins for. They're for childhood sins, the kind parents chasten you with or children sing rhymes for in the street.

Little Jack Horner,
Sat in the corner,
Eating a winter pie.
He ate all its meat,
For being a cheat,
And said, 'Now a good boy am I.'

The sin eater comes next, hefting her belly into the front room where the coffin sits, boards fresh and blunt from the saw, the nails placed but not sunk. She smells of wild onions already begun to sprout despite a full month until May Day. I feel ashamed at my small truckle bed in the corner, our house not fine enough for me to have a room of my own. The sin eater gruffs for a seat, and Bessie, our neighbour, brings her a stool. It disappears so completely under her skirts, I imagine her great buttocks swallowing it whole. A burp of laughter escapes my lips, and I clap my hands across my mouth.

Bessie takes me to the window. 'You're not to look,' she whispers in my ear. She pushes on, hearing my intake of breath readying for words, knowing I'm my mother's own little gabby goose. 'The sin eater walks among us. Unseen. Unheard,' she says.

'But I can see her—' I hiss.

'Unseen. Unheard,' she silences.

I've heard sin eaters have branded tongues, but this one hasn't opened her mouth.

Bessie speaks again. 'Sins of our flesh become sins of hers through the Eating, praise be. Your mother will fly right up to the heavens, May. Not a sin left to weigh her down.'

I go back and take my place next to my da. His face looks like sheets dropped off at the door for washing, hung with wrinkles that won't shake out.

'I'll wash your face,' I whisper. 'I'll hang it on the line.'

Da gives me the look he always does when I say something that doesn't seem right. His face widens open as if I've just told him good news. 'What are we ever going to do with you?'

Grapes, red and bursting. A loaf shaped like a bobbin. Crow's meat. They stick in my mind like porridge in the gullet.

NOW

1. ROAST PIGEON

THE BREAD'S STILL warm under my shawl, my heart echoing through its crust. I run, quick as I can, along the ditch beside the road.

A wide brown nostril swings into my face breathing hot horse breath.

'Get on!' calls the cart man, coming from a side lane, urging the mare into the mess of the main thoroughfare. She shuttles her head from side to side, the bit buckling against her yellow teeth. My way's blocked.

Too visible, I scold, even as I climb out from the ditch onto the flat of the road. I fold my prize into the hollow between my breasts and dart past the baulking horse and a hay wagon.

'Aye! That's her!' the baker yells. I daren't turn, just break into a run. I go down a narrow lane. At the crossroads I look to one side, hesitate, and go to the other, passing a stable and a smithy. But the baker's son tailing me doesn't hesitate. His hand cuffs my neck and knocks me to the ground. The side of my face presses into the mud. I can see the blacksmith's boots through his open door. My breath comes hard from running. I push the bread up with my hands and rip off the end with my teeth. *Might as well eat*, the thought comes. *If I'm going to the jail, might as well do it with food in my belly*.

———

May Owens. The turnkey calls me out of the cell. Calls me along with the other girls that came in my week. Twenty in all. Three girls who ran away from homes in other towns but don't have kin here or begging passports. Two whores without the chummage to bribe the constable to turn a blind eye. Five pickpockets. Eight cozeners and worse. One other goodly girl, like me. She killed a stray dog to eat, but turned out it had run off from a lord. Bad luck, that.

We walk in single file out into an early-spring morning heavy with mist. The damp creeps into my bones after the cell, where so many folk made for a comfortable fug. We march down the middle of the road, stopping carts and wagons, making carriage drivers call out in fury. The court-house is next door, but this is part of our punishment. All the eyes seeing our shame. They shout, calling us *wicked women* and *Eves*.

I wish you could show folk your insides the way you show your face. Then they'd know I'm not wicked at all. Or I wish that they'd see my hair and see how it looks just like the Queen's hair, the same black waves. Then folk would know I am goodly, like her. I am no Eve. Eve wasn't content to live in the heavenly plains with the Maker. She leapt to earth and sought out Adam, keeper of the fields and orchards, made him lead her to the Maker's tree and stole its fruit. When she ate all but the last bite, which she fed to Adam, the Maker cursed her for her treachery and sent her to be mistress of the underworld. She's purest evil. Even worse than Judas, who betrayed the Maker's son.

The turnkey takes us into a fine building with a roof so high even the tallest of folk couldn't touch it. We line a bench, twenty shivering girls. I guess some of us are women. I've been one for two years, though I don't know that I feel like one. Then again, I don't know what a woman is supposed to feel like. I twist my ring. It's thin and uneven and not real gold, but I like to imagine it is. It's the only bit left of my da. A token of him.

'What's to happen now?' I ask the dog eater, who's sitting beside me.

'Justice takes his decision,' says a dirty girl a ways down the bench. She stole a silver cup.

'Recorder is what he's called,' the turnkey says.

'Why a recorder?' I ask.

'My fate's decided,' says a ratlike girl who tried to sell the bastard she bore, mayhap trying to trade her soiled name away with it.

'Yeah, but it's got to be pronounced,' the dirty one tells the rat.

'Why is he called a recorder?' I try again. 'Does he record what happens?'

The turnkey shushes me.

'Sounds like donkey paddies to me,' the rat girl answers softly, an eye rounding the rest of us for nods. The others ignore her, so I drop my eyes too.

'When does the recorder come?' I ask the turnkey, but he's already starting to stand.

The recorder comes in by a side door. He walks to a high wooden table and climbs onto a high wooden chair. He looks for a moment like a child mounting his da's stool, and the laugh comes before I can stop it. The turnkey and recorder look over sharply, but I deaden my face, and the other girls don't give me away, even the rat. I feel bad I looked down earlier.

'Chasy Stow?' the recorder speaks. The turnkey waves for the girl to stand. 'Vagrancy and begging without a licence.'

'I'm from Chester Town,' Chasy says all quiet.

'This isn't Chester Town,' says the recorder without even looking up.

'But there wasn't any work, and I couldn't stay at home!' Chasy tries.

Even I know it doesn't matter the reason. Folk without a settled place to live are swept up by the constable for being vagabonds unless they've a special passport from the Queen.

The recorder's eyes stay on his parchment. 'Can you produce two credible witnesses to speak for you?'

It's a fool thing to ask. 'There's no folk here but us,' I tell the dog eater. 'Only the turnkey, and what's the chance he's her brother?' The recorder bangs a wooden mallet on his table, and I shut my lips.

The recorder pronounces Chasy's punishment, as the dirty girl said he would. She's to be whipped and then burned through the gristle of her ear with a hot iron as thick as a man's thumb. 'And should you come before this court again,' the recorder goes on. 'You will be hung by the neck until dead.'

This is foolish too, since when does a folk hang until not dead? But I don't tell the others. I just say it inside my head. Then I scold myself. Unkind thoughts: *The sin eater will eat parsnip on my grave.*

The recorder runs us down, girl by girl. Some get hanging, some get whipping. The rat-faced girl is to be burned alive. The recorder doesn't look at any of us. Asks no questions, except if we've got credible witnesses to speak for us, which he knows well enough we don't. Each time he asks it, I get star-shaped heat right in my chest where the rib bones meet. By the sixth or seventh time, I'm angry, and I'm not prone to choler. I want him to stop asking it. Or at least look at us.

'May Owens,' he calls.

'Yes,' I speak loudly, surprising myself as well as the turnkey, who gives me a scolding eye. But I've done it. I've made the recorder look.

He looks long. He stares, more like, his eyes turning to dark creases. The other girls raise their heads at the silence, broken out of whatever daydream they fell into. 'May Owens,' he says again, this time turning over each letter, running them across his tongue. 'Born Daffrey.'

'I'm an Owens,' I say, my voice coming sharper than I mean it to. My fingers go straight to my da's ring. I don't know how the recorder knows my mother's family name. His eyes don't even blink. Little moons of black, watching, watching. Mayhap he's seeing my insides like I wished for before, like a witch's spell.

Then, from nowhere, he calls out, 'Winnie Fletcher,' and the spell breaks. We all gaze at the recorder dumbly. 'Winnie Fletcher!' The recorder looks to the turnkey, who looks to us. Winnie Fletcher stands uncertainly. 'Picking a man's purse. Any credible witness to speak for you?'

After the last pronouncement, the recorder leaves through the same side door. The turnkey waves at us to stand.

'But I didn't get a punishment,' I say to him. I didn't even get a crime. All I got was my name. And that look.

We walk back through a dirty, wet midday to the jail.

'What about me?' I say again to the turnkey as I pass him at the cell door.

He shrugs as if to wash his hands of it and goes. I look at the other girls.

'What about me?' They avoid my eyes as we all did the rat's.

———

It's almost worse than a sentence, not having one. The girls set to hang are set to hang in three days' time.

'Am I to be hung with them?' I ask the turnkey through

14

the bars, but it's like he's turned to stone. 'Should I ready myself?'

Not that there's much for us to ready. Winnie promises her shoes to one of the whores if she'll eat her sins. Unless they're rich, folk in jail get the Simple Eating that's saved for those who can't confess before they die. The whore says no.

'But your soul is already lost,' argues Winnie. 'It can't do you harm. It's not much. Just the stealing and some lies; I swear it.'

The other whore shakes her head before Winnie even asks. 'No folk can look at a sin eater. No folk'll touch her. How am I to work if I'm not seen or touched?'

The rat girl is more successful. She offers a coin to the dog eater to bring a locket to her sister. She promises another coin from the sister when it's done.

'Won't be till next autumn,' the dog eater warns. She's in jail through spring and summer, which is as long as it'll take her family to pay off her fine.

'Not like to go bad,' says the rat of the locket, and places it in the dog eater's hand. I smile at the jest, but her eyes glaze past mine.

———

I pass the following day thinking on my da. How he lay on the bed with the blue patched quilt over him shaking and shivering after he cut his hand fixing the town's mill. How I called the doctor to come, but the doctor just looked him up and down and said there wasn't anything I had money enough for him to do. How Da asked me to tell him about what I saw from the window and didn't mind when I talked through my every noticing, even the ones like clouds that changed shape as they passed. How I couldn't bear to call the sin eater and so left it too late. One morning as I warmed the milk, Da shrank away from himself, leaving a husk and me all alone. His shadow stayed in the house for weeks. It wasn't dark like a shadow, just an empty place in the shape of my da. I would see it out of the side of my eye and turn knowing he should be there. But when I looked there wasn't anything.

The hardest was not having folk to say my noticings to, like if I saw a spider when I rinsed my hands in the basin. Or how I could make river waves by whipping the edge of dry bedclothes up and down, up and down.

I tried telling my noticings to our neighbour Bessie. She was welcoming when I first came to chat, laughing, calling me a gabby goose as my mother had done. But as the days went on, I'd catch her sagging a bit when she'd see me coming over. Days got to weeks, and she'd sigh loudly when I came, as if I wouldn't hear her sigh softly.

I tried speaking to the cat that liked to hunt in the weeds of my fallow garden. Or I'd speak to the sachet of flowers my mother had kept on the mantel. I'd trip over myself just to greet the few folk who still came for laundry. To hear their 'Thank ye kindly,' and say, ''Tis nought,' in return. Sometimes I'd speak to their clothes as I washed them, as if they were the folk who wore them. But I missed the answering back. So even though I knew she wasn't happy with me, I'd wait by my shutters, and when Bessie went out into her kitchen garden, I'd scamper over to share my news.

Then one day she was there on her knees, six dirty carrots at her side. One carrot, I remember, looked short and misshapen like a broken finger. I had come over to tell her about a crow that was pecking at an old bit of leather. She stood before I even got to the leather part.

'No, no, no, you don't. It's too much,' she cried. 'I'm not your ma. I've Lee and Tom to look after. Not you too.'

'You're my neighbour,' I said.

'I've done my neighbourly duty by you plenty.' Her words jumped all over me. 'What you need is kin, and you've got a whole lot of them down by the river. Go there with your chitter and chatter about what a dog smelled this morning and which cloud is shaped like a lamb.'

Kin was the last thing I needed.

—

Two mornings on, the hanging girls march out of the jail. The turnkey doesn't even blink when I say, 'What's to become of me?'

Just a few of us are left behind. It's better because of the piss pot. There's just the one, and when the cell is full, the pot fills so quick we have to piss in the corner. If I had known before how much piss there is in a jail, I'd have brought pails by to collect it. There's places will buy old piss. My mother and I used it for whitening laundry and fullers use it to clean new wool. Woad dyers use it too, but I don't know for what.

More girls arrive. The piss pot overflows again. Lots of thieves in the new lot, including four sisters who worked in the royal kitchen and had a good side custom selling the uneaten food from off Queen Bethany's tables when she and her court were staying in town.

On the hip bones of the year, spring and autumn, Queen Bethany and her court come up the river from the big city in great barges to live here. We all turn out to watch her arrive with her servants and ladies and trunks upon trunks of baggage. It means work and money. But the town sort of swells up in an uncomfortable way, the roads thickening with folk and carts and horses, pantoboys performing the news, tinkers and trinket sellers setting up stalls, vagabonds and beggars skulking about, like in the rhyme:

> *Hark, hark the dogs do bark,*
> *The beggars are coming to town,*
> *Eaters of sin, and drinkers of spirits,*
> *And players in velvet gowns.*

The four sisters who worked in the kitchen are a small society unto themselves, talking and laughing and sometimes holding one another through weeping. I sit on the fringes and pretend I'm a part. It makes me feel like I have friends. They seem not to mind.

'Selling leftover food weren't against the law in our mum's day,' says the eldest sister one morning. 'Was part of the job!'

'Everyone's feeling the squeeze now,' gripes a younger sister. 'Queen makes her court ladies pay their own keep, you know' – she speaks to those of us who don't – 'food, candles, firewood, even – though they serve at the Queen's pleasure. The spiteful Queen!'

'Hush, Lila!' scolds the eldest.

'Those are words to say inside your head,' I suggest aloud.

'Gemma saw the Queen stick a knife in a lady's hand for smiling at her favourite! The blade went clean through and got stuck in the table,' says Lila.

'You still don't say such things if you don't want your tongue cut out and hung up on the castle wall,' says the eldest.

'A wedding would solve it quick,' says another sister. 'No more favourites.'

'If the fighting over her hand doesn't bring us into another war,' moans the eldest.

'Oh, think of a royal wedding,' says Lila. 'Plenty of money and plenty of eating.'

'I hope she'll not marry a stranger,' says the eldest. 'Such a wealth of countrymen. From south and west and up north.'

'Up north's not strangers?' I say. Everyfolk knows Northern men wear skirts, eat nought but bag pudding and will fug anything, man, woman, even their own sheep. The sisters go on together as if I haven't spoken.

'Do you recall the young suitor with the red stockings?' says the youngest, and they all fall to laughing. Then a sigh settles over the group, and they nestle in together like doves in a cote.

Our neighbour Bessie would say it's just the way of queens and kings to make war.

'But they had a war,' I once complained to her when I was a girl. 'My grandsire died in it.'

'Aye, but that was the old king. He's gone and left a poor brood. Just the two daughters, Maris and Bethany, and all the land at arms over whose faith is better.'

'Isn't it who's eldest?'

'Shall you go up to the castle and tell them now? "Excuse me, your graces, the old faith and the new faith are no longer a matter for fighting. Call the royal wet nurse, who was weaned first?"' Bessie collapsed into giggles with her daughter, Lee. Lee still thinks anything to do with breasts is a laugh, even though she was born a whole year before me.

The faith bit is hard to sort out, but I know this much: the old king started the new faith, and while he was king, everyfolk had to be new faith too. If you were Eucharistian, or old faith, you could be killed. All the old-faith altars were destroyed and prayer beads burned in the rubbish field. But then he died.

Maris, his oldest daughter, was queen next. She was Eucharistian. She made everyfolk go back to the old faith and burned you if you didn't. She was known as Bloody Maris, even though it should have been Ashes Maris, since folk were burned not bloodied. Twice Queen Maris said that she was with child. And twice no child came. So when she died, her sister, Bethany, became queen. And what faith was she? Why, new faith. So she made everyfolk go back again to the new faith. Back and forth, back and forth. But it was no jest. Purgers came house to house to beat you if you didn't go along with the new faith. Though I notice folk don't call her Bloody Bethany. At least not aloud. And the fighting's still not done. But now it's for which suitor will win our queen, become king, and get his heir on her.

———

More days pass. I make my own nook in the straw. It's hard to sleep with so many breaths and snorings, but the company's a comfort.

'Jail's not so grim as you might think,' I tell a new girl barely bigger than a child. 'Though watch for bedbugs.'

She raises her shift and shows a smatter of bites. So she knows.

For two days it rains. A small stream comes through the roof. It digs a path down the centre of the earth cell, splitting all of us onto its two banks. Da could have mended the roof in a day.

Things just want to run right, he'd say. *Listen, and they'll tell you what needs fixing.* He'd hold a lock up to his ear. *A jammed pin, you say? Let's have a look.*

I remember one day Da brought home a wool merchant's necklace to repair. It was midsummer, and I was nine. The chain was broken, and while fixing it, Da showed me the red stone in its middle. So lovely. Then he showed me the back. It was made of paste. My face fell.

'Doesn't matter,' said Da. 'Still shines as nice.'

All the Owens could mend things. Owens. I pick apart each letter. The letters all sound wide and open to me. Like warm wind in spring. I am an Owens.

When I turned ten, Da told me it was time for me to take a profession. 'I wash clothes,' I said. 'Like Mother did.'

'Your mother washed clothes because she didn't know anything else,' he told me.

Da didn't know she knew lots of things. She knew how to nap like a cat in the fine sheets brought by the wool merchant's girl. She knew how to dress up in Goodwife Burley's nightgowns and pretend she was a queen with a badge and a crown. The nightgowns were silk, she told me, *pooped from worms*. When I heard that, I brought her a sack's worth of earthworms and presented them to her in our special crockery. I thought it was a fine gift, but she threw it back at me, worms and all, and sent me to bed with nothing to eat, unless I cared to eat the worms.

I imagine the worms in the earth all around my mother eating her now.

Thinking ill of the dead: *roast pigeon*.

My mother's folk were Daffreys. A name like the colour inside a bruised apple. All of us with the same hair, black and with the feel of sheep's wool bred for mutton not yarn. All of us with the same half smile and the same cleft in the cheek like a nail paring.

When I was small, I never much saw my Daffrey kin. Da said they weren't like us. He meant they weren't goodly folk. He didn't say it exactly, but I knew.

One year after my mother died, my Daffrey granddam arrived with two big men, my uncles. She pointed a finger warped like a birch twig at me. 'Learned something new about this one. We'll be taking her now.'

Da tried to fight them. 'She's mine by law.'

'Is she now?' said my granddam.

It was the only time I heard Da swear.

Grains of barley on the grave,
The blasphemer's soul is saved.

He was no match for my uncles. It took only one strike

for him to fall. And that's how I came to live with the Daffreys for the turn of a year. As black a year as ever there was.

The Daffrey house was down by the river on a spot where the earth sank and squelched under every step. The first week during my year with the Daffreys, my granddam kept me tied by a leash to the kitchen stove to be sure I didn't run away. She was turned in and hard like an old walnut, the meat all black and sour inside.

'Your uncle's going to get your sire to pay up and then we'll live high and fancy-like,' she said.

Da didn't have money for high and fancy, but I said nothing, just sank down as far from the stove as I could.

And then my cousins came. Two boys of an age with me. They came with a sack just the size for hoodman-blind. It went over my head, and the boys' hands were on me quick as a whip, pulling off my clothes, even my undershift. I yanked at the hood to get it off, but one boy held it in place. When I was bare, they put their hands all over, even between my legs. I tripped in my struggling, landing hard on the stove corner. It burned a *V* into my right shoulder. I heard footfalls, and my granddam's voice loud and rough, and then I was alone. The hood came off my face, tears and snot leaving two snail trails along the inside. My granddam cut my leash then, but promised she'd tie me up again and let the boys have at me if I tried to leave the kitchen.

I always hated the cleft in my cheek because of the Daffreys, hated having their mark on me.

'But you did them one better,' Da told me after he got me back. 'For you have a cleft on your chin too. None of them can boast that. It's a very rare thing, a cleft on the chin. Not two folk in twenty have such a thing.'

I turn my ring when I miss my da, sometimes so much it cuts the flesh.

———

A week passes in the jail and another round of girls go off to the courthouse. They seem hopeful, nervous, bewildered. I feel older, wiser. Then, just as the last one is leaving the cell door, the turnkey calls, 'May Owens.'

And suddenly I'm hopeful, nervous, bewildered, too. 'What news?' I ask.

The turnkey just looks away.

There's two new faith Makermen in black robes standing by the side door of the court today. I wonder if they're here to pray for us. The recorder runs through all the girls. Just like before, he says their crime and asks if there's any folk to speak for them. The sisters who worked in the kitchens have to pay a fine, but they'll go home today.

The recorder waits until the end, until all the sentences are pronounced, to call my name. This time he rushes it. He doesn't look at me. He doesn't even look up. He just says something about communion. Or commuted. My sentence is commuted. I only follow that I am not to be hanged or fined. I am to be given a different punishment. There's a murmur through the other girls. Blood thumps up the back of my skull. It thumps in my ears. A small, green hope buds in my heart. One of the sisters nods encouragingly, and I smile back. So I don't quite catch it when he says, 'To become a sin eater.'

'Pardon?' I call stupidly. As if recorders wait on girls' questions.

The recorder motions to the Makermen. Something glints in the first one's hand. The other carries a small box and a forked stick. They walk towards me, and suddenly I want nothing more than to pull a bedsheet over my face and hide. The first Makerman raises a heavy brass collar with a large sloping *S* hanging from its front and a thick lock in the back. Holding the collar above my head, he says old words:

> *The sin eater walks among us,*
> *Unseen, unheard*
> *Sins of our flesh become sins of hers,*
> *Following her to the grave*
> *Unseen, unheard,*
> *The sin eater walks among us.*

The Makerman places the collar around my neck. It's heavy and cold, except where his hands touched it, and I have a sudden image of a horse's bit, like he might slide it up into my mouth. But it's worse what happens next. The second Makerman takes hold of the collar's lock and shoves the shackle in. Even my guts feel the wards catch.

I grab at the collar. My fingers work their way around, feeling for the lock. I pull with all the strength I've got. With strong washerwoman arms. Thick, callused fingers. The brass cuts into my neck, but still I pull. I pull so hard I topple myself right over. It's stuck fast.

I start to cry out, 'Why me?' But the moment the words

take shape in the air, voices all around rise up together, saying the Maker's Prayer:

> *Maker mine, forever of the sun's light*
> *Miracles be wrought from your name*
> *Protect us sinners,*
> *Now and at the hour of our deaths.*

I try again, raising my voice against theirs, 'Please!' But I can barely hear the sounds in my own throat. They've been swallowed by the Maker's Prayer. None can hear me. None will listen.

The first Makerman's eyes are on the ceiling, but when he talks, I can tell it's for me to hear. 'The sin eater bears the sins of all folk in silence to her grave. She alone may never confess and be absolved. However, if she serves faithfully in true piety and obedience to the Maker's will, Eve will not be able to claim the sin eater when she dies. Her soul will rise to the Maker. But the Maker knows all. She must obey in every thought and every act her whole life through.'

'May it be,' says the second Makerman, and all the folk in the room say it too, like when you finish a prayer.

Then the second Makerman opens his box. Inside are a needle, a bottle of ink, and a pair of tongs like a smithy uses. I start to scramble off the bench, but the second Makerman takes his stick and catches my neck in its fork. He pushes me against the wall so I'm trapped like a scold in the stocks. The first Makerman picks up the tongs, prises open my mouth, and takes hold of my tongue.

It takes a good long while to ink the *S* into my tongue with his needle. Long enough for my tongue to get so dry I hardly feel the pricks any longer. Long enough for my sobs to fritter away into little gasps and then to hiccups. When they've finished, the Makermen let me go. My tongue is throbbing and thick in my mouth, and I can taste blood and the foul ink that has forever marked me as a sin eater. This is what I'll be until my death.

The girl next to me scoots away as if my flesh has begun to blacken and blister, like I'm plagued. The others, whose faces had earlier opened to me in wonder, encouragement, and envy, drop away like leeches full of blood. It's the last time they look at me. It's the last time nearly anyfolk does.

2. LAMB'S HEAD

WHEN I STUMBLE into the road, folk look and look away. Some scutter off. I scutter too. Down into the ditch, dodging puddles and beggars.

After the collar was placed on me, everyfolk in the courtroom turned away. All I could think on was the throbbing of my tongue, so it took a moment to know they were waiting. It took a moment more to know they were waiting for me. My feet were light as clouds and my collar weighted like stone. Tipping like a drunk woman, I walked by the other girls, their eyes on the ground. I walked by the recorder, his eyes on his parchment. By the Makermen, their eyes towards the sky.

—

Seeing my house after weeks away, a great lump grows in my chest. When did it get so run-down? The tiles are pebbled with rot, and the front shutter hangs askew. The garden weeds have grown nearly to the window ledges like they might eat the house whole. I laugh at the sight. Da always said, *Know where you're from*. Mine is shabby indeed.

I want to run away. Run off to another town where no folk know me, and pretend I was never made a sin eater. Could I do it? Brave the murderers and thieves along the roads? But anywhere I'd go, folk'd know I didn't belong. I'd be swept up by a constable to be whipped and burned through the ear like the girls in jail. Or worse, be swept up by folk like my Daffrey kin and tied to a stove or made to whore. Then I remember the collar and the *S* tattooed onto my tongue. I'm marked. No matter where I go, I'm a sin eater.

There's a scuffle behind the shutter as I step up to my old door. It's blocked when I try to push it open.

'This is my home!' I cry. In an instant, my tongue is throbbing again, and I taste blood. Whoever's taken over my home says nothing back.

Bessie comes out from next door to see what the clamour is. 'Why, that's May's voice, is it?' But when she sees me her jaw closes and opens like a newt eating a fly.

'Bessie,' I say, tears wetting my cheeks from the pain of my tongue.

Bessie shrieks and begins the Maker's Prayer. Her hand pushes out in front of her as if for protection.

Lee steps out of the kitchen door. 'But that's May,' she

says. 'She's got a—Mother! Do you see what's around her neck?'

'You do not see her, Lee!' Lee's eyes fall to the ground. 'If she speaks to you, you must silence her with your holiest prayers. No matter what she says.'

'But, Bessie,' I say. 'I don't know what to do.'

'What's wrong with her tongue?' Lee cries. 'There's a snake on her tongue!'

'"Maker mine, forever of the sun's light,"' Bessie chants. 'Pray, Lee!'

'"Maker mine,"' Lee says uncertainly.

'Bessie, where am I to go?' I plead.

I see Bessie hesitating.

It's Lee who helps, though I don't know if she means to. 'Where will she go, Mother?'

'Why, she'll go to the other, won't she. Now there's two. They'll be company to each other, I should think.' Bessie pauses. Waits for me to leave. 'Over in Northside,' Bessie prompts. 'That's where she is.'

——

It's always women who eat sins, since it was Eve who first ate a sin: the Forbidden Fruit. Some say that's why so many foods for sins are fruits. But there's other foods as well, like cream and leeks, that aren't fruit at all. There's some reason in it, for cousin sins will sometimes have the same foods, like covetousness and envy both being cream. But there's also some with no reason. Why are thieving and thinking ill of the dead both roast pigeon? It's like how there's two words *rock* and *stone* that mean the same thing, but the words don't sound alike at all.

There's also lots of dark beliefs about sin eaters. Folk believe a sin eater grows closer to Eve with every sin she eats. So looking at a sin eater opens you up to Eve's eye. And hearing her voice, you might be lulled into temptation, so you say the Maker's Prayer to drown out her voice if ever she speaks outside of Recitations and Eatings. To touch a sin eater is worst. It's a curse and burns the flesh of goodly folk. I touch the skin of my forearm, but it feels the same.

I think about Hans and Greta. In the fairy tale, Hans and Greta's parents send them into the woods to collect mushrooms and berries. The children leave a trail of acorns to find their way home, but squirrels eat them. It gets cold and dark, and Hans and Greta fear they'll starve or freeze, but then they see a light. It's in a cottage made of brambles, rose hips, cattails, and other things folk eat in lean years. It isn't theirs, but Hans and Greta are so hungry, they eat the rose hips and cattails anyway. The door to the cottage opens and an old sin eater comes out. She welcomes the children to warm themselves by her hearth fire. Hans and Greta go in and apologize for stealing food from her house. The sin eater just smiles. Hans curls up by the fire and falls asleep, but Greta stays awake and hears the sin eater singing:

Lost children roam,
I lure them home.
They steal and sin,
While I laugh and I grin.
I'll toss them in my fire,
On the morrow find their sire,
And eat roast pigeon on their graves, graves, graves!

In the story, Greta pushes the sin eater into the fire instead and they find their way home. When I heard the story I always pictured myself as Greta.

———

I make my way beyond the north wall of the castle, where winds come worst. Northside's the sort of place mothers use to scare daughters. *Any more of that lip, and I'll sell you up in Northside.* I never knew exactly to what a purpose a girl might be sold, but my fantasies were enough. Worse, mayhap.

The edge of Northside looks like the rest of the town, except a bit dirtier, a hair poorer. The homes all have thatched roofs, no tiles or slate. One even has a sheet of heavy felted wool instead of a wall that fills and snaps in the wind. In the lane I walk down, two boys run about in oversized men's clothes, like me playing dress-up with my mother's nightdress, but out on the road like it's their real clothes.

The boys use a stick to hit a pig's bladder. When they see me, they go to the side of the road, wanting to look but not nearly daring. Just as I pass, the larger one shoves the smaller at me. The smaller cries in terror and turns to beat the larger with his fists.

A row of taverns and alehouses signals Northside proper, whores in twos and threes standing at each door to wave folk in. 'Want a look? One bit. Two for a touch.'

They see my collar, and a whisper flies across the line. Eyes go every which way. But I feel them on my back when I go by. I still don't know where I'm going.

After the tavern row is a lane of fortune-tellers. Northside seems to be like the rest of town where lanes all have shops of the same trade along them, but here the shops are the kind folk don't want to be seen visiting. One fortune-teller has incense burning in the doorway. Mayhap Egypsies. Bessie said Egypsies are like witches.

Simple-makers and apothecaries are on the lane that comes next. Some windows have unnatural things in them like an unborn piglet in a jar and a tiny vermin with a caterpillar-like body and lots and lots of legs. This last one gives me a shiver in my guts.

The lane ends, but there's still no sign of the sin eater's house. The bottoms of my feet ache through my slippers. I'm accustomed to rough use on my hands from washing clothes but not on my feet.

An apothecary in a thin, black robe steps out of a shop. He looks greedily from my face to my chest.

Keeping my tongue as still as I can, I say, 'Good sir, where may be found—'

A great hissing cuts me short. He shrinks back into his robe, chanting the Maker's Prayer and crossing a hand about his chest and hips in the Maker's sign. 'Curse me not!' he cries, and goes back into his shop like he never meant to leave.

There's eyes on my back, but when I turn around to look, shutters clap closed. The lane's become empty. More than empty. An empty lane still feels alive. This one's become dead.

Inside me too. I've often been empty over the years. Empty, like alone. But now there's something worse in me. A deadness creeping into my heart. I look up at the sky. It's a high, white sort of sky that doesn't care two pennies about me. I don't know what to do.

Da's voice comes up from my guts. *Things just want to work right*.

I breathe in his voice. I breathe it out. I twist his ring on my finger. I am on the lane of apothecaries.

What kind of lane would a sin eater be found on? I ask a stone on the road.

One worse than the lane of apothecaries, it answers.

Who are more unfortunate than the apothecaries? I ask a beetle next to the stone.

Beggars, dung men, it lists. *Woad dyers*.

I remember there's a bend in the river known as Dungsbrook. The river widens and slows, and you can smell the rotting parts from the pig men who dump their offal there and the shit from the dung men who dump the town's shit there, all to be swept away by the river water. The land near the river bend is called Dungsbrook too. The rakers who collect the town's rubbish burn it in an open field there. And it's where the woad dyers must live too. Their work stinks so foully they're forced to live a certain distance from the castle. Dungsbrook is where all the worst smells in the world get gathered and dumped together. No place is as unfortunate as Dungsbrook. So I think I know where the sin eater lives.

It's not hard to find once I put my nose to it. The slaughter-house and rubbish field come first. Then I pass the dung dump and the lane to the woad dyers. I even pass the old Domus Conversorum, a big, stone dwelling crumbling like a biscuit where Jews were made to live by the old king while they converted to the new faith. It's no surprise to find it's in Dungsbrook too.

Beyond all this is a last, little lane. Its houses are close on one another, slouching towards the river like they're bent on drowning. In the middle of the lane is a house with an old brass *S*, just like the one on my collar, hanging above the door. Mouldering thatch, walls badly needing plaster, but a two-level house with shutters on the windows. The door's not barred, so I push it open.

She sits on a stool, a jug in her hand. She waves me away without looking. I don't know where to go, so I stay.

She's heavy with flesh. It makes her seem a giant, though I doubt she's taller than me. Middling height. She must have eaten a thousand sins. Her head pauses mid-drink like she's listening. Then she turns.

I dare not look direct at her, but I feel her eyes walking me up and down like houseflies. My *S* gleams with a spark from the fire. Her breath stops, then drops out all at once like a sack of grain hitting the ground. Then she turns back to the hearth and takes another swig from the jug.

'What shall I do?' I ask. I mean now, but also more widely. *What shall I do?*

Her head swings over again, loose like a marionette's. She's well into her cups.

I look down. Then up. Do I look at her? She's a sin eater, but I am too. I don't know the manners for this.

I take a peek. Her eyes are like chestnut moons. She has a nest of honey hair and her skin's honey, too. She's handsome, but with a look like something's been broken and won't ever be fixed. She hiccups and offers the jug. I catch a scent as she reaches out. Wild onions. And then there in my mind is the picture. Her. Younger. Smaller. She's the same sin eater as came to my mother's Eating.

She's still holding the jug. I've never tasted spirits.

What have you to lose? the jug asks.

I take it and tip it back. Warm liquid runs over my lips and down my chin. It burns my tongue so sharply, I shriek. Only a few drops get down before I'm coughing off the burn. She pulls the jug back.

'What shall I d—' I begin to ask again. Before the words leave my mouth, she leaps up, hands grabbing at my face. Her fingers dig all about my cheekbones, her thumbs under my chin. I think she means to put out my eyes. I bat her with my strong, washerwoman arms. But it's not my eyes she wants; it's my mouth. She clamps it shut, her nails biting through my cheeks and chin. I'm near as strong as her, but when she does no worse than hold my jaw shut, I fall still.

She gives my head a shake. A good, rough shake that would knock my teeth if they weren't held together. It's as plain as if she were saying it: *I am not to talk. Even to her.*

She returns to the stool. I find a dirty rug by the fire.

I'm a sin eater, I say to the red embers. *What does this mean?*

It means you'll never again see folk smiling at you with their eyes, the embers say back.

It means you'll never again feel the press of a chest against yours in a hug.

It means you'll never sit with Lee or Tom, giggling together, eating blackberries and watching the swallows dive.

The embers keep going, cracking and popping. I raise my hands to my ears so I don't hear the words they spit, but they needle their way straight into my heart.

You'll never marry.

You'll never bear a child.

You'll never have a lover or even just a good friend.

The only one you'll ever have is her.

I look at her, the Sin Eater, a wooden figure staring into the fire.

The deadness is creeping back into my heart. I hold Da's ring, wrapping both fists around it.

She's my kin now, I tell the ring.

I have a roof over my head. A fire to keep me warm. These are good things. I look again at the Sin Eater. Her flesh pushes against her clothes. I always dreamed of having such a beautiful shape. A body of plenty. *I'll have that too.*

The deadness slows its creeping. My hands soften around

Da's ring. My tongue's still throbbing as I fall asleep on the dirty rug.

———

She rouses me with her foot. It's morning. She wears her same clothing, but her hair's tied back. I sit dumbly, the rug about my shoulders. The fire's out, and early-spring cold nips in from all corners.

She walks to the door and waits. I hastily pull my shift down and my stockings up, my hair down and my collar up. I feel along my cheekbones. There are four half-moon cuts on each, made by her nails last night. My tongue feels swollen but less painful. I'm dreadfully hungry.

On the hearth is an old iron pot dressed in cobwebs. She looks at me and snorts. Again, she doesn't even need to say the words: *Eating's for work.*

Outside there's four boys trying to coax a beetle from under a stone. When the Sin Eater comes out of the door, they stand up like so many little soldiers.

'Recitation for Bernard Harrington,' says the plumpest one. He looks to the others.

They each give their message calling her to a Recitation or an Eating. The plump boy nods when they are done, and they go back to the stone. Must be a big beetle.

It's not plain I'm meant to follow her, but it's not plain I'm meant to stay, so I follow. She walks with long, strong steps, like the soles of her shoes are thick.

At the edge of Northside, along the tavern row, the whores sitting in the weak morning sun look down when she comes past and do not cast glances at her back. The same two boys in the same too-large men's clothes scatter to the ditch and don't play in her wake. No folk swerve out of her way because no folk get in it. It's like she's got a lamp shining yards in front of her telling folk of her approach. I try my best to keep up.

I'm out of breath when she finally stops at a fine house inside the town proper. There's glass in the windows and a metal ring outside the door for a lamp to be placed. I look for a ledge to catch my breath, but she goes in direct for the Recitation, without a call or a knock or a moment's rest.

Burning herbs cloud the stench of flesh and bowels, but I still smell them. The sweet mingles with the sour, turning my stomach. I'm glad there's nothing in it to spill.

A goodwife with silk brocade on her kirtle comes through a door. She keeps her eyes down but raises a finger to point the way up a set of stairs.

I've climbed a step here and there, at the Makerhall and the like, but I've never climbed a whole set. Ladders, sure, but ladders are easy. There's rungs to hold with your hands. The Sin Eater climbs these stairs like it's nothing. I wobble behind, trying not to tumble. Trying not to picture my head cracking like an egg if I do. The climb takes my breath away as fast as beating a soiled rug clean.

In the bedroom the smell's thicker. A maid's waving a smouldering bundle in the air. That's the herbs. Not thyme like we use when somefolk's got the farts. Something from a stranger place. At the bedside is a bowl of fat leeches. Willow bark too.

The Sin Eater goes to the bed and looks the man over. He's got a velvet dressing gown and cap. Velvet, heavy as it is, is one of the hardest to wash. Was. I guess I'm not a washerwoman any more.

The maid fetches a stool, placing it near the Sin Eater, and then ducks away with the goodwife, closing the door behind them. It clicks like there's a lock on it. I don't know why you'd need a lock on a bedchamber.

'The Unseen is now seen.' After her muteness it's uncanny to hear the Sin Eater's voice. It's rough and low, like you'd expect from her looks. With a start I see a sliver of black in her mouth. Her *S* brand, like a snake in the mouth. Like mine. She goes on. 'The Unheard is now heard. The sins of your flesh become the sins of mine to be borne to my grave in silence. Speak.'

The man breathes very shallowly. He struggles side to side as if speaking hurts him. A word passes his lips. Nothing I can grasp, but she nods along.

'Lying for gain or for protection?'

He says another half word.

'Mmm, mustard seed,' she answers.

His speaking gets better. I start to hear more. Placing wealth before faith. Disobeying his da. Pride in his wealth.

'Lamb shank, pickled herring, pigeon's egg,' the Sin Eater lists off the foods she will eat for those sins. I recognize some, but not the wealth ones. They're very particular and not the kinds of sins poor folk like me have the chance to fret much over.

Then the man gets quiet. I wonder if he's died. Then there's

41

a small squeak. 'Barrenness,' he whispers. 'I blamed my wife. I turned from her. I sought a lady. A . . .' He doesn't want to say the word. Mayhap ashamed.

'One who was not your wife,' the Sin Eater helps him. He's done adultery. I don't think she should make it easier.

'For years,' he goes on. 'But she, too, never conceived. I had blamed my wife. It drove me from her bed. But I fear . . . I fear all that time it was me.' He's talking quicker now.

'Barrenness is not a sin,' she tells him. 'But holding a grudge and faithlessness, yes. Oat porridge and dried raisins.'

He lies back, looking smaller than he did before.

'Last words for she who will take your sins?'

'I have no heir,' he says like it follows on her question. 'I have a cousin who will gladly inherit. But no heir of my body. I would even claim a bastard had I one to claim.'

Folk'll do all sorts of things for an heir, I think.

There's a long silence that comes up between him and us.

'When the food is et, your sins will be mine,' the Sin Eater ends the Recitation. 'I will bear them in silence to my grave.'

'May it be,' he says back with the words that finish all prayers.

The Sin Eater does the Maker's sign across his body, left shoulder to right hip, then right shoulder to left hip. It's the one time a sin eater touches you.

When the Sin Eater opens the bedroom door, it startles the goodwife and maid. They look to their shoes. The Sin Eater lists the foods to be got. The Recitation of sins is usually private, unless the dying wants it otherwise, but the food must be prepared by somefolk, so the sins come out, at least to the household. Sometimes the dying will ask that only a maid or only a husband hear the list of foods and prepare them. Of course then the gossip goes wild, everyfolk claiming they saw the husband buying fresh grapes for bearing a bastard or cooking up a pig's heart for killing.

The goodwife and maid nod along with the list of foods, but their nods sort of falter on the dried raisins for adultery. I take a gander at the goodwife. She's not supposed to look at me, but there's no rule about me looking at her. She has pimples on her chin, even though she's fully grown, and her eyes look like she's lost sleep. And for a fornicator.

Was it worth it? I want to ask. I ask it silently to the wall behind her head.

What choice did she have? the wall says back.

After the list is finished, the Sin Eater turns her bulk, lifts her skirts, and steps down the stairs as easy as if she were at a dance. I climb down each stair slow and wary, my heart in my throat, catching my balance with every step.

The door closes behind us. Behind me and my first Recitation. If I live a long life, I might have sixty years more of this. Sixty years of hearing folk's sins. Not their joys or their blessings, just their sins. I stand outside the house, while this knowledge digs down into my heart.

I'm there but a moment before the Sin Eater reaches back and pulls me by the ear down the road.

—

We go next to a lane where guildsmen live. Houses neat and clean, you can tell even from the outside. I know which one we're heading to because a man stands in the doorway openly weeping like I don't know what. His smock's white with flour and brown with blood. The Sin Eater goes right past him into the house.

A midwife kneels next to a woman on a bed, one of the midwife's hands on the woman's chest, the other squeezing a bundle between her legs. Everything smells like blood. An infant squalls suddenly off in the corner where an old body hushes it gentle-like.

The Sin Eater sits down. The midwife manages not to touch her but keeps to both her tasks: feeling the heart beating, staunching the blood flow between the legs.

'The Unseen is now seen,' says the Sin Eater. 'The Unheard is now heard. The sins of your flesh become the sins of mine to be borne to my grave in silence. Speak.'

The woman's chest barely rises, and her lips only make hollow sounds.

'I sent a boy to the midwife and the sin eater, as you do,' says the smocked man from the doorway. The husband, he must be. 'I never thought she'd need it.'

'My own girl, don't leave us,' cries the old body holding the babe. The granddam. The baby shrieks in agreement.

'I never thought she'd need it,' says the husband again.

The Sin Eater waits, her ear by the new mother's mouth, but the lips don't move.

'She's passing,' says the midwife.

So the Sin Eater names the foods for the Simple Eating, the one for those who depart before the sin eater can hear the Recitation. 'Salt for pride, cream for envy, leeks for lies of omission, garlic for miserliness and bread for the sin we are born with. When the food is et, your sins will be mine. I will bear them in silence to my grave.' She starts to make the sign across the woman's shoulders and hips.

'Must add dried plum,' the smocked husband says quick. 'She was my brother's wife before mine.' The Sin Eater nods. It's incest, even if they are married kin, not blood kin, and just as sinful in the eyes of the Maker. Most folk's eyes too. I've never seen folk who've done it. I made jests, same as all the other children, when Lee or some other would do something foolish. Made jests about how her parents must have been sister and brother. I look down at the mother, newly passed. This is what incest looks like. The granddam stares dumbly at her daughter on the bed.

——

On our way down the road, a boy runs up alongside us. He keeps his eyes straight ahead. 'Sin Eater's called to Caris Cooper in Southside,' he tells us. The Sin Eater huffs her breath. It's not talking exactly, but it tells the boy she heard. The boy scampers off.

The Sin Eater turns off the main road. We walk until houses get scarcer and gardens commoner. Soon we are in the country. I'm so hungry I feel like a hard fruit's lodged in my belly. I knot my hands and rub it.

She looks at me and nods with her head towards the road ahead. Mayhap there's an Eating coming. Just thinking of the word eating, I drool so much I have to clamp my lips shut and swallow. Then I remember the food will be somefolk's sins, and the drool reverses, and I have to keep my jaw shut so as not to retch. I want to eat so badly. Yet the cost.

The sin eater takes on the sins of others, so says the Maker's Book. (Or, so the Makermen say the Book says. I know some letters, but only how they fit to make two words: May and Owens.) The Maker's Book says the sins are lifted from the sinner and placed on the sin eater's soul. I always pictured that my own coffin would be nearly bare. Even when I stole the bread, it was only roast pigeon added to the Simple Eating on the pine board.

And now . . . The thought stops me short, right in the middle of the road like an ass. Whatever sins we'll find at the Eating, if I eat, will become mine. And I won't shed them. I'll take them to my judgement. How has it taken me so long to see this? There's a choking sound behind me. I start to turn, but it comes again, closer. It's not behind me. It's my own throat, closing up. My rib bones shrink in, too, like a too-tight shift with no place left for breath. The Sin Eater looks at me again – at my eyes, my lips, my throat – like a cunning woman assessing which herbs she might need to heal me. Then it comes, her hand straight across my cheek with a great smack. I stumble and nearly fall. She doesn't pause to see if I right myself.

━━━

The main room's been cleared for the coffin. The goodwife stands by the wall, a neighbour's hand on her for comfort. The coffin's well joined. On it are bowls of porridge, cream, and boiled eggs. There's a plate with leeks, a pile of salt, a small loaf of bread, and a pot of honey. In the moment it takes my eyes to see the food, my belly makes the choice. I will eat. It's not the choice I want. A small voice says, *Think of your da. He would never.* But then the other voice, shouting through my belly and up into my heart drowns out the little voice. And I know that questions about sin and souls are for Makermen, not hungry girls. My soul will pay whatever price it must, because that price is later and eating is now. Shame blooms across my chest.

I remind myself of the Makerman's words when I was made a sin eater. If I serve faithfully enough, I might join the Maker when I die. The words rub up against the shame but don't much ease it.

A stool has already been placed in front of the coffin. The Sin Eater sits down and begins. No words. No nothing. Despite her girth, she eats carefully, cracking the egg, peeling it with nimble fingers, until it's glossy and white. She dips the small end into the salt and takes a tiny bite, chewing so long it must be mush in her mouth. I summon the courage to reach out for the bread. No, the porridge. No, the honey. The goodwife sweeps behind me, and a stool hits lightly against my knee backs. A seat for me.

'Thank ye kind—' I start out of habit. The Sin Eater wheels on me with bullish eyes. I clench my jaws together. She turns back to the coffin. I pull my stool nearer. I reach out for the bread, but the Sin Eater's hand stops mine. She gives me, instead, the other egg.

I peel it badly, stripping the wobbly white along with the brown shell, until an irregular round remains, the pale yellow yolk peeking through on one side. I dip it shakily in salt and stuff it between my lips. My tongue burns with its touch, so I chew roughly with my side teeth, swallowing before it's half mashed. I can feel the Sin Eater's disapproval, but I eat it in just the one bite. Then wait, my hands shaking, ready for her to tell me what's next.

She finishes her egg. She sits on the stool. She takes a breath. The moment seems like it will never end. Finally, her hand goes out for the bread. Thank the Maker, the bread! She rips it in two, then lifts the lid on the honey pot and drizzles half on my bread and half on hers, spreading it so thin that it coats it all without even dripping off.

My whole body shivers with the sweet, and I feel an itch inside both ears. I eat it like a dog eats meat, in great swallows, then wait, while she chews bite after tiny bite.

Think of your da, the little voice starts.

I will never have another hungry day! my belly screams. *I will never spend another gnawing hour!*

Next comes the leek, stringy and sharp. Finally the porridge, spoonful by spoonful. I scrape the bowl of every last oat. When I'm done, I sit back like her. She takes a breath and says, 'The sins are now mine. I bear them in silence to my grave.'

She stays as still as a picture. I wait. Her hand rises and lands atop my leg with a slap, and then I know why we wait.

'I . . . The sins are now mine . . .' I begin, my voice sounding high and faraway. 'I bear them in silence to my grave.'

I expect to feel something, a change. Same as when I got my monthly courses. Then, all I felt were cramps. Now, it's much the same, a cramp in my belly from so much food after so little. And a stinging on my tongue. I fear I may retch. She eyes me when she stands and barely shakes her head, but I see it. I must keep the food down.

The goodwife drops a few coins into the Sin Eater's hand as we go, careful to avoid her touch.

Two steps outside, I'm puking by the road. She takes hold of my ear again.

'I can't help it!' I squeal as another retch rocks up from my guts. Her fist hits my chin on an upswing, and my teeth slam together so hard, I fear they will shatter.

I must not speak.

She pulls me on down the road, and I have to swallow half the mess in my mouth. The rest dribbles down my chin as I bob along behind her.

She lets me go when we are back in town. By then, the waves in my belly are no longer crashing upward. She looks me over again, eyeing me fully, but this time waiting. I sniff and nod. She nods back. It's the first care she's shown.

—

'None knew the old woman,' a neighbour says too loud. Perhaps to explain why the body's started to rot. Or why there's no coffin.

'If only we knew who her folk were,' another neighbour says with wide eyes, but I can tell she's not honest. It must have taken them days to find the body. And then only by the stream of rats and other vermin filing in. It's her funeral procession.

All about the room are the signs of a cunning woman –

marjoram and sage drying in the window, a clyster pipe for constipation on a little wooden shelf, mandrake root and a dead dove for a love charm it looks like the dead woman was lately making. Gracie Manners said some cunning women use baby's blood in love charms, but my mother told me that was all donkey paddies. *Love charms are white magic*, my mother said. Only black magic uses blood. Blood and other nasty things like hairs plucked under a full moon or wax poppets. I look for signs of black magic in the room, but don't see any.

The neighbours have laid out the salt, leek, garlic, and bread for the Simple Eating. None brought cream.

'I brought the salt,' huffs one neighbour through a kerchief pressed to her nose. 'And the leek.' She eyes the others. Who eye her back. Cream comes dear in early spring.

Finally a neighbour goes and collects a saucer of milk.

Miserliness: *garlic*.

When we sit, the neighbours take their chance to leave their guilt behind with the ants. It's good they leave because I puke over and over at the foot of the body just from the smell. Only greenish-yellow bile comes out, speckled with blood from my branded tongue, yet my guts go on. In between, the Sin Eater hands me bites of food. It's a fool's show: bite and puke, bite and puke. All the while, she licks every drop of milk from the saucer, chews every crumb of bread. The crush of the leek between her teeth, dry and shrivelled as it is, sends me into greater retches with its onion stink. Finally she says the words to end and makes the Maker's sign over the rotting body.

We climb down two sets of stairs. I never knew you could climb so many stairs in a day. A neighbour holds out a penny as we go into the gathering dusk. My legs wobble like a newborn calf's, but I follow. Because where else can I go?

——

I nearly weep when she stops at a merchant's house. We aren't done. *Why must we do so many Recitations and Eatings in one day?* I ask the house.

Because souls do not wait upon young women like you, it says back. *You wait upon them.*

Red hangings line the hall like long tongues. It's a colour I've never seen in cloth. The woad blue woven around the red I know well. Woad blue is the colour of common folk's clothes because woad dye is cheap and bears up through years of washing. But this bright, rich red. I thought it was just a colour of the body – the inside of an open mouth, chapped lips, a cunny.

The coffin sits in a large wood-panelled room hung with paintings and lit by sconces of fat, beeswax candles. I startle when one painting moves, before I see it's just a looking glass. My black hair is slack. My eyes are small, black stones. But my square face is pink. My lips too, bright as the hangings on the walls. Must be the retching.

Fetching retching, I tell the looking glass.

I open my mouth to see my tongue. A black *S* weaves down it like a snake, just as Lee said. The tongue around the *S* is red and puffy. It's monstrous. I'm monstrous. I turn away from the looking glass.

Then an odd thing happens. A maid comes into the room to dust, as if it were an ordinary day. She finishes one sconce and moves to the mantel. Even at the cunning woman's Eating there was some feeling. The feeling was guilt felt by miserly neighbours, but it was feeling. Here, none attend the coffin. None cry in the corner. There's just the maid, going about her duties. I look at the Sin Eater. She's looking at the food.

Spread on the coffin are some foods I know: mustard seed for lying, gristle for wrath, bitter greens for not saying your prayers. There are also some sins I don't know: what looks to be a dried crab apple stuffed with mushrooms. But to one side is a sin I know because it's whispered about in haunting stories told to scare folk. A lamb's head, stewed in its mother's milk. *Forcing oneself on a child.*

I begin to shake again. From somewhere deep. If I knew where my soul lived, I would say it comes from there. The Sin Eater pauses too, but her pause is quick. Then she sits on the stool and eats.

I watch as she works through the mustard seed, crunching the tiny shells. She saves the last several. Holds them out in her hand for me.

I should run. Run out of the door and go back to the jail. Beg to be hung with only my own sins and the few I've eaten today to weigh down my soul.

Instead, I stand like a wooden post, so she grabs me easily, pulling me across her body like a child to be spanked. She digs fat fingers into the corners of my lips, and prises my jaws apart. And then she feeds me. Me coughing as the mustard seeds catch in my throat, her holding my mouth and nose until I swallow. Then the stuffed crab apple. Then a slab of lamb's head she rips apart with her own teeth. Milk dribbles down my chin, down the same curves the puke traced before, the same curves the puke will follow after. She holds my nose and mouth. And, weak, I now know, truly weak, I swallow. I swallow, instead of letting her pinching fingers kill me. I swallow. And now I am what he was. His sin is mine.

3. BREAD

THIS TIME I sit with her, but on an upended split of wood because there's just the one stool. We're at her home. She passes the jug. I drink. It doesn't matter that I'll puke it up. That seems to be the way of things now. Enough gets in me that my thoughts glaze over now and again before snapping back to our poor, grey truth.

We took it from him, I say to the fire. *We should not have done!*

Great sobs quake through my ribs. She passes the jug.

Why would he admit it? I ask the hearth stones. *Why not just take the Simple Eating and be forgiven pride, envy, miserliness, lies?*

The stones answer, *The Maker would know. The Maker would punish him to live in Eve's land under the earth.*

Why would the family cook the food? I ask the wood floor.

The wood says back, *A family's duty. They deliver him out of this world as he was delivered into it: as blemishless as can be.*

The jug hits the floor, fallen from her hand. I turn to it, then her. She is badly drunk. Or mayhap I am. Her eyes flutter like a toad's in the sun. They flash open suddenly, and her hand shoots out to my cheek, pushing my eyes away.

It's me, I think stupidly. She growls, then laughs. She grabs at my collar, her thick fingers following it around until they find the *S* in front. Her face gets calm. Then she hiccups and falls off the stool.

She's laughing. Her humping body shakes and cackles. Her great breasts heave above her belly. Yes, she is broken in a way I think even Da couldn't fix. I touch his ring on my finger. With what I've done can I still call myself his daughter? Mayhap I'm something different now.

I lie back on the wood floor. The ceiling is wooden too. Am I on the ceiling or am I on the floor? I try to lift my head, but it falls back with a crack. My feet are very warm. They must be close to the hearth. I'm still asking my questions, mumbling them to the wood planks, when I fall asleep.

Sometime in the night after the fire's gone cold, I feel her against my back. My eyes are wet, and my chest aches with ragged breaths. I must be crying. Her arms come around mine, cradling me. She holds me there, like you do an animal when you want to make it calm, soft shushes coming from her lips. My breath comes smoother, and I fall back into sleep with her holding me.

———

In the morning we stagger about like lepers, unsure our limbs will hold. My belly is empty and nettled. She drinks a gallon of water direct from the ewer in unending gulps. It turns my belly just to see. Only horses and pigs drink plain water. She burps and gropes for her woollen shawl. But she waits for me. Hands me my own shawl. Something has changed. We're together now. We are us.

The boys outside call their messages until there's just one small boy left. 'The great mill,' is all he says. He's lost the rest of his words. His eyes look up, as if to find his message on the roof. The Sin Eater and I start down the lane. As we near the turn, finally, a reedy voice follows after, 'By the great mill, Eating for Goodwife Stow!'

We go to a Recitation straightaway. A nervous-eyed house-keeper answers the door to a cluttered two-storeyed home. She makes the Maker's sign across her shoulders and hips when we pass as if we're a catching illness. It sours me towards her.

We follow a loud, wet cough to the hearth where an old body, hair tucked in a brown coif, sits before the fire. On the wall is a shelf with more books than I've ever seen in one house. Eight, I count. I can't even fathom the number of words it'd take to fill them. Or how many years to read them.

'Miss Albers, the sin eater's come,' says the maid, as if the two of us weren't standing there, filling up the room.

The old body turns her neck and shoulders, all of a piece. 'I never called her, Nellie.' She's got an accent like from a stranger country and talks in a sharp way that makes me cringe for her maid, Nellie, despite my earlier sour towards her.

'You're poorer and poorer with each day, Miss Albers,' Nellie the maid says back.

'It's you wants to see me in the grave!' her mistress spits with more venom than you'd think such an old body could muster.

'Maker forgive you, Miss Albers, for saying such a thing, when I do nought but care for you!' The maid makes the Maker's sign across her shoulders and hips again.

'I'll none of your sham piety, Nellie.'

Nellie whispers something under her breath before she goes. The Sin Eater stays where she stands.

'Still here?' the old body says. 'Shame to waste your coming. On with it.'

'The Unseen is now seen, the Unheard is heard,' says the Sin Eater.

'She thinks me a witch,' the woman cuts in. 'I'm old, and I enjoy reading in stranger tongues.'

A good start for a witch, I think. *Add to it the eight books . . .*

The woman goes on, 'Nellie's a ninny who hears a stranger tongue and thinks it a witch's incantation. Sees no husband and conceives I must be wived to Eve.' She pauses for coughing. 'I keep to myself and won't suffer fools, that's the only pact I've made. My sins are thus: pride, miserliness,

58

wrath, coveting my neighbour's property, slandering my maid, trying to breed animals of different kinds together, intentionally letting a goose bite my maid.' I look to the Sin Eater, but she nods along, as if the sins were no more peculiar than forgetting your prayers.

Everyfolk knows the foods for the commoner sins just from living. Parents threaten 'Don't make me see herring on your coffin!' for disobeying. Neighbours gossip about who'll make the sin eater eat raisins. And of course there's nursery rhymes:

> Jack and Jane went up the lane
> To fetch a pail of water,
> Jack fell in and couldn't swim
> And Jane had a picnic after.
> What did she carry in the hamper
> To eat and save Jack's soul?
> A herring, a pickle, a cracker with treacle
> And a spoonful of salt in a bowl.

I used to spend hours with Lee parsing out the sins: Jack disobeys his father (herring) by going to the well. He's prideful (salt) about getting near to the well. He's lazy (pickle) in not learning to swim. We never agreed on what the cracker with treacle was, but Gracie Manners thought it was an old-fashioned way to say bread (the sin we're born with). But breeding animals together and setting a goose on your maid? I have no inkling of the foods for them.

All at once the old body's finished her list. She looks us

each hard in the eye, 'Say your words to end it, sin eaters, but come back not on the morrow for my Eating, nor the day after that, for until Nellie calls the witch finder to prick me with a bodkin or see if I burn, I'll be here, hale and hearty, sitting a piece in my chair.'

Nellie shuffles us out with one more Maker's sign across her body.

———

We go on to two more Recitations and two more Eatings. The Sin Eater feeds me only the tiniest morsels of each food, and I manage not to puke.

On our way back through the town square towards Northside and Dungsbrook, we find folk gathered for a newspanto. We stand in the front, where I've never been. Usually I'm hopping up and down behind some burly apprentice hoping for a look at the playacting newsboys, but the older Sin Eater pushes through, folk's sharp words dying in their throats when they see it's us.

It's a fair-sized crowd. Among them I notice three stranger men. I don't know how exactly I can tell they're strangers. Something about their clothes or the look on their faces says they're not from here. Two of them carry what look like long lutes, as if they're musicians. Before I can think on it more, one of the newsboys dances out in front of the crowd and announces a countess has been arrested for plotting against Queen Bethany. Behind him, the other boys act it out. One's made up like the countess, lead paint rubbed into his cheeks to make them white like highborn ladies'. Another plays a guard.

'Of what am I accused?' cries the countess.

'Sending spies to murder Queen Bethany and put her Eucharistian cousin on the throne instead,' answers the guard.

'Oh, Maker mine!' says the countess. She pulls out a string of prayer beads and begins to pray. It's a very daring bit of playacting, since prayer beads are from the old Eucharistian faith and were outlawed when Bethany became queen. But it's also clever, I think, because it says the countess is Eucharistian without saying it aloud. Every folk knows the Eucharistians want Bethany dead and her Eucharistian cousin on the throne, or at least for Queen Bethany to name her cousin as her heir since she has no children of her own.

One of the pantoboys with a fine voice begins a song:

> *The Dame of Pikes,*
> *Brings her spies*
> *To take our ace of hearts.*
>
> *But her vile knaves*
> *Will never trump*
> *With their veiled arts.*
>
> *With clubs and tiles,*
> *We'll seek these spies*
> *And chop them into parts.*
>
> *On their coffins*
> *Will be et beefsteak,*
> *As well as cock brain tarts*

The song sounds like it's about playing cards, but I think the dame of pikes is meant to be the countess and the ace of hearts Queen Bethany. Beefsteak is et for treason and cock brain tart must be for spying, though I'm not sure. It gives me shivers to think there might be spies hidden in town. I look for the three stranger musicians I saw in the crowd, but they've gone.

The panto ends with the guard pushing the countess off as if towards the dungeon under Queen Bethany's castle. Folk clap, but there's a mutter here and there too. Queen Bethany's hard as bone with rivals. They don't live long.

'Tempered choleric, like a man,' I hear a folk say.

'Unnatural,' inkles another.

Just then a different newsboy comes out dressed like Queen Bethany herself. His crown has paste jewels and trailing after him are four little boys, baby fat still cupping their chins. The boys are all made up as the Queen's suitors. Three are meant to be Anglish lords bearing their little coats of arms. One has a stag on white, another a blue boar, and the third, a golden ship. The fourth boy's dressed as the Norman prince, who's Eucharistian and a stranger but would become an ally through marriage. There's hissing from the crowd as he goes by.

A man nearby spits in the dirt. 'Heathen prince would make us all into Eucharistians.'

'Dirty Normans,' says a goodwife. 'Their women are whores.'

Before the crowd gets too rowdy, a final boy comes out. He's a sweetie barely past toddling, with a quill in his plump, little hand – the Queen's secretary, who folk all say is her favourite at court. He's an Anglishman, new faith, and of good family, which calms everyfolk. This is when the bigger newsboys swing through the crowd with their hats in their hands for coins. There's no news, this part of the show's just to make us all cluck and coo over the sweet babes and dig into our aprons for a penny. Not that I have any to give.

The sun's set, and I think we're done for the day, but the Sin Eater takes us to one last Eating. It's for the new mother who did incest by marrying her husband's brother. When we arrive, we find a second Eating's been laid out too. Just one roll of fresh bread atop the smallest of pine boxes for her babe. It's expected for babies to pass, still it catches my breath to see the little roll. Then my belly rumbles. Shame spreads warm and sticky into my heart. I pray to the Maker that the folk come to witness didn't hear the rumble.

We eat the baby's bread, for the sin that we're born with, Eve's original trespass, along with the sins of the mother. I eat slowly.

I will not puke, I tell the coffins. Not just to do the Eating right for the mother and her babe, but because I need food that sticks.

—

In the evening we pass the jug between us before the fire. When it burns low, she points to a door out to the garden, where I find a small pile of firewood neatly stacked.

As I kneel before the hearth with an armful of wood, a thick, black spider scuttles out and over my hand. I shriek before I know it. I catch a motion from the side of my eye and brace myself for a cuff from the Sin Eater, but it's the spider she's after with her heel. She grinds it into the floorboards. Later, after the fire has gone cold, I feel her cradle around me again. It feels good.

See, it's not the worst of the worst, I tell the deadness still lodged in my heart. *I have a roof over my head. A fire to keep me warm.*

And us. Against the grief and the loneliness and the sins heaped upon our souls, I remind myself, *we have us.*

Even though I'm not crying, she shushes me softly. Mayhap it's more for her than me.

4. POMEGRANATE

DAYS JOIN TOGETHER into weeks. Early spring becomes late spring. The Sin Eater's nothing like my mother. The Sin Eater is silent and steady and ready with a slap if I, say, sleep past dawn or don't do the words right at the end of a Recitation. But when she holds me sometimes at night, it feels like I belong. Her house becomes our house. Our house becomes home. Me on my rug by the hearth. Her in the loft I've still never ventured into. She's not my kin, and I'm not hers, but we're something to each other. *We are us.*

—

Light comes through the edges of the shutters, and there's a sloshing sound. She's gulping down water. I roll away from the sound, sorting dream from waking. She's on to tying back her hair, readying to leave.

I sit up. I should comb my hair, I think, suddenly sure that this is what should happen. But then she pulls open the door, and I'm running after, my unkempt black hair bobbing along with me.

I pat it down as the boys call out today's Eatings and Recitations. I'm accustomed to at least a splash of water on my face, some marker between day and night. But in this new world there's scarcely any.

One of the messengers, I notice, is not a boy at all but a proper servant wearing the Queen's badge, a falcon and a rose.

My own mother knew all the royal heraldry even though the old king had six wives. She'd draw the queens' badges over and over in our hearth cinders until they stuck in my mind too. A crowned swan for his first wife, the mother of Queen Maris. A crowned falcon for his second, who was Queen Bethany's mother and killed for treason, fornication, incest, and witchcraft. A phoenix for his third wife, who died in childbirth. This one was my mother's favourite because the phoenix, she said, rose from cinders to greatness. After that was a plain golden badge for the fourth wife, a plain crown for his fifth, and, finally, a maiden rising from a rose for his last wife, Queen Katryna. She lived longer than the king and was Queen Bethany's stepmother, raising her up in her own household.

I'm brought back by the older Sin Eater starting off down the lane. The boys have finished their messages, and I heard not a one.

The Queen's messenger accompanies us at a distance, so we must be going to the castle. I've never been inside the castle, only seen it from a distance. I have to take two steps for every one of the older Sin Eater's. I keep my eye on her skirts swaying across her jiggy-joggy buttocks so I don't lose her on the busy morning roads. As we approach the queue at the castle gate, the carts and carriages slow. I can see the stoppage ahead: a young farmer driving cattle across the road.

'Get out of the way!' cries a cart man.

'Got the same right as you,' the farmer calls back, trying to move his cows along. He sounds uncertain. Mayhap it's his first time to town.

'Slaughterhouse's in Dungsbrook, back behind you,' the cart man tells him, and not kindly. 'Follow the stink if you can smell it above your own.'

'Going to the bull, not the slaughterhouse,' says the farmer, nodding to his cattle.

'Heifers, are they? Young'uns going to meet the bull?' says the cart man with a lewd nod like they're young ladies.

The older Sin Eater doesn't wait to hear the end of their talk. She pushes right past the farmer and his heifers. Then she goes up the side of the queue, cutting in front of all the folk waiting to enter the castle. A salt man is just stepping up to the guards when she makes it to the front. He swallows his surprise and moves aside. Even the castle guards turn away when we go in. I have never felt so important.

The messenger leads us through a courtyard to the castle's heart. Just the heart is bigger even than the great Makerhall in the centre of town. We go to a heavy, wooden door with carved stone above it made to look like a scroll. I want to touch it because it curves almost like water, but the Sin Eater doesn't stop, and it's too high to reach anyway.

Inside is a passageway lined with doors. I try to imagine what might be behind each – kitchen, scullery, larder, buttery, storeroom, servants' chamber . . . The messenger leads us to a set of stairs. I give a small prayer for protection going up. On the next level, there are even more doors – linen closet, herb dispensary, silver room . . . My mind falls short of imagining what could be inside. Then we go up yet another set of stairs. We're higher in the air than I have ever been. We must be as high as starlings fly. My head feels light, but I still wish there were a window for me to see out of.

How does the town look from a starling's range? I ask the terrifying stairs. *Could I see my old house?*

I get my wish soon enough. We pass a slit window in the stone. All I see is east out of the castle: pasture and farmland. Still, the houses look like miniatures and the sheep! As small as ants. The older Sin Eater pulls me by the collar. I think I hear a stitch tear.

A great ham of a woman awaits us in a doorway. She seems to be a woman, though she is so painted she could well be a picture. Her face has been covered in white paint. Her eyebrows are drawn into narrow arches. Each cheek is marked with an oval of red, and her lips are painted into a small bow. Across her bosom is the same white as her face but with blue veins painted on top. Only a nervousness that makes her mouth pucker and tremble shows she's a breathing lady and not canvas. I can tell she's rich beyond rich because her enormous skirt's embroidered with jewels. Then I notice her stomacher. Tawny orange like her skirt and hemmed with cloth of silver. The only folk allowed to wear cloth of silver are the ladies of the Queen's bedchamber. There's rules about it.

This Painted Pig has to sidestep out of the doorway while we pass because she and the Sin Eater are both so plump. She's surprised to see a second sin eater, I can tell, but I wear the *S*, so there's nothing for it. The Painted Pig leaves us and takes the news of our arrival through an inner door flanked by guards.

We come into a sort of presence or sitting room. At least that's what most of the ladies are doing. They must be the ladies-in-waiting or privy ladies. I know there's many levels, but not all the names for them. There's chambermaids and washerwomen at the bottom. There's the Queen's bedchamber ladies at the top. And then there's all the other ladies in between. Gracie Manners's sister, who worked as a chambermaid, said Queen Bethany even keeps a few daughters of old Eucharistian families like hostages among her ladies. That way, if any of the families try for a rebellion, she's got heads to cut off. Except for them, it seems a great advantage to wait on the Queen. When there's a position that opens up, it's like a fair in front of the castle, highborn folk all coming to squeeze in a daughter or sister or wife with the Queen's ladies.

We wait. The rushes under my feet have been trod down, and the stones are hard through my slippers. I shift from foot to foot, the ache building in each sole until I find myself looking hungrily at the cushions two young ladies of an age with me – one pretty, one plain – sit atop nearby. Even with the cushions both sit like they've sticks up their backsides. I swallow a little laugh at the thought.

The fair one is dressed almost as well as the Painted Pig, but with an open partlet up top, showing some of her bosom. She's truly beautiful and has thick gold hair like in songs about pretty girls. Her sleeves, I notice, are of a new fashion, brought in at the wrist instead of open.

'Have you an extra candle for me?' the fair lady asks the plain one. The plain one's face is the kind that's hard to remember, like there's nothing there to notice. A face like a bowl of mush. Her dress is dark, simple wool, and her sleeves are wide like mine. From the way she holds her arms down, she's trying to keep attention from them.

'Haven't you any candles of your own?' Mush Face asks back. 'I saw a whole sconce in your chamber not two days ago.'

Fair Hair smooths her partlet awkwardly.

'How now?' snorts Mush Face. 'Have you used them all?'

Fair Hair doesn't answer.

'Then you've either taken up books or a lover.'

Fair Hair tries to hide it, but her eyes say Mush Face got one of her guesses right.

I shift again from foot to foot. Fair Hair looks up at me, then hastily at a tapestry. It's got a picture of a naked lady in a wood under a full moon on it. It's different from the naked-lady pictures my Daffrey uncles paid a printer to ink up and sell on market days. On the tapestry, tree branches cover all the naughty bits. Also, one of the naked lady's hands is on a trunk of a tree that has a winged fairy coming out of a flower in it. The naked lady's other hand's on her belly like she's got the guts gripes. That's what my mother called it when your belly gets sore and cramped from too much yellow bile or worms. In the weaving there's not all the details of a true woman, like the belly's all one smooth plain, and the toes are all the same length. At the foot of the naked woman are fierce creatures like you'd never want near in real life: a yellow lion, a big stag, and a blue boar. They're all at her feet like dogs.

'Has Diana in the Wood become so absorbing?' Mush Face asks Fair Hair.

'I heard Lady Corliss commissioned it for a thousand pounds.'

'A thousand pounds,' repeats Mush Face. Her eyes get dull. 'It's nothing compared to the gifts the Queen showers on her favourites.'

I look at the tapestry woman's face. Something niggles. She looks just like the Queen. The same hair and eyes. Surely there's something wrong about that. A weaving of the Queen without her clothing.

I look over the rest of the tapestry. There's a border of vines and leaves all around the edges. But in one place, the vines are uneven. Mayhap they're letters. Two of them look like little *N*'s, which I know from my own name. The middle one I've never seen, but then there are probably hundreds of letters I don't know. This letter looks like a skinny boy leaning over to study a stone in his hand. Or a small tree leaning under the weight of an apple. There's also little letters underneath the big ones. One looks like a gallows. Another looks like the littlest of worms. Mayhap these letters explain why the tapestry is so costly. I look at Fair Hair. She's still looking at the tapestry too.

'I heard the Queen's favourite was married once,' Fair Hair says so quietly I barely catch the words. 'But just after he joined the Queen's court, his wife took a nasty fall down a stair and broke her head like an egg.'

Mush Face crosses herself across shoulders and hips, 'Maker save us from such misfortune.'

'Misfortune, was it?' Fair Hair's tongue darts against her upper lip, letting her words sit.

The ladies are so intent on their talk, they don't notice the Painted Pig come back into the room and cross towards them.

'You're suggesting she was pushed?' Mush Face plants her leather slipper like a mule. 'The Queen'll take your tongue for slander.'

'Don't chastise me,' Fair Hair says. 'Your mother's dead and your father was executed for treason. His badge of golden wings was taken from the banner room wall. If not for the Queen's mercy, you'd be a beggar.'

All at once, there's a loud slap. The Painted Pig stands above Fair Hair, her face so fixed you'd never know she'd just struck the blow.

Fair Hair looks like she'd like to stick her thumbs through the Painted Pig's eyes.

'Wipe off that sour face,' the Painted Pig hisses. 'There are ladies clamouring for these positions.'

Fair Hair's eyes get sharp. 'Ones without Eucharistians

perched in their family trees?' She says this direct to the Painted Pig, nasty-like.

The Painted Pig's face gets so still it seems she's become wood. After a long, quiet moment, she finally turns her broad body towards the Sin Eater and me and points to the chamber's inner, guarded door. All the while her eyes stay on Fair Hair.

—

An old body bowed like a gnarled willow tree leans over a lady on a couch and sniffs at a bowl of urine. He's got bulgy eyes and a cracked face. Over his flat-backed head he wears a white doctor's cap.

The Painted Pig has followed us in. 'Is this the appropriate place for a Recitation?' she asks. 'The Queen's privy chamber?'

The Willow Tree doctor answers, 'The Queen asked for Corliss to be treated here so she can remain nearby.' He nods to an inner door where the Queen must be. It's like a fairy mound, this castle, door upon door upon door, going on forever.

'The flux is catching,' the Painted Pig says as if the doctor doesn't know. 'Can this truly be the most appropriate place?'

'Flux only passes at night when mists are about to transport it,' answers the Willow Tree. His claw-like hand goes to the couch to help himself to stand. I see that he's got something silver covering his smallest fingernail. It's a witch pricker, a thimble with a long, thick needle on top used to test witches. True witches don't feel pain.

The Willow Tree hands the bowl of urine to the Painted Pig. She takes the bowl, not knowing quite what to do with it.

'Lady Corliss,' the Willow Tree prompts gently to the lady on the couch.

Corliss turns her head and sees the older Sin Eater and me. She darts her eyes away, then laughs softly. 'Past that, I suppose.'

'Shall we leave you, Corliss?' asks the Willow Tree.

'A swallow before you go? My mouth burns so,' Corliss says.

The Willow Tree fills a cup and pours a few drops into her mouth. Then he and the Painted Pig leave for the outer sitting room.

Corliss looks the Sin Eater in the eyes. 'I'm ready.'

The older Sin Eater searches for a stool but there's only a wooden bench by the wall. She nods at me, which I guess means go and fetch it. The bench is heavy built, so I drag it. It makes an awful scraping noise and takes half the rushes on the floor along with it. The Sin Eater gives me a hard look, but Corliss seems not to have noticed. The Sin Eater says the words to begin.

'Maker forgive me,' Corliss starts. 'I have many a sin. I am vain; not as charitable as I should be.' She waits, and I think from the way her eyes move that she's in pain. Bad pain. 'Lying. Envy.' She suddenly pitches to the side, retching. The Sin Eater passes a bowl in time to catch the puke. I pick up a cloth and wipe Corliss's lips.

'Thank you,' Corliss says to me like she means it.

The Sin Eater names the foods she'll eat for the recited sins, then waits.

Corliss takes a ragged breath and swallows, 'I should get on with it. Nothing to gain by hiding. I've, oh. I've used my favour with the Queen for gain. Took money from folk who had too little to spare and promised them the Queen's ear.' Corliss breathes like the air's heavy. 'The Queen ever had her own mind. I wasn't like to sway it.' She takes another breath and says softly, 'But that's not what I said to those who came to me.'

'Roast peacock,' the Sin Eater answers.

Corliss looks as though she'll puke again, so I lift up the bowl, but all that comes out is a little choke and a sick-sweet smell. Her lips've turned a bluish colour, and something niggles in my mind. I try to catch the thought, but it flits away, too quick to grasp. Corliss lies back with a sigh. 'I fornicated with a man. He was a wolf. A wolf with women. I knew better. And he was married.' Her eyes close. 'But we shared . . . an ambition.'

'Dried raisins,' says the Sin Eater.

Corliss's eyes go from the Sin Eater's to mine. 'I cast horoscopes and other auguries.'

'Pomegranate,' the Sin Eater says.

My breath pulls in. Pomegranate is for witchcraft.

Corliss seems taken aback as well. 'But horoscopes are white magic.'

'Trying to know the Maker's plan is spell casting. Spell casting is pomegranate,' is all the Sin Eater says.

Corliss is quiet. When she speaks again her voice is high,

like a girl's. 'I believe I have one more thing to recite.' She chooses her words. 'I sinned to protect a folk I dearly love. I swore never to speak of it. But if I am to die, the Queen should know. Well as I taught her, she may not decipher the pictures.' She shudders, but this time I can tell it's not from pain, it's with feeling. 'I was the Queen's governess. I've lived with her since she was a girl, when she was no more than a cast-off in her stepmother Katryna's household, long before her fortune turned and she became queen.' Corliss speaks quicker. 'Maker help me, I only wanted to protect her. But if others discover what we've done, the Queen will fall.'

Corliss shudders again, but this time it seems to linger. No, it begins to grow. The shuddering turns to shaking. Then it's like she has the falling sickness, she's shaking so badly. Foam comes to Corliss's blue lips. The Sin Eater nods me towards the sitting room where the Willow Tree and the Painted Pig went.

All the eyes in the outer sitting room shoot to me when I open the door, then fly away at angles like a clay pot dropped on the floor.

The Painted Pig twists a ring and calls to the room, 'How now?'

The Willow Tree grasps why I've come and sweeps through the door without pause.

He goes direct past Corliss, to the innermost door and knocks. A low murmur comes back through. I have a feeling like water running down my back. Then the inner door opens and in walks the Queen.

I want to drop my eyes, and I want to look. It's like five

folk have walked into the room, but it's only her. Barely thirty years of age but with as much presence as a granddam. She's magnificent. I could work all the years of my life and not afford a yard of her skirt. It's stranger silk, with embroidered birds in gold and red. Her stomacher is gold-embroidered black velvet that highlights the black of her hair. Her curls have been brushed up to give her even more height than she already has, parted only in front to reveal her gold crown.

'Your Grace.' The Willow Tree and Painted Pig bow.

The Queen steps forward, but just before she sits, she starts to back up. 'Is it catching, this flux?'

The Painted Pig takes the smallest of pauses, then answers, 'No, Your Grace. Your physician declared so himself.'

'No danger, Your Grace,' agrees the Willow Tree.

The Queen sits down beside the shaking Corliss. 'My dear one?'

Corliss's eyes shift to the side.

The Queen whispers, 'I forbid this. I forbid you from leaving me.' Then, from nowhere the Queen gives a fierce shriek that startles us all. 'Who shall sleep at the foot of my bed? Who shall share my meals? Who shall take care of me?' The Queen takes the cup by Corliss's couch and throws it wildly. It hits the Painted Pig's skirts. A stain blooms across the orange fabric.

The Willow Tree bows low as a dog. 'Your Grace, I beg you to guard your temper.'

'I shall do as I please!' the Queen spits back at him.

The look between the Willow Tree and the Painted Pig is small, but I see it nonetheless. Choler must be common in the Queen's privy life, like her father, the old king, who married and killed wife upon wife.

'Corliss is beyond help,' says the Willow Tree to the Queen. 'You who loved her must witness her passage to the Maker. It's all that's left.'

The Queen holds still a moment, then takes a breath. The air goes straight into her back, raising her up, and all at once she's the sober Queen again. 'Did she finish her Recitation?'

The Sin Eater, who's been like a stool or a tapestry, comes back to life. 'I say the words to end this Recitation: When the food is et, your sins will be ours. We bear them in silence to our grave.'

'I will take the list of foods to the kitchen,' the Willow Tree says.

———

The Willow Tree stands before us in the corner, breathing noisily with a musty mouth-smell that hits me in waves. The Sin Eater names the foods, and he scratches them on a parchment. His brow furrows once at the pomegranate for witchcraft but then goes back to flatness. With a last smelly breath, the Willow Tree finishes his writing.

Back in the corridor, we turn down one passage and another. We go down a set of stairs. It's colder farther away from the Queen's rooms. I wrap my shawl close around me. The Sin Eater pauses at each turn as if she's remembering the way. I've never been inside any house large enough to get lost in. I look to the tapestries along the wall. I suppose they could be like particular trees in the wood that you recall to

retrace your steps. This one's got unicorns on it. Farther along
the wall is one showing a rich lady with a goat in her lap. I
think it's meant to look like a deer. That would be more
fitting.

When I look up from the goat-deer, the Sin Eater's disappeared around the next corner. I hurry after, but she's gone
from sight when I get to the corner. Left or right, I can't tell.

Behind me I hear boot steps. I move to the side, and a
man of an age with me passes by. Not tall, but built broad
and strong and wearing sleeves slashed to show burgundy
silk. He's dark-haired and dark-eyed and as handsome as
you've seen.

He goes to the same corner the older Sin Eater disappeared beyond. Just as he turns, something small and bright
bounces from his hand and onto the rushes on the floor,
landing as silent as a shadow. A ring, gold like the one I
wear for Da, but thick all around. I pick it up and follow
after to return it

He hears my steps and looks back. I drop my eyes and
raise the ring.

'What's this?!' he says sharp-like, but doesn't move to take
it. Mayhap he's discovered my *S* collar. Mayhap he's afraid to
touch the ring now that I've soiled it. I didn't even think on
it, I just picked it right up. But when I look up, his face is
open like a sheet.

'I must confess to you,' he says. 'A moment ago I wouldn't
have believed any folk in this castle honest enough to return
a gold ring.'

I'd never steal, I think. Then I remember the bread. *But that was because I had to*, I remind myself, *not because I'm dishonest*. My face must show my thoughts knocking about, because he goes on.

'I don't mean to cause insult. It's just I'm not from here. And since I've come I've not met two in twenty who wouldn't sell their mother's soul to Eve for their own advancement. The ring is a token from a friend back home.'

My hand goes to my own ring.

'You have one too,' he says in a sober way. 'So you know.' He waits as if it's my turn to speak. If it were a week before this, I would tell him that I do know. I would tell him about my da. But why is he talking to me? He must see what I am.

I feel for my *S* collar. I find my shawl wrapped over the top of it. That's why he's still looking. When he discovers what I am, he'll hate me. He'll think I hid it from him. I drop my eyes.

'What?' he asks hard. 'Even a maid won't speak with a Northern lord, is it? This whole court is so puffed up none will deign to keep company with a country mouse raised by rustics. I've not a soul to speak to.'

There was an old rhyme about a country mouse and a town mouse, but all I can think on is what will happen if he finds out what I am.

He speaks again. 'I would welcome a kind word. Excepting my father, all the world knows my suit for the Queen is fruitless, and they haven't minced words in telling me.' He pulls at his ruff. 'And these pleated collars you Southerners wear are uncomfortable, useless, and take an awful lot of starching.'

A laugh comes out of my mouth before I can help it.

'And now you laugh,' he says as if I'm mocking him, but then he starts to laugh a little too. 'I've told you something about me, and now I've ferreted out something about you. You know about washing clothes. Look at that, we're nearly old friends. Perhaps you can help me pass the time until the Queen declines my marriage suit and I can return home. How about it, old friend?'

A thought comes, *Mayhap he won't mind. Mayhap I could show him my S, and he would still want to know me.*

I reach for my collar, but slapping footfalls in the passage turn his head. A young man appears wearing scarlet hose that make him look like a rooster. 'Dallying with a maid? Not a means to ply your suit with the Queen. Your father would be' – but he cuts off his words because my collar has come free of my shawl – 'that's a sin eater!'

I look to the Country Mouse. His colour drains away. The Rooster tugs on his sleeve. The Country Mouse drops his eyes and follows him away down the passage. I hear the old rhyme in my head:

> *Said the Country Mouse to Cousin Town Mouse,*
>   *'Adieu,*
> *Town life may do for you,*
> *But I prefer bacon and beans secure from harm*
> *To feeding on fine cakes in fear and alarum.'*

The older Sin Eater's not happy when I finally catch up to her in the courtyard. I think on the Country Mouse all the way back through town. How his cheek had little pins of dark hair that needed shaving. How his voice got happier when he learned I knew about washing. Imagine, a rich folk who cares that a girl knows about washing.

We make one more stop, at a merchant's house. In the kitchen there's a small box, a roll atop it. The cook and steward, the only folk to witness, stand with heads bowed. Such fragile things, babies. How can there be so many grown folk, when so many babies die?

—

After the Eating, the older Sin Eater's steps take on the heaviness of the walk homeward after a day's work. In the town square she slows for a newspanto but doesn't stop, so I catch only snippets. A poppet was found by the castle wall under the Queen's windows, the newsboys tell. Not a white magic love charm, but dark magic made to curse folk. It was fashioned from yellow beeswax and made to look like a highborn woman. Worse still, whoever made the poppet stuck pig bristles through its belly and nether parts.

I feel a clench in my own cunny just thinking on it. What a dire thing, not just to curse a woman but to curse her baby parts. Of course, the newsboys don't shy from playacting it. For them, the more terrifying, the better the show. A witch with a devil's teat on his cheek holds a little poppet in a blue dress. The witch mutters in a stranger tongue and pushes a pin into the poppet's belly. An actor dressed in blue like the poppet clutches at his belly, for everyfolk knows what's done to a poppet is felt by whoever it's fashioned to look like. Stick pig bristles through the poppet dressed like a lady, and the lady feels the pricks. The newsboy playing the lady howls and howls.

Well past the town square, I can still hear the howling. *The lady in the panto died just like Corliss, clutching at her guts*, I think. The thought gives me a cold dripping feeling in my neck.

Soon the sounds of the show get swallowed up by the bump and din of Northside. My feet are like ants, marching one in front of the other, towards home. I put Corliss and the poppet out of my mind. Instead, I piece again through my moments with the Country Mouse up until the footfalls of the Rooster. I stop just before then.

5. DEER'S HEART

WHEN I WAS a little girl and Maris was Queen, the Makerhall had great stone altars with pictures and statues of the Maker's son, the angels, and the hagis all around. But the new faith doesn't hold with decorations, so when Bethany became queen the altars were changed to wooden tables with nought on them but the Maker's Book in plain Anglish, instead of the old tongue. The Anglish is supposed to make it so we common folk can read the Word of the Maker ourselves. But as I can't read to start with, it doesn't make a lick of difference to me.

The only decorations left in the town's Makerhall are the stone carvings of Hagi Saul and Hagi Gabriel cut into the very walls beside its doors and the coloured glass windows.

During services, I would sit in a pew where the sun cast coloured light, so I could lift my hand and see my skin blue, green, gold. It seemed as true a mystery as the Maker's miracles.

—

Corliss's Eating takes place in the Queen's private Makerhall at the castle. Lots of folk come to witness, their heads sitting above their ruffs like roast meat on platters. Among them I find the Country Mouse, looking ill at ease in his pew. His eyes pass my direction, and I'm sure he sees me. Before I can help it, I smile, but his eyes have been pulled by the folk beside him, whispering and pointing to the coffin. I look around at the rest of the folk. A fair number are murmuring and pointing towards the coffin too. Must be the pomegranate for witchcraft. A frightful sin, to be sure.

Suddenly there's squeaks and scrapes of pews moving as folk stand. Then the Queen comes in. The gnarled Willow Tree doctor walks behind her, and she has a dog at her side. Not a real dog, a man-dog. He wears a neat beard and a thick gold chain around his neck. His fingers are stained black with ink. The chain and ink are because he's the Queen's secretary. He's the one folk say is her favourite.

Once the Queen takes her seat in the front, it's our turn. The Sin Eater and I walk up the aisle towards the coffin at the front. The pews to each side are so polished that the wood looks like water. I brush them as I go by with my fingers, sliding callus to callus along the cool and smooth of it. I'm so intent on the feeling that I bump full into the Sin Eater's

rump when she stops a step from the coffin. I peek around
to see why she's halted.

The deer heart is dressed in truffles and oil. It must have
been a huge animal. It sits like a centrepiece between the
roast peacock and the pomegranate. I go over the list of foods
in my head, but Corliss never recited a deer heart. And it
isn't a sin to forget. This is why all the folk were whispering
and pointing.

The Sin Eater gets still. Not like an ass that won't go,
digging in its feet and eyeing you from the side, but wood-
still like the pews, cool and smooth.

The folk sitting are a different matter. At first none notice
the Sin Eater's stopped, for a little pause here and there is
usual. But then time stretches out and becomes something
to note. It stretches further and becomes something to
unsettle. That's when all the motion no longer in the Sin
Eater seems to jump to the other folk. The longer she stays
still, the more they need to move about, shifting and looking
and peering and whispering.

The Queen herself sits not four paces from us. 'The sin
eater stopped. Is it a portent?' she asks the Willow Tree.

The Willow Tree talks louder than he should, but more
like because he's unaware than that he means to be loud. 'I
saw no such signs. Perhaps she trembles at the gravity of the
sin.'

The Queen signals her black-fingered secretary. He goes
to the front of the Makerhall. The Willow Tree hastily follows
after as if he doesn't want to be left out. They talk a bit as if
they're arguing. The secretary's hands move as he speaks, and

his black fingertips look like charred tinder. I swallow away the giggle that comes into my throat.

Black Fingers addresses the hall. 'The sin eater will proceed with the Eating of Corliss Ashton as is the sin eater's duty, conferred by the Maker and his agent on earth, Her Majesty, Queen Bethany.'

The Sin Eater doesn't move.

I know it's the deer heart. She vowed to eat the sins Corliss recited. The deer heart is a lie. She won't break her vow. I feel like a squirrel seeing the shadow of a hawk. I dread what's coming for us.

Black Fingers waits one more breath and then speaks. 'If the sin eater refuses to eat, she disobeys a direct order from the Maker as it is written in the Maker's Book.' Every breath in every body stills. As if following my thoughts, he goes on. 'To disobey a direct order from the Maker and his agent Queen Bethany' – his own voice quiets – 'is treason.'

Treason is death. And under Queen Bethany that's not by a noose and the gallows but by gutting or burning or worse. I wait for the Sin Eater to move. When she doesn't, I do something plain foolish. I take my hand and place it on hers. I expect it to be cool and hard like the wood of the pews, but heat pulses off it. I squeeze. I don't know what I mean by it. Only that something must be done. Something other than stillness and treason and death.

'Guards!' Black Fingers's voice echoes in the hall.

I wait for the guards to come and haul me away like the constable who took me to jail. And the guards do come, but they stop a pace away. They don't want to touch a sin eater.

The Willow Tree comes into the aisle too. He gets so close to Black Fingers they look like they might kiss. I swallow another miserable giggle.

They're near enough I just catch their words. 'Shall I do your work?' the Willow Tree says. 'The Queen is distressed enough.'

'I am the Queen's favourite,' Black Fingers says back through his teeth. 'I'm an earl now, and may soon be more. And you will be the first to go, you charlatan.'

'You are a dog in lion's garb, and your pups will never sit on the throne.'

Black Fingers tugs at his own ear. He turns to the guards. 'Are you men?'

One guard, then the other raises his sword, but it's only the older Sin Eater they push out of the Makerhall with the flat of their blades.

Black Fingers stays behind. 'The sin eater will do her Makergiven duty.' He can only mean me. 'She will execute this Eating, and all future Recitations and Eatings, or also be charged with treason against Maker and country.' Two more guards come up the aisle, their swords at the ready. The cutting edge of one has a small brown stain on it.

When the purgers came in the night to our home, Bethany had just been crowned queen. I was seven. She made it treason to be Eucharistian, but Da hadn't yet destroyed our family altar. How the purgers knew it, I don't know. Some folk must have told them.

My mother urged Da to burn the altar. 'Bend in the wind, don't swing in it,' she said.

Da had shaken his head. 'What we do shows who we are. I cannot change my faith one day to the next.'

But when Da left for work, my mother sent me to fetch her brothers. I found them in the road by the town square, idling and taunting folk who came by. They waved me away like a fly. I told them, just as my mother instructed, that Da 'hadn't cleaned the house proper and guests were coming'. When I said that, their ears perked up like dogs after a squirrel. They followed me home. Mother sent me to the kitchen while my uncles made a mess in the garden with hammers.

When Da came home at sunset, Mother gave him supper but no words. He had only finished his meat when there was a knock at the door. Faces were covered by hoods, but I heard the smithy's voice and saw the dark, hairy hands of Gracie Manners's da. I can still hear in my mind Da saying all calm-like, 'Come in, would you like some small beer?'

The smith stood over me smelling like vinegar and fear. 'We're going to all the houses,' he said.

Da was quiet as the hooded men walked past him into our home. I don't remember where Mother was, but I remember she was weeping.

When they left, the smith said, 'Barely in time.' It was like a storm that passes without a drop even though the clouds were dark and low.

'Where is it?' Da asked Mother when they'd gone. 'Where is our altar?'

Mother just said, 'Dust to dust.'

'What have you done?' Da whispered. He wasn't angry

exactly, but there was none of the soft that was always in his voice.

Mother looked him in the eye then. 'You say it shows who you are. You're nothing if you're dead.'

Black Fingers, the Queen's secretary, is weary of waiting. The guards feel it and raise their sword flats to my shoulders. In the end it's this: the metal pushing through my shift, pushing pictures into my head of the brown stain on the blade digging into my guts, spilling my insides onto a block. The blade sawing at my hips until the bones give way and my legs are dragged off for dogs. My head stuck on a spike and posted on the castle gate so crows eat my eyes and lips.

I can't help the Sin Eater if I'm dead, I tell the deer heart as my teeth tear into its flesh.

I'm a goodly girl, I whisper to the coffin.

I look up just once, to see the Country Mouse at his pew. His face is dropped, but on it is a plain look of disgust. Is it for me? For eating a lie? I hear a sort of choked sigh. My eyes skip without thinking to its maker. The Queen. I don't know what it signifies, only that it seems to be made of both grief and relief all at once. And that a heart on a coffin is for killing.

6. CAKE BREAD

I CAN TASTE THE deer's heart in my mouth as I walk home alone.

How could this happen? Why would an unrecited heart be placed on a coffin? It takes a moment for the answer to come up from the road.

To put blame for a killing on Corliss.

Somefolk placed the heart there to make us all believe Corliss had done a murder. But she never did. And I partook in the lie.

My steps come harder against the road, but words I don't want to hear rise up. *The Sin Eater's in Queen Bethany's dungeon. And you're free because of a lie.*

But why didn't she eat the heart if refusing meant torture and death? I ask back. Queen Bethany's command to eat was the Maker's command, that's what Black Fingers said. So obeying and eating the heart was the Maker's will. When I became a sin eater, the Makerman said the only way I'd escape an eternity by Eve's side was to obey the Maker's will. Surely the other Sin Eater knew that too.

But the heart wasn't recited, the road says. *It was a lie. How can a lie be the Maker's will?*

Was it the Maker's will for us to refuse? Is that why the other Sin Eater wouldn't eat the heart? Did she trade a fearsome death for an eternity of peace? Did I forfeit my own salvation by eating the heart?

Did I obey, or didn't I?! I scream in silence.

I have no notion of the right answer, but all my thoughts are coated with a sticky shame. It feels like the oil on the deer heart.

I look down at the wheel ruts. *Traitors must confess before they are killed*, I tell them. *It's law. The other Sin Eater'll say there was no heart recited.*

The bony grooves arch into the bottoms of my feet through my leather soles, up through the bones of my legs. *Will she break the sacred rule and speak?* the ruts ask. *She swore to carry the contents of Corliss's Recitation in silence to her grave.*

I daren't think on what will happen to her if she doesn't confess. I look at the sparse clouds at the top of the sky, so far away they won't bother to tell me. But it comes into my head anyway. They use stones, some as wide around as cartwheels to make traitors speak if they refuse to confess.

They lay the man or woman on a bed of wood, then pile stones onto their chest, stopping only if a confession is made. Speak or die. It can take hours to crush an able body. The newsboys have performed it in pantos before. Lee and I shrieked with the rest of the folk watching as a bladder of pig's blood sprayed us when the traitor was crushed in the show. That will be her end. There's no way through I can see.

But mayhap I could speak, the thought comes. If folk knew the deer heart wasn't recited, the Sin Eater might be let go. And surely saving a life is a goodly act. I could tell somefolk – Black Fingers, the Queen, the Willow Tree.

An awful twitching seizes my guts, like my bowels might empty right here in the road. What does it mean that I'd consider breaking a sin eater's rule of silence? It's like breaking a vow. Da said if you break a vow, it cracks your soul. I'd never escape Eve then.

I think of my da. What it was like to be known and seen and heard by him. And how each year since he's been gone I've lost more of my place in this world until I don't know who I am or where I belong. But I could sort things out, I think. I could mend things. I could get the other Sin Eater back. I could be us again. And mayhap, Maker help me, if I make things right, I'll be forgiven for eating the unrecited heart, and when I die I can go to the Maker. I turn on my toes back towards the castle. Mayhap we can both be saved.

———

The castle guards don't know what to do with me. They look at their parchment list, then at one another. Never at me, except a first, startled half look. I wait, and they wait. But in my chest I remember the cold dark of a cellar and wonder how much worse the dungeon must be for the Sin Eater. And then I just go on and slip between the guards through the castle gate into the courtyard. I expect a cry behind me, but it's quiet as I cross the stones.

The Makerhall is still. The folk've all gone. I walk up the centre aisle, the padding of my steps disappearing into the large emptiness. Near the front is a small, carved door, but it only goes to a vestment room, hung with Makermen robes. Where now? The only other place I know in the castle is the Queen's rooms, where we heard Corliss's Recitation.

Back in the courtyard I find the door with the stone scroll above it. There's a guard, but he seems as confused as the gatekeepers at my approach. I take a gamble and walk with purpose. Just before my toe strikes the door, the guard pushes it open, sliding to the side to avoid my touch.

There's plenty of folk to be found in the passageways of the Queen's quarters, maids and grooms and guards, guards everywhere, but they look away when I pass. If only my uncles knew what a thief a sin eater could make, they would fashion a brass *S*, don skirts, and forgo their other games.

I climb the castle stairs as quick as I dare, keeping my hand against the wall to be sure I don't fall. Somewhere near, Maker help me, is the Queen. I will tell her that Corliss recited no killing. I will make it all right.

As I turn the next corner, I see a maid, head bowed,

coming out of a smallish door. A store closet, mayhap. But it's not a maid. It's one of the young ladies from the Queen's chamber, the pretty Fair Hair, wearing a butter-yellow dress and straightening the coif on her head.

A voice calls to her. 'I wondered where you had disappeared to.' It's Mush Face, coming from around a turn.

'I told you I needed candles,' Fair Hair answers. 'I was looking for a maid to fetch some.'

'In the herb dispensary?' Mush Face eyes Fair Hair. 'Did you hear about the Eating? The Queen's dearest Corliss was a witch.'

Fair Hair's mouth works like a newly caught fish. 'There was pomegranate on the coffin?'

'And a deer heart as big as a rabbit,' Mush Face says.

'Witches kill for their magic, I've heard tell,' says Fair Hair. 'We should return to the presence chamber.'

'Where are your candles?' Mush Face asks without moving her eyes.

'My what?'

It's then Fair Hair sees me, still as a bird in a bush, at the passageway's turn. She starts twice when she sees me, first to find folk there and again when she sees my brass *S*. Her eyes drop, and both ladies make the Maker's sign across their shoulders and hips.

'She's the one who ate the deer heart,' Mush Face says. 'It's poor luck to see her after the Eating.'

'Why, that's old-faith mummery,' says Fair Hair. She puts her hand on Mush Face's arm and leads her towards the Queen's sitting room.

Just as they disappear down the way, the door to the herb dispensary opens again and out comes Black Fingers, the Queen's secretary. It's odd that two folk came from the same, small closet, but mayhap the oddness's a sign from the Maker. Black Fingers has the Queen's ear.

I summon my breath. 'Sir!' I call to him. Even though I haven't been a sin eater long, my voice sounds wrong and at the same time welcome like warm water. Black Fingers hardly takes me in before he's begun the Maker's Prayer. I try to raise my voice over his. 'There was a misdeed committed, Sir! It must be set right.' But he only speaks louder, drowning out my words, turning to go on his way.

I run after him, my collar bumping hard at my neck. I need something to catch his attention. I call louder still. 'A killing's been blamed on the wrong folk. The Queen must be told.'

His change is so sudden I think he must have tripped until I see the blade in his hand. Then he comes at me at a run. I stumble back, but in moments his neat beard is right over me, and the knife is digging into the flesh below my left ear. My hands catch his, fighting against the blade's tug as it tries to carve its way across my throat.

A burble of laughter comes out of the Queen's sitting room as the door opens. Nimble like a Northside cut-throat, Black Fingers slides his blade out of my neck and into his sleeve. He's walking coolly away, bowing to three ladies coming from the sitting room when I fall against the wall. My heart thumps in my ears. I grab at my shawl to staunch the warm stream at my throat.

The laughing women have nearly reached me, but so accustomed are they to servants hugging the walls at their approach, it's not until they are within arm's reach that they see who I am or what's happened.

The nearest lady gives a mighty shriek and steps backwards, treading on the woman behind her. They fall together, cries joining the snapping of wicker skirt hoops. The third woman furiously speaks the Maker's Prayer, an echo of Black Fingers:

> *Maker mine, forever of the sun's light*
> *Miracles be wrought from your name*
> *Protect us sinners,*
> *Now and at the hour of our death.*

I saw a pig man at work once. He held the sow in one arm and with the other he cut across its throat. You'd never guess how much blood was in the one animal. It bled and bled in bulging pulses and then in a steady stream. I remember it took longer than I could stand and watch for it to drain. I grew tired of the sight and went on about my day. Mayhap I will die in the same fashion. Mayhap I'm doing so now. This is what comes of a sin eater speaking.

If I live, Maker mine, I pray, *I will do my duty. I vow never to speak again outside the Recitations and the Eatings. I will obey.*

I venture a small breath. I look down to see black blood soaking through the woad blue of my shawl. There is only one way I'll live. I need to find a healer.

The courtyard is shadowed by evening when I stumble out of the scroll door. There's a spike of cold where the shawl is wet with blood. A giggle comes out of my mouth, there's so much blood. I make my way to the gate. Mayhap I'm swaying. I can't rightly tell.

I've only ever gone to a cunning woman for healing and only for household ailments: warts, charms, constipation. I've no notion where to go. In my mind I see black robes. Curiosities in windows. Apothecary lane.

I make it to Northside, passing the whores and taverns. The apothecary shops are just shuttering. I'm very tired, and when I shift my shawl, there's no more dry to staunch the wet. I step into the path of a man in apothecary robes with a small, curled beard. I raise my hand for help.

He rears back like a horse, hands crossing himself, and goes around me. Like a drunkard I turn in slow steps after him, but he's too quick. Across the lane, another robed man stops to gape. I raise my hand to him. He hisses as if across a great distance, and the ground moves under me like water under a river wherry. By now folk have gathered in a wide circle around me. No, an egg. An egg is the shape they've made. It seems suddenly important that the shape they've made is an egg and not a circle. And none in the egg will help.

The ground moves again, this time in a sudden jolt. I feel a smack against my temple. I lick my lips and taste cold earth. There's a white mist rising from my lips. Mayhap it's my soul fleeing my body. My soul melting away into the air. Why doesn't it take me with it? I try to go after my soul, but my legs don't answer when I call on them to move. I am the sow who was cut open by the pig man. I shall be butchered and strung up in the marketplace. I see faces dimly in the distance. And then the mist comes and swallows me whole.

7. PIG'S HEART

'STILL WARM.' A dream voice hardens into waking life.
It's night. Deep night. My shoes are gone, and somefolk's digging in my sleeve. I shudder.

Two figures jerk back above me. Vagabonds. Two women.
No, a man and a woman. I'm still on the apothecary lane. I
must have fallen.

'We're mere beggars, not rogues,' the man says with a
Northern accent. 'We would never have molested your person
had we known you remained among the living.' His face is
clotted with earth or clay, and his speech is fancy like an
actor's. I lift a hand to my neck. My shawl is stuck about my
neck in a wet lump.

'If you have a penny . . .' says the woman. She's curled

in on herself under a blanket. 'We've not et since a week past.'

I dig under the shawl to feel my wound, but my fingers find metal, hard and cold. It takes a moment to remember it's the brass sin eater collar. My thumb catches on something along it. A nick or a notch, not far from where Black Fingers's knife dug in. My collar stopped his knife. Or hindered it. A laugh starts, but what comes out is a sort of gasp and choke.

'Oh, look now. She's cut, Paul. Badly at the neck,' says the woman.

'Shall we wait for her to die?'

'Never such a soul as you,' scolds the woman. She must not have seen the collar yet, covered as it is by the bloodied shawl. She comes closer. I try to pull back, but my body won't obey. 'Now, now,' the woman shushes. 'Would you rather I do as Paul suggests and play at bone dice until you pass?' She has a smell about her. It takes a moment to name what it is. Rotting meat.

She tugs at the shawl, but it's my flesh that's pulled up as if cloth and skin are stuck. 'Not so big, but deep. A stitch or three might do.' Her fingers don't find the collar. 'Have you a home, dearie? Paul's a knack with a needle if you've a hearth fire for two honest beggars.'

Honest beggars. One thing you can't trust about beggars and vagabonds is that they're honest. They've no kin and no home. No folk can speak for them. They could be thieves, murderers, heretics . . . but what choice do I have?

Once they know I'm a sin eater I figure they'll surely desert me, so I'll get what I can before they do. It's not lying, just not telling. My arm is heavy as stone as I raise it up. But raise it I do, and point the way to Dungsbrook.

The man, Paul, carries me. He's younger than his rags suggest, and strong. There's something about his face I can't quite figure in the dark. Like clotted cheese stuck in his beard. They both go about silently, and we stop once in a doorway as a warm lamp and its constable sway past.

I point the way at each turn till I can tell by the smell we've reached Dungsbrook. As we get close, I'm a girl again in Da's arms, letting my full weight rest against his warmth, feeling the bounce of his step. I want to fall fast asleep here in this moment, safe in these arms.

'Where now, dearie?' comes the woman's voice. We're a stone's throw from the Sin Eater's house. Perhaps I can crawl there. 'Where, dearie?' she asks again. They'll flee from me when I show them, but there's nothing for it. I raise my finger and point. The woman starts like a horse.

'Oh, Maker mine,' says Paul. He half drops, half places me down. I can see him wrong way round above me. 'Did I touch her skin? I surely did. I surely did!'

'Are you sure she's a . . .' asks the woman.

The man's fingers feel about my neck. He jerks back when he finds the collar.

'Does your flesh burn, lovey?' calls the woman.

'She was light as a child,' is all Paul says. I can't fathom why they haven't yet fled.

'Mayhap new to it. Hasn't had time to fatten,' the woman says back. 'Can you get her inside?'

'While avoiding touch and direct gaze?' Paul asks.

'Lodging for the night out of the cold,' says the woman. 'And no constable chasing us down.'

'What have we come to?' Paul grabs hold of my skirt and drags me in the door without touching my flesh.

Just before the door shuts, a piece of moonshine falls across Paul and the woman. And suddenly I know why they dare come in with me. What looked to be clotted cheese in Paul's beard are pocks and patches of grey, hardened skin on his face, as if he was burned, but a little different. And the woman. Her rags have fallen open. Inside is but half a body. A shoulder caved and drooping, a rib cage with an unnatural cant, a cropped and misshapen arm. These are not just vagabonds. They are the unseen too.

—

I'm stuck like a beetle on my back, too weak to turn myself. Paul's left me just inside the door and is now building up the hearth fire. The woman, called Brida, I learn, settles down on the Sin Eater's stool. As the flickers of firelight grow I see fully what she is. A leper.

There's old stories about lepers, of how they banged clappers when they walked through town to warn folk of their coming. How they were forbidden from using the well for fear of contagion. How, like a sin eater, none looked upon them lest they be cursed. But I must have heaped lepers in with goblins and hog boons and other fables because, seeing Brida before me, I can't countenance she's real.

'Don't fear, lovey,' she says to the ceiling as if she knows my thoughts. 'The sickness doesn't pass so easy as that. Paul, here, hasn't caught it, not in a handful of years. We won't share food and drink or sleep close, and you'll be right as rain.'

A corpse she is, rotted and caved at the edges. Her nose is a stub and on one side where there should be the square of a shoulder there's a bowl-shaped hollow. One arm comes to its natural end, but the other sheers off like a shard of bone just past the elbow. She is grisly and repugnant and rightly unseen.

And then Paul turns round from his fire making. What his malady is, I cannot tell, but the skin on his face, neck, and the backs of his hands has been deeply scarred. The rest of him seems untouched.

I wonder if they'll leave me here by the door until I die. Or mayhap I already passed into death on the apothecary lane, and this is the underworld, Paul and Brida two demons. If so, they are curious. I hear Paul behind me picking up the piss pot, the ewer, the broom, then climbing the ladder to the loft.

'A dung heap. Floor hasn't been scrubbed in a month of Makersdays, and nary a crumb to be seen,' he says, coming back down with something in his hand.

'What do you expect?' says Brida. Then, 'What's that?'

'Better than crumbs,' he answers, and I hear the slosh of liquid. The jug of spirits.

All at once Paul's dragging me towards the fire. He lets me down so close, I can feel my hairs burning. Does he mean to scar me like himself?

'Brida?' Paul says, impatient-like.

'Just here,' she answers, and I feel a cool rush, then burning about my neck. She's pouring the spirits on my wound. 'Hush, now,' Brida soothes. 'Will loosen the thickened blood. The cloth's stuck in there fast.'

'Stop your mouth!' Paul's curdled jaw is set. 'You should not speak to her. We should have nought to do with her.'

'Very well, I shan't speak,' says Brida brightly. 'But do stitch her up, dearie. She can't be worse than me, and you haven't been cursed by our association.'

'I very much beg to differ, you old sack of pus,' spits Paul. 'I was not born to coarseness. I have gentle blood. If my life be not cursed, you have surely begun to lose your wits along with your limbs.'

There's a wet snorting sound in response. Brida is laughing, a bubble of snot blooming out of the hole where her nose ought to be. 'Oh, you.'

A glint catches my eye. Paul's threading a needle in the firelight. 'I shall repair her wound. And, Maker help me, this act of charity will prove powerful mitigation for my past sins.' The needle stabs into my neck, and I mewl like a rat dying in a trap.

'She could eat your sins,' suggests Brida.

'Indeed,' says Paul. 'She shall eat my sins gratis, I hope.'

'All the dried plums in town.' Brida smiles. Plums are for fornicating with those you should not, like in incest. I wonder if they are sister and brother. He sounded like a Northerner, after all.

Paul tugs the thread through my flesh, and I feel warm, new blood. Still, he's clever with the needle. I never feel his skin against mine. Brida presses a soft cloth to my neck. It's blood moss for between your legs when you've got your monthly courses. Paul must have found it up the ladder in the loft. Another prick and tug, and another. I seem to be in a river wherry again from the way the floor tilts and turns. And then somehow I'm back in my truckle bed, the one I had as a small child. The sound of my parents' breath soothes me to sleep.

—

When I wake, there are three stripes of daylight on the far wall. Brida appears above me. Through her gaping nose hole I see the white of bone.

She leaves the old black pot from above the hearth at my side. It's been cleared of cobwebs and warmed. I lift it and pour weak broth into my mouth. It tastes of sharp onion and mould.

Brida sits on the stool. Paul's sleeping hump rises and falls beyond. I finger the cloth at my neck. It's dry. Then sleep swallows me back.

When I wake again, the light says it's afternoon. Paul's peering out of a crack in the shutters. 'A whole group,' he says.

'For us? Have they come for us?' There's fear in Brida's voice. 'It's the witch who made that poppet they want.'

'One of the Queen's own ladies died just after that poppet was found. They'll sweep up any they can easily lay the blame on,' Paul tells her. 'And if you don't look like Eve's own hand-maiden, who does?'

'I thought she might be a victim of the witch.' Brida points towards me. 'Terrible thing.' As if they hadn't been ready to rob my dead body.

'There's no constable with them,' Paul assays through the shutters. 'It looks to be merely a pack of dirty boys, Maker help us. I hope they don't want food.'

Messengers. I rise, my neck burning, and swoon back onto the rug.

'Oh, now, it's too soon for her to be up and about,' says Brida to the room.

My head conjures an image of the Sin Eater beneath the castle in some hell.

I could still tell the Queen of the deer heart, I think. But, no, I vowed to the Maker I would not speak if he spared me, except to do my duty as a sin eater.

I stand and wait for another swoon to pass. I stagger to the window. Six, no eight messengers. *I must do my duty. I'll help the Sin Eater when I think of a way.*

My shoes have reappeared by the hearth. That's a kindness, though just pulling them on makes the stitches at my neck ache and sting.

Brida looks to Paul. 'Surely she can rest a piece more.'

'I couldn't care less what she does,' Paul says.

'She's sharing her home with us,' Brida says.

Paul snorts, 'And I risked my own flesh to save hers. As I see it, she is in my debt.'

'She should rest a piece more,' Brida says again.

'The boys are likely the heralds of her trade, each one from a soul dead or dying,' says Paul.

Brida sighs wetly, 'Then she must go.'

When I open the door, the boys come forward, messages flying. It's like crows fallen on a dead rabbit in a field, the larger ones pushing out the smaller, who squawk all the louder for it.

I pick out the name Fletcher and Smithy Lane and start on my way. I nearly fall when a spell of faintness takes me by the town square. The boys kick at the dirt till I find my feet under me again. Messengers get their penny only after I arrive.

—

John Fletcher lies on a bed of straw in the corner of a two-room cottage. He's young enough, but his breathing comes hard, like his lungs are closing in on themselves. His wife clutches her hands at her middle.

There's one stool placed beside him. It takes a moment to remember it's just me for the Recitation. Only me. Shame swells in my chest, so I hastily say the words to begin.

My voice is so low and broken, it startles me. It startles the goodwife too. I notice her skin is chapped from a long winter, and there's a red sore on her bottom lip. 'The Unheard is now heard. The Unseen seen. Your flesh—' How does it go? I've never properly learned the words. 'I will bear your sins to my grave. Speak.'

'All what you do as a boy,' John Fletcher wheezes. 'Teasing and brawling and scrumping from gardens.' There's a whistle that comes when he lets out his breath. Like blowing through your thumbs on a blade of grass. 'Told a pack of lies every which way; forced a girl with two other fellows.' His eyes dart towards his wife. One of her shoes scrapes against the floor. 'Nothing boys won't do. Was a beggar girl. Nothing you can blame boys for. She wanted it anyhow.'

He's inventing this last bit. I don't know how I know, but the lie is like a smell or a taste you know right away.

'Disobeyed my da and ma,' he wheezes on. 'Failed to say my prayers. And I killed a man.' The goodwife's shoe scrapes again. 'It was not with intention, only mischance. I . . .' The whistle when he breathes gets louder. 'I hit him just the two times. Never thought it'd do him.' He wheezes hard now. 'A man . . . shouldn't be brought down . . . by just two blows . . . Like a woman, he was . . . Was never my fault.'

When he finishes, I go to the goodwife, her hands still clutched at her middle. I name the foods to prepare huskily. Gristle and roast pigeon. Pickled cucumber and mustard seed. Bitter greens. Pickled herring. Capon's head for forcing oneself on a woman.

But the killing. I don't know what kind of heart to eat. This is why folk are apprenticed to masters. But I've lost mine. All I know is the story of Mr Fox.

Clever Mary marries the rich Mr Fox. He tells his new bride she can go anywhere in his grand house, but she must never look in his cupboard. Of course one day, curiosity gets the better of her, and she opens the cupboard. Inside are the seven corpses of Mr Fox's seven previous brides. Clever Mary hears Mr Fox behind her. He says now she must go into the cupboard, as well, to keep his secret, but she runs to town to tell what she found. Of course no folk believe her because

Mr Fox is rich and respected. They drive Clever Mary back home to him. Mr Fox is waiting to kill her, but just as he's pushing her into the cupboard, she breaks a rib bone off one of the corpses and stabs Mr Fox with it. At his Eating, seven pig hearts sit atop his coffin, and the whole town finally learns of his crimes.

But pig heart isn't right. There are some sins so terrible they're divided into different foods depending on how it happened. Like forcing oneself on a woman (capon's head) is different from forcing oneself on a child (lamb's head). Likewise, killing folk purposefully, which is a pig heart, is different from killing folk without intention. In my head I see the deer heart from Corliss's Eating. What kind of killing was it for?

The goodwife's waiting, so I name goat heart, since goats are a kinder sort of animal than pigs, and killing without intention is kinder than plain murder. The goodwife nods, and John Fletcher does nothing but wheeze. Mayhap they don't know either.

Just as I'm leaving, a whisper slips from the goodwife's lips. At first I think it must be thanks, but the words come out with different shapes. 'He'll go now,' is what she says. She hands me two coins, looks at her husband and whispers it again. Like a prayer.

—

The messenger boys await me outside. Two play a throwing game with a bit of wood. Another stamps on ants. A curly-haired boy about as high as my breast has gathered some of the others with a story. 'And Corliss, the Queen's governess, was the witch that made the poppet!' the curly-haired boy finishes. Some of the boys nod solemnly.

The ant stamper pauses in his stamping. 'No, it was the Queen's governess got cursed by the witch. That's why she died. So she can't be the witch.'

I remember Corliss clutching her belly, just where the poppet was said to have been stuck with pig bristles. If a witch is at work in our town, no folk is safe.

'The newspanto said the governess was a lamb among wolves,' a boy with two missing teeth joins in.

'It's a wolf among lambs,' bites back the curly-haired boy. 'I saw the panto. The Queen's secretary said she was a murderess and traitor. He said her crime was treason against the crown and against Queen Bethany, and there'll be an inquiry into it because the governess was a wolf among lambs.'

'Who'd she kill?' asks the ant stamper. 'Who got murdered?'

'Sin eater ate deer heart on her coffin,' is all the curly-haired boy says in answer.

To be treason, Corliss would have had to kill royalty. Is that what the deer heart signifies? There hasn't been royal folk who died since Queen Maris. And none before that except the old king. Unless you count Queen Maris's babes that were lost in the womb.

Was Corliss a killer and a witch who didn't recite her sins? Who would dare such a thing if her soul's endless torment was the cost? No, somefolk falsely blamed Corliss for murder.

But the ant stamper asks a good question. If there really

was a murder, who got killed? And if everyfolk thinks Corliss did it, then the true killer must still be out there. The thought makes me cold and hot in the same moment. Trying to shake the feeling off catches the boys' attention.

The ant stamper gathers himself quickest. An Eating near the Great Makerhall, he announces. The others come right in, all their words heaping atop the others. Recitation for an ailing child south of the river's bridge. Recitation for Goodwife Miller. Eating at Spring's Meadow Farm. Eating for the second son of the chandler near the guild house. And on and on and on.

—

At day's end, I make my way back to Dungsbrook. The Recitations melt together into one lumpen bit inside my head, but the tastes of other folk's sins are still on my breath. Bitter greens for not saying prayers. Barley grains for cursing. Stewed gurnards for tale bearing. Hippocras for drunkenness. They make me feel melancholic and gassy. My neck aches. I want my rug by the fire. I want to sleep.

As I get close to home, the smells of burning rubbish and shit and woad overcome the tastes in my mouth until all that's there is the Dungsbrook reek. At least the sins are gone. Mayhap Dungsbrook has a useful side.

Brida's on my rug when I arrive. Paul stands before a low fire, wrapping his rags around him like he means to go out. I suppose hog boons and goblins keep their wanderings to the night.

He gets still when I come in but doesn't look to see who

it is. Then he goes on dressing, taking care with each fold and wrap of the fabric. It takes a moment to realize he cares what he looks like. A vain monster! I laugh so loud Paul jumps. He recovers, wraps his face hastily, and hurries out of the door.

'Tsk,' Brida clucks at me from the rug by the hearth. Mayhap she doesn't find it comical.

—

For the first time, I take the ladder to the loft, though the climbing pulls on the stitches in my neck. I look about. There's shelves with wooden boxes on them all up and down a wall, and, thank the Maker, a mattress. It's been a good long while since I slept on one. I drop onto it, pretending I can't smell that the ticking's gone too long unchanged.

But tired as I am, sleep won't come. My mind is aflutter with pictures and thoughts. Why did Black Fingers knife me? Is he the witch who killed Corliss? Did he plant the deer heart on her coffin? All I know is that he hurt me because I spoke out about a murder. To stay safe, I must keep silent.

A slice of moonlight comes in through the shutter. In its dim light, the wooden boxes on the shelves look like overlarge bricks. One box sits open at the foot of the mattress. I pull it into the moonlight for a look.

It's like a picture of a person. Not a real picture, but a likeness made up of what's inside. There's a copper band as is worn on the finger to signify marriage. There's two bone pendants of the kind mothers give babies to protect against Eve's eye, even though Makermen say it's heathen. The leather strings are unworn. Babes that didn't last. There's a kerchief made of fine linen with two embroidered letters I don't know. There's a book bound in calfskin, mayhap for prayers. The prayer book brings a different picture to my mind: a dungeon, Black Fingers at the Sin Eater's side, holding up a stone to crush a confession out of her.

I never even learned her name.

Quick-like, I replace her things, for they must be hers. I shove the box back at the foot of the mattress. But then Paul's voice comes up the ladder. He's returned. It gives me a notion.

Box in hand, I climb down the ladder, careful not to strain at my stitches. Brida eyes me from the side like I'm an unbroken horse who's bolted. I place the box by the hearth and hold up the Sin Eater's kerchief.

Paul looks away, but Brida half peeks.

I point to the embroidered letters.

'I don't know what she wants,' Brida tells Paul.

I want so much to speak, a huff comes out of my lips.

Instantly Paul turns away and urgently recites the Maker's Prayer. I clamp my lips closed, but he goes on. I place my hand over my mouth.

'Paul,' Brida prompts above his prayer. 'She won't speak.'

Paul stops short. 'I want nothing to do with her.'

I wish I didn't need his help, but there's no folk else. I hold up the kerchief again and point.

'She's just indicating the letters,' Brida says.

Paul lets his eyes graze over the cloth, '*R. G.*'

And now I know the letters of her names. *R* for her given name. *G* for her family.

'Wasn't so hard now, was it?' Brida scolds.

'What would you know, you nasty corpse?' Paul barks at her. 'The indignities I bear! Travelling only in the night, blenching from constables' lanterns, supping on other folk's discarded filth, and closeting myself in a squalid little shack with this pollution!' He waves towards me.

'We could return to the sheepfold,' Brida offers as if she's accustomed to such rudeness.

Paul begins to wrap his face as if he means to leave again. Which is just fine by me. He may have saved my life stitching up my neck, but he's tempered like a goose. As he dresses, he catches sight of the book in the Sin Eater's box. He gives a short laugh.

'What is it?' asks Brida.

'*A Compendium of Diverse Sins Both Large and Small and Their According Foods*,' Paul reads the words pressed into the book's cover. 'But our young sin eater hasn't her letters. What a comedy!' A few moments later the door slams shut behind him. Good riddance.

Back in the loft the old ticking pokes at my hips as I crawl onto the mattress. Her mattress. *R . . . Rose?* I let my body soften into the packed places where her big body once rested. *Rebecca?* I find the dip where her head used to lie. *Ruth? Ruth*, a solid name.

And the name of the folk she comes from? Glover? Granger? Garrington? I try all the names I know, but none seems right. My eyes go to her box. I still haven't found a way to help her. It keeps me shifting and turning for hours in the nest of her imprint.

8. PIGEON PIE

I T'S STILL DARK when I'm woken from my fitful sleep by a rapping sound. Somefolk at the door, I think, then sink back into sleep. I dream I'm at home, my true home, and my mother's making fine cakes for Makersday dinner. She keeps knocking the wooden spoon against the bowl. *Thunk. Thunk. Thunk.* Then I'm awake again, the rapping at the door coming harder.

Out of the shutter, I see a pale, little messenger boy, a long woollen nightcap atop his head, calling me to a Recitation that can't wait till morning. I grab my shawl and crawl down the ladder. Brida and Paul are both gone, and the hearth is cold.

'A Recitation for Tilly Howe,' the boy tells me. 'Tilly Howe at the castle.'

The castle. I don't want to go back. Black Fingers is there.

But the castle is where the Sin Eater is too. Ruth, I christened her last night.

You must go, says the still-dark sky. My throat tightens, and my stitches burn.

It's your duty to obey, say the stones on the road.

Their voices grow as loud as the messenger's and finally there's nought to do but go.

—

By the time I reach the castle gate, morning's come and the roads have filled up even though it's Makersday and folk are meant to rest.

Once inside the gate, I follow the messenger to the scroll door. The scroll door again. The castle is a large place with all sorts of rooms and all sorts of folk, so it gives me a cold feeling along the back of my neck to have returned to the same door.

I'm terrified of coming upon Black Fingers. *As long as I'm not alone he can't harm me*, I think, stepping quicker after the messenger ahead. *And as long as I stay silent, I'll be safe.*

We pass the tapestry of the goat-deer, its wefts made of rough wool. Then the one showing unicorns made of finer wool and so brightly dyed the trees behind the creatures look real. I pass more tapestries, each more valuable than the last, so I know we're returning to the Queen's own chambers. Behind the messenger, I trail my fingers across the hangings, feeling the weaves grow finer and finer without even needing to look.

I'm left in the Queen's sitting room again. The Painted Pig who was at Corliss's Recitation is atop a stool embroidering a red figure on a yellow field. Her ruff today is so large I don't know how she sees over it to make her stitches. Above her on the wall is the naked-lady tapestry that looks like the Queen. *Diana of the Wood*, Mush Face had called it.

Mush Face herself is nearby, looking at drawings in a book. I can see shapes with horns and crosses.

The Painted Pig pauses to wave her embroidery at Mush Face's book, 'In plain sight? With the Queen's physician even now interrogating suspected witches?!'

'The ancient scholars were witches, were they?' asks Mush Face, not looking up from the book.

'That is no Greek scholarship, I know that much,' mutters the Painted Pig.

Mush Face turns a page. My slippers are uncomfortable. I look down to find I've put them on the wrong feet, and the left foot, which is longer, pinches in the toe of the right.

'Womanly arts like stitching are too good for you?' the Painted Pig goes on, raising her stitching. I see now it's a badge she's making, most like her family heraldry.

'You're uneasy,' says Mush Face to the Painted Pig, eyes still on her book. 'I could fetch some wine to calm your nerves.'

'I don't need wine,' snaps the Painted Pig. 'There are queer happenings these days. Poppets, pomegranates, deer hearts . . . We are in danger. And you' – the Painted Pig looks at Mush Face – 'sitting there with your books thinking yourself so clever.'

'Perhaps it is because I am.' Mush Face finally looks up. She catches me from the side of her eye but doesn't startle. 'Shall I fetch that wine?' Mush Face offers again.

At that moment a maid arrives. 'Begging your pardons, great ladies,' she curtsies. 'The guards were meant to show the' – she stops and clears her throat – 'the sin eater to the chamberers' rooms.'

'Who is it she's called for?' asks the Painted Pig.

'Tilly Howe, milady. Old Doctor Howe's daughter.'

Like a great tree yielding to a woodcutter, the Painted Pig shrieks once, then faints dead away off her stool.

———

It's her belly that's brought Tilly Howe to bed, something painful that comes in waves. A woman of an age with Tilly, perhaps forty years, sits nearby. 'Tilly, to think, you were right as rain not one day ago.'

'Oh, Meg,' Tilly says to the friend, 'I never felt the like. You must send word to my father. He's only a day's walk away.'

'Let me call the Queen's physician,' Meg offers. That must be the Willow Tree.

'He's a conjuror,' spits Tilly.

'He's not your father,' Meg says. 'But he's learned.'

'A sham, the belly knows,' Tilly mutters. *The belly knows.* My mother would say that sometimes. It's for when you know something deep, deep in your guts, even if reason says it's wrong.

'The Queen sent lemon balm,' Meg says, I think to cheer Tilly.

Tilly smiles a small smile. Then a wave of pain comes, and it's almost like a fit the way Tilly's body seizes. Her breath quickens, 'Has the . . . has she come?'

Meg looks my way. 'Yes, she's here.'

Tilly looks over, and her head jerks back. 'Not her! The Queen. I had hoped she might . . .' Tilly braces for another wave. When it passes, her face's gone slack, like a sheet dunked in water. 'Is it time for the sin eater, then?'

Meg says nothing.

'Don't leave my side.'

'Won't never, Tilly. Won't never.'

I bring a stool to Tilly's bed. Meg clutches her hand. 'Think, you'll soon join the Maker.'

'I don't know, Meg,' Tilly pinches the bedsheet. 'I've my sins.' Tears well up in Tilly's eyes, and another painful wave shakes them loose.

'You helped bring enough souls into this world to balance whatever sins you carry,' Meg clucks. Tilly nods, and then there's silence.

'The Unseen is now seen. The Unheard is now heard,' I begin. 'The sins of your flesh become the sins of mine to be borne to my grave in silence. Speak.'

Tilly turns her head. 'Well, what have we got?' Now that she can look at me, she assays me good and proper. 'Just a young thing. What are you, fourteen? Of an age with the Queen when I first met her, oh, what a time!' she says. Another wave of pain takes hold, and she waits for it to pass before sinking back into her memories. 'My da worked for the Queen's stepmother Katryna. He was her physician, my da. Katryna wasn't queen any more by that point, of course. Katryna wasn't royal blood, so when the old king died, the crown went to his daughter Maris. Bethany was just a girl, living in Katryna's household.

'Oh, but Katryna was kind to my father, let him bring me along when he worked. She was the one who warned him to burn his books when Maris came to the throne. A true believer in the new faith, he still is.' Tilly holds herself still a moment, waiting for the pain to come and go.

'Should get to it, shouldn't I?' Tilly gathers herself. 'Goodness me. Here it is: I always liked a sweetie, I did. I fret my mother so, like as I was to pluck a plum from a pie before it was served,' Tilly breaks again for the pain. But her story brings faint pink to her cheeks, and she seems to fare a little better than before. She goes through gluttony (her love of sweets), drunkenness (her love of wine), white lies from helping mothers in childbirth ('the worst is past, now's just pushing'). Like her father she had the knack for healing. She takes me through her life, sin by sin, pausing for pain.

My own mind wanders back to when I was young. When you're little it's like each moment is its own lifetime. I remember collecting leaves just past dawn one morning, brown, orange, yellow and soaked with rain so they stuck in great, flat cakes to the rake. Da and Mother came outside ready for the Makerhall, steam coming from their mouths like two pots on the fire. It was after the purgers came, but I still had the prayer beads Da had given me hanging from my apron.

'Must throw them on the rubbish heap, May.' Da's eyes

were full of brown leaves as he said it. I didn't understand why a pretty gift from my da could matter to grown folk. 'Do it now,' he said while my mother stamped her foot to loosen a clod of mud from her shoe.

I threw my rake to the ground and refused. Mother had to hold me while Da took the beads. Later I understood folk were killed for such things. Wars were fought for such things, and might be again. Maris's burnings, Queen Bethany's purgers. Faith is a bloody business.

'And then, well,' Tilly goes on. 'Seeing as I never married, I kept assisting my father in Katryna's household. Katryna was still young. Oh, and clever. She and the Queen's governess, Corliss, and the other ladies all at their books, studying, studying, all the time. That sham of a doctor here in Bethany's court was about then too. Not a physician yet, but a tutor. He taught the ladies the old tongues, Greek and Hebrew. Spoke three languages, Katryna did. Knew mathematics. Astrology, too. Mmm.' She smiles at the memory. Then a grimace passes over her face. 'But she chose to remarry, Katryna did. To Baron Seymaur. A wolf, that man. Katryna was blind in love. And you couldn't say they weren't a hand-some couple. Good families, both with claims to the throne. Of course, the baron lost his head for such ambitions. But back then, before all that, they married, and Katryna was with child before you could blink.

'My father served her through her confinement. Died not long after giving birth, she did. Her wolf of a husband betrayed her. That's why she died. Not her body, but her heart broke.' She squeezes Meg's hand and waits for a wave to pass.

'And little Bethany, barely past childhood, living in the same house. Never imagined she'd be queen, what with her married sister on the throne sure to soon have an heir—' Tilly suddenly pauses, and not for pain.

'But then,' she says. 'But then.' Something's stuck in her thoughts. 'I shouldn't speak of it. I spoke of it once and I fear . . . But I must, mustn't I?' She looks at Meg.

'Cast off your burdens,' Meg comforts.

Tilly looks away and takes a ragged breath. 'Is it treason to deceive one of royal blood?'

'Why, Tilly!' hisses Meg.

'Oh, now, Meg, I've lived a life.'

'But, Tilly, you surely did no such thing,' Meg's eyes are wide and white in her face. 'As I heard it, when Katryna went into seclusion for the birth, she was already doing poorly. Whatever you told her as she lay dying was surely not deception.'

Tilly shakes her head. 'Wasn't her. I made a promise to Bethany.'

Meg's head bobs in hesitation like a cat sniffing about a new room. 'Tilly?'

Tilly grasps suddenly for Meg's hand, her eyes closed tight. 'Coming quicker now,' she whispers. More tears well up. 'We all made a promise to Bethany, but we broke it. What could we do? We wanted her to be queen. Oh, it burns so!'

'Your belly?' asks Meg.

'My lips,' answers Tilly. 'Give me the cup, I'm like to die of thirst.'

Her lips, I see with startlement, have turned bluish. I feel

126

the same niggle as when I saw Corliss's blue lips. But this time, the memory comes into my head, the picture clear and well lit. I know what makes lips turn blue, the body shake, and foam come out of the mouth. It's not the falling sickness or the flux, though it looks the same for most of its course. That's why the herbs are so dear to purchase. And why, when the gallipot described them to my Daffrey uncles, it was safe inside their house in the black of night. Corliss and Tilly were poisoned.

———

I tried my best to forget every moment from my dark year at the Daffreys. But it doesn't mean I managed to. My uncles were upright men, which in thieves' cant means top-of-the-heap rogues. Before going to the Daffreys I hadn't known that rogues and other crooked folk have ranks and orders just like nobles do, with the most cunning of the rogues right at the top. My uncles were the rulers, my granddam the dowager queen.

All manner of rotten men tramped through the Daffrey house considering themselves lords and dukes of roguery. Highway robbers who would kill a man for his calfskin boots, priggers who thieved horses, jarkmen selling begging passports. There were others, but their names I forgot. Or at least tried to during those nights when they'd fill up the kitchen. Me cooking them supper. Them eating my pottage, looking at me through my clothes, though I was only a girl, so I'd shiver even beside the fire. But I do remember a certain type. Gallipots.

Gallipots were men who would have been apothecaries if the herbs and concoctions they sold ever helped a body towards health. Their wares nudged folk the other way. How plain or subtle the nudge was a difference of price.

One night when I'd been at the Daffreys a few months, the rogues came one after the other, first filling the twin benches of the kitchen table, then the stools from the hearth, then the two pails, overturned, then sitting atop the firewood placed on its end, and finally standing all along the wall over to the stove where I was stirring the soup. It was a meeting to divide out territory and collect duties for the right to work it. Rogues pay duties too. But not to the Queen. These duties went to Misgett, my elder uncle, the king rogue.

Uric, the younger uncle, more silent, but frightening in his silence, drew the map of the area in oat flour on the table. When it was done, and everyone knew their place, Misgett banged his cup on the table and called attention. A new peer was joining the ranks, and it was time for his baptism. The men pushed to the side so there was a place for the new man, Barnabas he was called, to kneel before Misgett. Misgett rose from his seat. 'We see you be a man, is it so?'

Barnabas answered, 'As I've handled a woman, I say so.' The rogues all cheered.

'We see you be an Anglishman, is it so?' said Misgett next.

'As my mother was an Anglishwoman, I say so.' More cheers.

'We see you be a rogue, is it so?'

'As I pay allegiance with this purse, I say so.' Barnabas raised a little sack to Misgett, who shook it all around the room, spilling the coins for the men to grab for.

Uric banged the table for quiet. Misgett raised his cup. 'I

welcome you as a man, an Anglishman, and a rogue!' And with that he poured his beer over Barnabas's head right at the kitchen table, leaving a sweet puddle for me to mop up later.

Then, it was time for Barnabas to share his 'game' with his new peers. He took out a leather box. Then he brought in the dogs.

There were three of them. Not skinny, little mongrels that root around in rubbish, but sturdy farm dogs. They were nervous to come into a room full of men, but Barnabas had them muzzled and leashed so in they came. Two were of sound health, the third doing poorly, its breath coming hard and whining as if pained.

Barnabas opened the leather box. Inside were three glass jars wrapped like new babes in wool fluff. Inside the jars were his poisons, for Barnabas was a gallipot.

The third dog, the one doing poorly, Barnabas told the rogues, had been given poison that worked in small bits each day from one of the jars. Over a month, it'd kill a grown man with none the wiser. Barnabas kicked the dog hard in the gut. It fell with a howl and couldn't get up. The men cheered while the dog tried to crawl to the door. Misgett waved, and a lower rogue dragged the dog out into the yard.

Barnabas brought the second dog forward. Then he opened one of the jars from the box and poured three drops into a bloody slurry in a bowl. He let the dog at it. It dived for the bowl, lapping up the blood. The other hale dog barked and leapt for the bowl. Barnabas must have been starving them so he'd be sure they'd eat.

It took only a moment for the poison to work. The yelps of the dog were so piteous, I covered my ears. 'Burning a hole right through the dog's throat, it is,' said Barnabas. 'In a man, you can see it more plainly because there's no fur.'

The dog's yelps frittered into whines. Misgett waved his hand again, and that dog was dragged out too. Not long after, its whining stopped.

Barnabas removed one more jar from his box. This one had a powder inside. With a gloved hand, he took several pinches and mixed it in a pan of offal. The last dog gobbled it down.

'A pinch'll take a day or two to do its work,' Barnabas said. 'But I've given more so as to see the effects quicker.' The men filled their cups again, but they weren't halfway drunk before the howls began. The dog shook and howled and howled and shook. When its bowels opened, Misgett had the same lower rogue take the dog outside.

'Looks like the bloody flux,' one of the other rogues said.

'Indeed,' agreed Barnabas. 'But it can be known for a few moments just before death by blue lips, foaming mouth, and great shaking.'

It was one of the worst nights at the Daffreys in a year of worsts.

Bastard Daffreys. They gave me something useful after all.

—

I'm snapped back to the moment by Tilly moaning. She's growing more senseless by the moment. She curls to her side and whispers something to the bed curtains.

I lean forward but I've missed the words. 'What did you say?' I urge her. But Tilly doesn't reply.

Meg squeezes Tilly's hand and looks away. 'She said there'll be deer heart on her coffin too.'

9. MUTTON CHOP

IT'S LIKE SEEING a big, clawed print in the mud. The first time you see it, you think, sure it's bigger than a dog's, but mayhap the mud was soft, mayhap the dog's foot was swollen. But after the second print, you know it's wolf.

Two ladies poisoned. Two deer hearts on coffins. Something dark's afoot. Surely others must have noticed. I name all the folk who saw Corliss and Tilly in their final moments and might have witnessed the signs of poison.

Healers? The Willow Tree, the Queen's physician, saw to Corliss, but not to Tilly.

Maids? Folk like Tilly don't have chambermaids.

Who might have come and seen the prints in the mud?

Me. I'm the only folk who saw how both women died.

The only folk who heard both Recitations. What do I do with this knowledge? I know I should tell somefolk, but how?

Da said things just want to work right, but they're getting more broken and muddled. There's only one thing the poisoning has shown: it wasn't the witch's poppet that killed Corliss. I know that much for certain now. There's another fiend at work as well. A witch and a poisoner. I wish the other Sin Eater were here. *Ruth, I named her*, I remind myself.

Meg's waiting for me. I list off the foods. Clotted cream for gluttony, plain cream for envy, hippocras for drunkenness, mustard seed for lies, whipped syllabub for deception, until there's none left, only Tilly's last whispered words hanging in the air between us. Meg's eyes stay keen on the floor rushes, waiting to see if I add the heart.

Beyond us, on the bed, Tilly begins to shake again. White foam comes to her lips.

I close the Recitation. 'Any last words?' But Tilly is beyond that.

When I come out of the scroll door, for a moment the sunlight warms away the muddle. I take a deep breath. The air is still just air. The stones are still just stones. The day is still day. If I walked away now back to Dungsbrook, mayhap I could leave these grim dealings behind.

But then I look out across the courtyard and see the tower. Underneath it is the dungeon. That's where Ruth is.

My guts say, *Flee.* They say it loud and plain so I barely

even notice the uneven cobbles beneath my thin slippers, still on the wrong feet.

It takes fewer steps than I think to cross the courtyard, fewer steps than I want to reach the dungeon. There's no guards to block me going in. It's only going out that's forbidden.

Ten mouldy, green stairs take me down into the earth. At the bottom is a doorway guarded by a lumpy man on a stool with a beard as furry as the mouldy steps. Beyond him is a stone hallway that's wet like it's weeping. The hallway has wooden doors every few paces along it until it's too dark to see. It's not like the jail I was in, a big, earthen room with a lock on it and everyfolk crowded in. This one's only for traitors and highborn folk.

'Who's been granted a visit from a sin eater?' Mouldy Beard says aloud. His voice echoes down the passage.

An older guard wearing a neat, grey beard shaped like a spade comes out of the dark corridor. He lets his eyes rove across me without settling. 'None to die today. Send her away.'

'How?' asks Mouldy Beard like he's been asked to remove a snake.

'None to die today,' Grey Beard says louder.

Like a squirrel, I make a dash around them, expecting their pull at my clothing. But all they do is yell. At each other. 'You let her pass!' scolds Grey Beard.

'What was I meant to do?' says Mouldy Beard.

'What does she intend? Follow her!'

I hear their footsteps behind me as I peer in a small hole

cut into the first door. Inside the cell's a young man on his knees in prayer.

Inside the next is a large man lying on a dirty pile of rushes, still as the dead.

'She's looking for somefolk,' says Mouldy Beard.

The following cell is larger. It has a bed and a table. There's a woman in a fine dress writing on a parchment, a nub of a beeswax candle lighting her work.

'She's looking at the Eucharistian countess,' says Mouldy Beard.

'You needn't recite what we both see plainly!' curses Grey Beard.

The countess looks up at the voices.

'Have you a parcel for me?' she says to the guards in a tired way. 'I was to be brought one by my kinfolk.'

There's some quiet, and then Mouldy Beard calls, 'There was, milady.' His footsteps go and come back. He unlocks the countess's door, a basket in his hand. It's covered in a yellow cloth embroidered with a red badge like the Painted Pig was stitching.

'And would you have given it me had I not asked for it?' says the countess like she's in her own home, addressing a servant. 'Or kept it for yourself?'

Mouldy Beard looks at his shoes and locks the door again. But Grey Beard says, 'You're a traitor to the Queen, so mayhap you shouldn't complain.'

'Perhaps you should not address me so boldly!' the countess says back through the door. 'I may be Eucharistian, I will not deny my faith, but I have never plotted to overthrow

Queen Bethany. My own cousin serves as a lady of the bedchamber! We are loyal.'

'Eucharistian spies all over Queen Bethany's court like vermin. Eve's own daughters,' says Grey Beard, nasty-like.

'I was a dear friend of the dowager Queen Katryna, Bethany's stepmother, and lived in her household the same years Queen Bethany did. She should recall as much and take care lest the cuckoo call too loudly.' Then the countess sings a rhyme:

> The cuckoo is a sly bird
> It never builds a nest
> It will not claim its hatchling
> It leaves it to the rest.

'You speaking riddles now? I'll call the witch finder,' says Grey Beard.

The countess doesn't answer him. 'There's only candles and cakes in the parcel. My cousin was to send me ink.'

'So you can write your spy letters?' asks Grey Beard.

'Give me my ink!'

Grey Beard says nothing back.

After the countess's cell, the dungeon's weepy walls disappear in a long, dark curve. There's a sudden howl, like from an animal, coming from the black that makes my guts drop. What will I find if I go on?

But she's here. And she's the only folk I've got left.

'She's going to the interrogation cells,' Mouldy Beard says. I hear the sound of Grey Beard's fist hitting Mouldy Beard's flesh.

A few paces into the dark curve I see a whisper of light. It's another several paces before it brightens into a lamp lighting a second row of doors. A low howl comes from the first door. A bitter taste comes up into my mouth as I step to the peephole.

Inside is like a shadow image of a picture I've seen before. The Willow Tree, the Queen's physician, is there. He's leaning over a bowl of urine, just like he did when he tended to Corliss. But this time he's next to an ancient, shrivelled woman, and he's not trying to heal her.

She's dressed in rags, and her face and neck have small burns and needle pricks all over them. The Willow Tree sniffs at the urine. 'Inconclusive, again,' he says. 'You carry your secrets close, mistress.' He places the bowl of urine on the cell floor. As he does, there's a glint from his hand. It's the witch pricker on the nail of his little finger. He lowers the thick needle towards her. Its tip doesn't shine because it's dark with her blood.

I remind myself the old woman may well have made the poppet that was found, the one fashioned to curse a highborn lady with bristles stuck in the belly and cunny. That's blackest magic. I hurry to the next cell door and look in.

A whimper escapes my lips when I see the Sin Eater. It's dim in the cell, but I see her nonetheless. She's sitting on the floor, facing away, hanging over herself. The stones that will press her are in a pile nearby.

I gruff to pull her attention. I sound like an animal, a horse or a cow. But the Sin Eater is as still as the stones. She must be drunk. But no, there's no drink here. Not in a dungeon. Only cold stones and waiting and the much worse that comes when the waiting ends.

I don't know what to do, so I wait too. I wait with her. Mayhap my breaths in and out will take the place of words. Mayhap she'll hear the catches in it and know I've come to comfort her. That I've given her a name. That I'm sorry. That I miss her.

And then I see the blood on the floor.

It's under the pressing stones, a dark carpet that I missed at first because of the dim light.

Mayhap it's old blood, but even as I think this, I know it's not true. *Oh, Ruth.*

I look closely at her hands. The fingers are dark and blistered. No, not blistered. Burst. Burst from blood being squeezed until her fingertips split. She's not waiting. She's dead. I'm looking at the memory of her, the husk that was discarded to the side after the stones pressed the life out of her. I'm too late.

Grey Beard's voice makes me jump. I forgot the guards were behind me. 'Was good fortune the little sin eater had sense enough to eat when the big one didn't.'

What must Ruth's face look like? Her big chestnut eyes?

Grey Beard's voice goes on. 'If the little one had baulked too, they couldn't have put the elder sin eater under the press. The Queen's secretary would've had to do something else. Can't have a town with no sin eaters.'

A drum thunders in my ears. It's my own blood coming hard. Could I have kept her from dying? Did I make her expendable by choosing to eat?

'Couldn't they just make another sin eater?' asks Mouldy Beard.

'It's not like being made apprentice to a smithy,' huffs Grey Beard. 'Making a new sin eater takes care.'

'Just need a girl, don't you?'

The guards go on talking like their words haven't grabbed hold of my heart. Like they're talking about crops in the field or if it's like to rain.

'Not just a girl,' says Grey Beard. 'Think on it: if the recorder pronounced a girl of your own blood and kin to be the next sin eater, what would you do?'

'I'd never let them!' spits Mouldy Beard.

'You'd be shouting in the road in protest!' agrees Grey Beard. 'As would every honest man. So the recorder has to choose with care who he makes a sin eater. Our recorder is vindictive.' Grey Beard nods towards Ruth, dead in her cell. 'His wife lost two babes one after another, then had one that was simple. So he cursed her back, made her into that sin eater there.'

I remember the two bone pendants from the box at the foot of the mattress. Her two lost children. Is that why she sat on the stool before the hearth? Is that why she moaned and drank? Mouldy Beard's feet shift on the stones. 'And what'd this young one do?'

'How the fug should I know?' says Grey Beard. 'Why's the body still here?'

Mouldy Beard passes me, key in hand. Then there's a grunt and Mouldy Beard's heavy breath as he drags Ruth's body out. Two dragging sounds for each of his footsteps. Then a rest. Two drags, then a rest. A word in each drag. I try to catch the shape of the two words. You . . . ? No, one word:

Judas.

Her body says it as he drags her from the bloody cell. Judas, the betrayer. I ate the deer heart that was never recited and so Black Fingers, the Queen's secretary, was free to kill her.

My head shakes like a dog shaking its wet fur, but the name won't shake off. Mouldy Beard drags her body past me. There's mud at the sides of her mouth and eyes, mud caked into her nail beds. No, not mud. Blood.

'Oh, Ruth,' my lips trace. My breath fritters away into a howl. A howl at her pain and my sorrow and the loneliness that presses on my chest like the stones that killed her. My lips grab at the sounds coming from my mouth, making them into whispers. *'Forgive me, forgive me!'*

It was right that I was made a sin eater. I am vile. I am filthy. I turn from the cell and run past the guards, up, up and away, trying to outrun my guilt, my regret, my grief.

10. BITTER GREENS

I run out of the castle. I run through town and don't stop until I reach the great Makerhall in the town square. I think somehow if I can hear the High Makerman's prayers or dip my hand in the light from the coloured windows, mayhap I can be clean again. I don't know what else to do.

The road is full of folk in their white clothes on their way to noontide service. I push straight through, my breath all caught up in my chest. *Forgive me, Ruth.*

Ahead of me, I see the statues of Hagi Saul and Hagi Gabriel cut into the stone beside the Makerhall doors. I hear folk saying, 'Peace to you,' and the Makermen just inside the doors answering back the same way.

But before I make it in the door, there's a sharp hiss in

my face, then the crook of a Makerman's staff an inch from my nose. 'The sin eater will not defile the Maker's house!' a voice shrieks.

Folk stutter and spin away all around me. The Makerman jabs his staff forward, hitting me hard in the pocket of my shoulder. Another blow strikes my ear from the side. I look up to see a second Makerman raising his staff to strike. 'Sin monger!' he yells.

I turn to flee, but there's too many folk coming in for me to move away. A man nearby starts yelling along with the Makerman, 'Sin monger!' Then, somefolk's hat whips at my back, hard enough to bite. Another folk takes off his hat and hits me with it too. The cries of 'Sin monger' get louder than the 'Peace to yous' until they're all I can hear. It seems every-folk is yelling and hitting, shoving and herding me back from the door. I can't see through the bodies and hats striking me, but suddenly I lose my footing, and I'm tumbling along with a young girl down into the ditch beside the road. The girl's mother screams and pulls the girl up by the arm, swatting her across the bottom for shame and hugging her for comfort all at the same time. I wait in the ditch with my hands covering my head until I'm sure no folk are still striking me.

The crowd has gone quiet. I look up at the line of folk outside the Makerhall. They have turned away, shading their faces with their hands. None cry 'Sin monger' any more. A moment passes. I start to hear quiet 'Peace to yous' up by the door again. The queue begins to move. The folk file into the Makerhall until the road above me is empty.

Dirty water's soaking up into my shift. I feel it cold across my left thigh and bottom. What I think is, *I've no soap at Ruth's house.*

The other thoughts of guilt and regret and grief are there too, but for some reason it's the soap that sticks. I swallow a little giggle. Soap.

I climb out of the ditch. I can hear the High Makerman starting the service inside. 'O Maker, have mercy upon us miserable sinners.'

My lips move without thinking, along with the response, 'May it be.'

I always loved saying 'May it be' at the end of each prayer. Hearing everyfolk uttering my name, May, like I was part of the Maker's prayers and mysteries.

Outside the door, I look at the statue of Hagi Gabriel. His face is kinder than Hagi Saul's, and his hands open at his sides in welcome. But there's nothing welcoming here.

The High Makerman goes on. 'Dear brethren, we assemble to give thanks for the great benefits we receive at the Maker's hands.' What benefits have I received? I can't think of a one.

Every folk answers again, but this time, like Hagi Gabriel, I'm quiet.

—

The graveyard has lots of markers, some worn down, some with edges still square. One marker has a picture scratched on its back in white chalk: an *x* with eyes on either side. Witch's markings, most like.

There's just a small stone for Da. It was all I could pay for. I lie down on the green shoots of grass over his grave.

My shift sticks to the back of my legs, and my cunny is wet with dirty ditch water. I lie for a long time. The sky above me becomes dark and cold. Stars come out through clouds that look like carrot tops. Lying above Da's bones like on a bed, I understand why sin eaters were made. Carrying such feelings is too much for one little heart, too much for one body. There must be some hope of shedding regret, grief, sorrow, sloughing them off like a skin and going into death free and light. Else we'd never be able to live.

Night airs bring fever. I'll wait for them to seep into my nose and eyes and ears. They'll dry up my life, and I'll leave this world. Whether I'll go to Eve or the Maker, I don't know.

The moon passes above me, lighting a beech tree thick with new leaves. I wait. But nothing happens. After days of filling my belly, I'm coursing with life, warm and sound, and itching to move. The Makermen wouldn't help me. Now death won't either.

I roll over so I can see Da's stone. I stick my finger in our etched name. *O-W-E-N-S*, I trace the letters over. Grey grit gets caught in my fingernail. I trace the letters again. The wide *O*. The doubled-up *W*. The *E* and *N*. The *S* to finish. I do it again. And again. Over and over until my thoughts get plain. If I'm to live, then I need to fix this mess. I fold my hands.

Ruth, I pray, *I vow to make this right.*

I will prove myself Da's daughter and repair things.

May it be.

May it be.

May it be.

11. NEAT'S TONGUE

I'S WITCHING HOUR. Even the whores are tucked away when I walk down tavern row towards home. I feel a swell of relief when I smell the first stink of Dungsbrook. Soon I'll be tucked away in my home too.

I turn onto my lane. I pass the path to the woad yard and the Domus Conversorum. For a moment, I think I hear a flute coming from the old, stone ruin where Jews had to live until they converted to the new faith. My guts get light thinking about unconverted souls that might be trapped in the building, but it's not spirits I hear, just wind passing through its crumbling chimney.

I'm still shaking off the shivers in my guts when I step up to my door, so I don't notice the shadows coming round the side of the house. One slips between me and the door, one blocks the road, just like rogue cut-throats. Which is what they must be. Black Fingers's men sent to finish what he began.

Only a little while ago, I was wishing for death to take me, but now that it's come knocking, I want none of it. The cut-throat in the road is a thick man with a kerchief across his lower face. He raises a short sword. Without thought, I barrel into the second cut-throat standing at my door. His own sword's in his hand, but still at his side. Though I'm smaller than him, he stumbles back. The shoddy doorframe gives way, and the two of us fall through, landing hard in the main room of my house.

I scramble off the second cut-throat as quick as I can. He's scrambling too, his breath coming heavy.

'Stick her!' yells the first cut-throat through his kerchief. He's blocking the doorway. The second cut-throat is back on his feet a few paces from me. He raises his blade. I dart towards the back door, but he cuts over in front of it before I get there. I stumble back towards the hearth. A cut-throat at each door. I'm trapped.

I grab wildly behind me. My hand finds the old pot. I fling it at the second cut-throat, but he ducks easily.

'Stick her!' the first cut-throat yells again from the doorway, and the second cut-throat takes a step towards me.

As I shrink back in the corner waiting for his blow, my foot treads on something. Suddenly there's movement behind me. I cry out in startlement, but I'm not the only one making noise.

'What the fug is that?' the second cut-throat cries. He raises his sword, but in protection not attack.

I wheel around to see a misshapen horror rising inches from me. Black, looming eyes. A sunken hole for a nose. A wrinkled maw with shattered teeth. Brida.

'It's the very devil,' whispers the first cut-throat from the doorway.

Brida's ragged shawl falls from her body. The low hearth light flickers across her sunken pit of a shoulder. She raises the shaft of bone that finishes one arm and aims it at me. 'She cursed me,' comes Brida's little voice. 'I was once a man like you. I came to do her harm, but she cursed me so. Look at my man parts now.' Brida lifts her skirt to show her cunny.

The second cut-throat begins to pray. Brida staggers towards him on legs wet with weeping sores. 'If you harm the sin eater, you will share my curse.'

The first cut-throat has already fled the doorway, leaving it open for the second cut-throat to follow. He wastes not a moment thundering out in his heeled boots.

—

'Broke the doorframe entirely.' Paul climbs down the loft's ladder.

'Run off like rabbits,' an unfamiliar voice sounds from behind him. 'Good show, Brida. Inspired improvisation!'

My heart is thumping, and my arms feel light and tingly. Still, I note that my vagabonds have returned. And increased, like mould or toadstools.

'My apologies,' the new man says. 'Paul and I violated the intimate chamber. We heard a scuffle at the door and fled.'

'You waste words, Frederick,' says Paul. 'She's a sin eater; she doesn't speak.'

'But she can hear, can she not?'

'What does it matter?' Paul says back.

'Beasts are calmed by the voice,' says Frederick. 'Even pig men speak to their sows before the slaughter.' He bites playfully at the air. 'I'll keep her from gobbling us up.'

Brida sets herself down by the hearth. Paul goes to build up the fire for her. After the unkind way he's spoken to her before, I'm surprised by his care.

Brida's spent by her act. As my heart calms, I find I am too. But I look over this Frederick before I go to my bed. He's older, the age my da was when he passed. But he's healthy and better dressed than Paul and Brida. Working at some trade. But not a reputable one or he'd be at an inn. I don't expect any more notice from a man who likened me to a sow, but as I cross to the ladder, Frederick calls out, eyes looking past my shoulder, 'I solicit pardon for our poor manners. Paul has Saturn's spleen. We do her wrong that would be, should she deign to accept us, our most gracious host.'

An actor. One, I suspect, who's mocking me. I need quiet for my nerves to settle, not a house of rude vagabonds and grown pantoboys. I climb the ladder to the loft.

There's still a little tingle left in my arms. Cut-throats are as suspicious as any folk, I reassure myself. They aren't like to come back. And yet what Grey Beard said in the dungeon wasn't true. Black Fingers is willing to murder the only sin eater. I am expendable. Mayhap he's having the recorder make another sin eater right now. My heart starts its thumping again. How do I stop Black Fingers from coming after me?

He certainly could be the one who poisoned the women and placed deer hearts on their coffins. Mayhap if I sort out the mess, he'll be executed. My heart thumps soften a hair. I just need to sort out this mess.

If it were a jammed lock, how would Da fix it?

Let it tell you.

I lie back and wait. My stitches itch. I do my best not to touch them. My shift is stiff from the dirty ditch water. I crinkle the cloth with my hand to soften it. Then my foot starts to jiggle. I take another breath and try to listen to the lock again.

Finally, finally, something speaks. But it's not the lock, it's my noticings from the past days. The noticings I told to walls or stones or swallowed whole. Corliss and Tilly were both poisoned. What have they in common? Not much. Corliss was highborn and Tilly hardly more than a servant. But Corliss was a governess, so she would have lived in the household with the Queen when she was a girl. Tilly said she did too. So they were together in the house where Bethany lived growing up. It was Bethany's stepmother's house. The old king's last wife, Katryna.

I wait for more noticings to come. Instead, Frederick's voice comes through the floorboards like bees. It's bothersome. But then it's calming too, the chitter and chatter of a home. I stick my hand in between my thighs where it's warm, and the flesh feels like bread dough. There's more flesh there than before, I think, as I listen to my vagabond squatters.

It sounds as if Frederick and his acting troupe have come to town to play in some revels. The Norman prince, who is a stranger and an enemy, is sending an emissary to ask for Queen Bethany's hand in marriage to make an alliance.

'She'll never marry the Norman prince,' says Paul. 'He's Eucharistian.'

'I would put money on the Queen's secretary,' says Frederick. 'I heard the Queen stabbed a serving girl's hand for batting eyes at him. She's said to be quite the jealous lover.'

'You don't believe she's a virgin?' Brida asks.

'They say the Norman prince sent a doctor here to perform a test to see if she is,' answers Frederick.

Brida clucks her tongue. 'She'd lose her throne if she's not a virgin. She's unmarried.'

I hear Frederick's laugh. 'Then no folk better find her out. It's all a great pageant anyhow. Pageantry is power. The Virgin Queen. Now that is quite a role,' Frederick laughs again. 'If she were clever, and I believe she is, she would encourage her likeness to the Holy Virgin and convince everyfolk she has divine right to the throne. Why would she want to marry anyhow? All she'd get is a king to take all the decisions himself and leave her sewing in the corner.'

'Then why the suitors?' asks Brida.

'Why, Brida,' says Frederick saucily. 'How does the courtesan keep her conquests happy? By making each and every one believe he has her heart.'

'Oh, Freddie,' chastens Brida. Likening the Queen to a

courtesan is a fine way to lose your head. 'But she needs an heir.'

'Mmm,' agrees Paul. 'Or the throne goes to . . . well, now, who does it go to?'

'There's a question,' picks up Frederick. 'Let's see. Maris and Bethany's father had six wives. All the children are now dead, except our dear Queen, Maker keep her.'

'What about the king's last wife?' asks Paul.

'Katryna.'

'Didn't Katryna have a daughter with her next husband, the Baron Seymaur?' says Paul. 'Surely the daughter has a strong claim.'

'No, you see, the old king had royal blood,' Frederick's voice gets louder like Gracie Manners's would when she knew something none of the rest of us did. 'His wives were only queens because they were married to him. When he died, Katryna wasn't queen any more. She became the dowager queen, which is simply an honorific that means next to nothing. The moment the king died, the throne passed to his eldest child, Maris.'

Brida speaks, 'So who's next in line?'

'No folk knows,' Frederick answers. 'Queen Bethany must either produce an heir or name a successor. The Eucharistians hope she will name her Northern cousin. The Norman prince hopes to wed and get a child on her, as does every lord in Angland. The only thing we know is that once Bethany has an heir, she will lose a good part of her power. Everyfolk will be wanting to charm the heir instead of her. That's why I wager she doesn't accept any of her suitors.'

'At least the Norman emissary will have the revels to enjoy before bringing Bethany's refusal to his prince,' says Paul. 'Poor bugger.'

'It will be splendid! A feast with jugglers and music and our little play as its capstone.' Frederick goes on. 'Paul, you would not believe the production. They've demanded we build an entire stage with multiple scenery panels and a device to raise and lower them!'

'Multiple panels?' asks Paul.

'It seems some Anglish lord or other witnessed the Italians changing the scenery from act to act during their plays. I suspect the scenery did not move at all; the lord was simply drunk.' Brida snorts in laughter. 'But jests aside, the lord provided drawings of a rope and pulley system fitted to drop a flat panel from above the stage into a groove on the stage floor. Imagine, a scenery panel hanging above the stage as you are performing. Sword of Damocles, indeed.'

'And what will you play?' asks Paul.

'Something diverting, but not too taxing, composed by the Cambridge wits,' says Frederick.

'And who will play the young ladies?' asks Paul in a tight kind of way. 'Is it Andrew? It is, isn't it?'

'Do you remember when you played Dame Custance?' says Frederick, as if it follows on Paul's question. 'It was in Leicester Town, where the mercers' guild was defiling the *Fall of Man*, have I got it right?'

Paul laughs. 'The mayor asked if we had anything that "skirted the faith" as he put it.'

'Skirted the faith?' says Brida.

'All were afeard of the faith plays at that time,' says Paul. 'You never knew who you might offend.'

'It was a reprieve, in truth,' says Frederick. 'After years of arriving to town, appearing to the mayor, and having him ask if we might play a little interlude entitled *The Second Shepherd's Play*.'

'How many times did we perform it?'

'A dozen times a summer. Two dozen! And when new plays abound,' says Frederick. '*Ralph Roister Doister* we chose in Leicester Town. Heavens above, you were a good player – are, you *are* a good player.' Frederick corrects. 'Apologies, that was thoughtless of me.'

'No, no, you have the right of it. That life is done,' Paul answers quick, but the happy in his voice is gone. There's a sound like drinking and the clunk of a jug being set down.

'Oh, I haven't told you the best part,' Frederick says like he's trying to cheer Paul. 'The revels, including our play, are meant to take place inside a great tent pitched in a field east of the castle.'

'In a field?' asks Brida. 'Whyever would they do such a thing?'

Frederick's voice gets louder again. 'It's plainly meant to recall the exquisite spectacle of the Queen's father. The old king once had a great tent of gold cloth built in which to meet a Norman ally. He hosted the most magnificent revels ever witnessed on these shores.' Frederick drinks, then sighs. 'I've witnessed a tent atop a stage, but never a stage within a tent. It beggars belief!'

'I've never heard the like,' Brida says.

Frederick's voice gets softer. 'Paul, you could find work. You are still strong, and we'll need folk who know how to build a stage and arrange a tiring room. And we could always use a good dresser backstage. You are a knack with a needle.'

'I have descended to such a state,' Paul says. 'I could not . . . I would not wish to be seen.'

'You are not the first to be so scarred by painting his face. Why, it's practically a badge of the trade. And you know all those highborn women suffer too. It's why their layers of paint grow thicker with each year they age – to cover their scars.'

'None are so awfully disfigured as me.'

'You were beautiful,' Frederick says, gentle-like.

'I was irresistible,' says Paul. 'I was given a ruby ring. Did you know? A true gem, and I would know. I have gentle blood.'

'You were loved,' Frederick agrees. There's a scraping sound, like somefolk getting up from the stool. 'Where are you going, Paul? Good company is the only balm for hard living.'

'I'm not distressed, I'm just fetching more wood,' Paul says back, and the door to the yard opens and shuts. It's plain he's lying.

'He's a fair piece worse than last I saw him,' Frederick says almost too low for me to hear. 'He sweats melancholy.'

'He's of a fickle humour these days,' Brida says back. 'He calls me such things! Eve's handmaiden and, what is it now,' Brida searches for the words, 'foul Mefite?'

'Mephitis, the goddess of sulphurous stink,' offers

Frederick. 'Paul's the bastard son of a lord, you know. His sire educated him. Refused him his name, but equipped him with a ranging knowledge to call upon when cursing his companions.'

'All the same, he cares for me as kin,' says Brida with warmth in her voice. 'So there you have it.'

'He ever had a kind heart,' sighs Frederick. 'Bruised and beaten as it is. Justice would see that villain whipped who stole his heart and then cast him off when he was no longer beautiful.'

The yard door opens. Frederick's voice gets louder again. 'Paul! You must read the lines I've been given. The scholars who wrote it read Aristotle and believe that makes them poets, forgetting as they always do that wit must be accompanied by irreverence, lest the audience succumb to sleep as the verse is spoken.' As he says this bit, a new thought brings me fully awake.

I'm down the ladder in a moment. Frederick and Paul scoot away as I near the hearth, while Brida does her best to make herself smaller on the rug. I hold out the book I found in Ruth's box. Frederick and Paul have their letters. I can learn what kind of killing the deer heart signifies.

'You told me the sin eater didn't trouble you!' cries Frederick, tensed like a rabbit against the wall.

'It's the book from the box,' Brida sees out of the side of her eye. I turn the cover and indicate the first collection of letters. Brida grasps my meaning. 'She wants you to read it.'

Paul pulls his hands back. 'I told you I'll have nought to do with her!'

I need their help, so I hold my ground a pace from them, the hearth embers crackling in the quiet.

Finally Frederick mutters, 'If the book's verse hastens her retreat, then I yield.' He reaches out to take the book, careful to keep from touching me. He clears his throat. '*A Compendium of Diverse Sins Both Large and Small and Their According Foods.*' He takes a breath. '"In which it is set forth the foodstuffs accorded each sin and by which means the sin eater may verily cleanse the sins from the soul."'

'A tale of intrigue and feeling,' Paul says like he doesn't mean it at all, settling his back against the wall by the hearth. And so we begin.

Frederick reads from the beginning of the book. It's just a list of all the sins and their foods. Adultery, assault, arrogance, and many more, but no deer heart. I guess it will be under the sin of killing, but I don't know where killing comes in the book. I keep waiting, hoping it will be next.

What Frederick reads is still useful. I knew before that adultery is dried raisins and bearing a grudge is porridge, but bigamy is orange marmalade and blinding folk is pork pie. Hippocras, I knew, was for drunkenness, but it's also for blood sacrifice. And there's six kinds of coveting, and they're all different creams: plain cream, clotted cream, curdled cream, posset, butter eggs with cream, and whipped cream.

Frederick's only a short way through the book when he yawns and rubs at his eyes. 'Regretfully, I must suspend this edifying labour for the evening and rest my eyes.' He holds out the book. 'I have surely more than met this creature's demand.' I take the book from Frederick and try to ignore how his hand jerks back at my nearness. I'll have him do more another night.

—

I'm woken before dawn by yelling outside the house. Sleep drunk, I first think somefolk's come again to do me harm. But then the sounds shift into two men fighting. I think it's Paul or Frederick, but the fighting men's words are too rough, like clods of earth.

'Got nought against her,' says one.

'Old bitch,' says the other. Mayhap one is a woman, but with such a low and gravelly voice as to be taken for a man. I peek out of the shutters. A constable and an old body.

'Saw you drawing a devil's sign on a house,' says the constable.

'Was nought but scribbling!' The old body is tied at the waist. She does her best to hobble away from the constable, but she's so ancient, the constable doesn't even need to run after her. He catches the rope and drags her on towards town.

'Burn you like the devil fugger you are,' he says.

'Haven't done nothing!' shrieks the woman.

They turn a corner, and the house sinks into quiet for a moment. Then low voices come up the ladder.

'Everyfolk's on the hunt for witches because of that poppet,' whispers Frederick.

'Could have been me,' I hear Brida's little voice.

'She was making the marks,' Paul says. 'Should know better than to get caught.'

Brida speaks again softly, 'Could have been me.'

12. HUMBLE PIE

I N THE MORNING when I climb down the ladder, my squatters are asleep. The house smells of farts and Brida's rot. The broken doorframe's been hastily repaired. The ewer is filled with water, and they've piled more wood near the hearth. I best get used to the noise and funk. They hope to stay.

Outside I find a sky threatening rain and three messengers. Two are using sticks to poke at a frog half-eaten by some night-time fiend. The other is picking his nose with spirit. The nose picker sees me first. 'Eating for Tilly Howe at the castle.'

The frog pokers are next. 'Milly Beane's labouring with child in Northside tavern row.'

'I got a Recitation for a lady in child labour too,' says the second frog poker. 'Goodwife Twarby. There's a witch's mark on the door.'

It takes me a moment to hear the last bit. I turn to my door, but there's nothing to be seen. The second frog poker uses his stick to lead my eyes to the lower corner down by the ground. It's a small marking in charcoal that nearly disappears into the weathered wood. The marking has two eyes on either side of a shape that looks like a woman's skirt. Keen sight, that second frog poker.

I squat and try to rub the marking out with my fingers. All I get is a splinter.

Why is my door marked? The thought drives me to a shiver. Everyfolk knows a witch's mark's a curse.

———

The rain holds off as I walk to the first Recitation. *It's not that I'm putting off going to the castle*, I tell the road before it can say anything. I've promised I'll sort this all out, and I'll keep my word. *It's just the dead have time the dying don't*, I tell it. *So Recitations come first.*

The first frog poker leads me to an alehouse in Northside.

'Well, that took a fugging long time,' says a fat woman in an apron to the first frog poker. 'The babe could've been born, raised, and shrived in the time it took you. Fortunate my sister is a slow birther. Don't be expecting a penny from me.' The frog poker cries out an excuse, but the woman waves him off.

She leads me up the stairs to a family bedroom above the

alehouse where Milly, also fat, lies abed, her belly swollen with child. There's a toddler asleep at her side and an older child whose eyes match hers holding a mug of small beer at the ready. This isn't her first time reciting before childbirth.

'How's it down there?' asks Milly.

'Folk drink just fine without you,' says her sister.

'You tell Carter Parris he owes me for three pints. Don't you let him run any stories at you.' Milly waves at the child for the small beer and takes a drink.

'Carter Parris isn't going to run any stories at me,' the sister answers.

'Bring us a light, would you? Dark as Eve's heart in here,' complains Milly.

The sister nods at the child, who finds a rush candle and lights it from the hearth fire. Milly peers over at me. 'A new sin eater.'

'The Unseen is now seen,' I say. 'The Unheard is now heard. The sins of your flesh become the sins of mine to be borne to my grave in silence.'

Milly's eyes go to the ceiling. 'There's scolding, vanity, not saying my prayers as I ought, putting money before goodliness, more scolding. Fanny, what all have I done?'

The sister puffs out her lips. 'Quarrelling, miserliness. You smacked Carter Parris a good many times.'

'Miserliness? I never!' cries Milly. 'I watch my pennies. That's good sense's all.'

'You're the one asked,' says the sister, Fanny.

'Wait till you're doing the reciting: ill-temper, churlishness, scolding . . .'

'That's all the same sin!'

'Being moody all the time,' adds Milly.

'You just said that,' says Fanny.

'Being a sourpuss,' adds Milly.

'I'm leaving,' Fanny announces. She looks at the older child. 'Call me up when your mother's too pained to talk.' She disappears down the stairs.

'Don't let Carter Parris drink!' Milly yells after her. She looks in my direction. 'Let's be done then.'

'When the food is et, your sins will be mine,' I say. 'I will bear them in silence to my grave.'

The next Recitation is for Goodwife Twarby. The second frog poker follows me close by. When I near the merchants' row, he comes to my elbow and guides me not to the front of the houses, but around the back. We go down a little lane and then through a garden gate past pretty boxes of spring flowers.

A maid lets us in the garden door. She nods her head up the stairs just as a moan comes down it. I've become accustomed enough to steps that I barely even need to hold the wall as I climb.

On the second storey, another maid waits outside a shut bedchamber with a brass ewer. 'Madam?' she calls through the door. 'I brought cool water for you.'

A voice comes back, 'Leave it outside.'

The maid notices me behind her and knocks again. 'Madam?'

'You may not enter!' urges the voice.

The maid holds out the ewer for me.

Inside is Goodwife Twarby and her daughter, a girl no older than me. But it's not Goodwife Twarby who's labouring, it's the daughter. There's a wooden spoon between the girl's teeth. Her mother wipes her brow as the labour pains come.

Goodwife Twarby wears a loose gown of the sort women wear when they're with child, but as she takes the ewer from me, the bulge under the gown squashes under her elbow like it's made of blood moss or wool batting. The daughter whimpers through the spoon, and the mother takes up the moan loud enough to carry down the stairs.

I wonder if the housemaids have fallen for this ruse. The goodwife and her daughter are not the first to try. Even the rumour of lost virginity stains an unmarried girl for good. There's girls cast out of their own homes for less.

The daughter's Recitation is quick. Fornicating, it comes as no surprise. Not much besides, not even disobeying her parents. So many with such worse sins, yet this girl's the one who's stained.

———

Finally it's time for Tilly Howe's Eating. I look for more messengers as I make my way to the castle, just to be sure there aren't any more Recitations to be done, but none find me. The Eating it must be. With luck, it will be too small an affair to draw the likes of Black Fingers.

A maid guides me through the servants' quarters. Grooms carry parcels and guards pull at their stockings. We stop for a moment for porters bringing in ale barrels. There's one shaft of sunlight coming in a window along the passage, so I take a peek while we wait.

The window looks out onto a garden where some courtiers play at bowling. The sky's lightened some, at least enough for the bowlers to make a go of it. They strut and scratch like cocks on bony legs. Beyond the bowling on a stone bench, I see a man alone. There's a tingling in my guts. The Country Mouse.

What is he doing on the bench alone? Mayhap he dislikes bowling. Then I remember he said the other highborn folk look down on him for being from the North. The porters behind me are still loading ale barrels, so I settle in for a gander. He's looking at something in his hand. A coin? A pocket clock? His ring. Thinking of his friend from home. I wish I could keep him company.

I drop into a little daydream. *The courtiers decide to jape the Country Mouse for being a Northerner. They take a ball from their bowling and plan to knock him on the head with it. From here, at the window, I wave to him. He spies the movement and stands, moving out of the ball's path. He rounds on the courtiers and they scatter in shame. He finds my face, like a picture in the window . . .* all at once the Country Mouse's face does rise. I feel when his eyes arrive at my face. There's a quick look of startlement. Without knowing why, I raise my da's ring into the sunlight and twist it to send a sunbeam to him. It hits his chest. He looks down at the white circle of light hovering on him like a moth. Slowly, he raises his own ring and catches the light with it. Sends it back to me. It makes me laugh as it pricks at my eyes.

There's a rough cough beside me from the maid, pulling me back into the servants' passage. Everything seems dim and sunken after the bright garden light. The porters are gone, and the maid wants to go.

He sent the sunbeam back. The thought bounces down the corridor. I tuck my little sunbeam memory into my heart and follow the maid to Tilly Howe's Eating.

—

It's warm enough in the small hall where the coffin's laid out that the oil slips down the deer heart like water. I suppose I shouldn't be surprised to see it. Tilly warned me.

But the folk who've come to pay respects weren't warned. In their faces I see the reflection of the deer heart, like a pall. Many come, some women with grown children and some of the Queen's ladies too, but none stay to take one of the stools. They are aghast at the crime. Tilly was a midwife as well as a healer. Supposed to bring life into the world, not end it. And so soon after Corliss's Eating.

The only one who stays is the Willow Tree. He stands in the corner, his eyes glancing off the coffin like a fly after a pie. Mayhap he's checking to see if I'll eat the heart.

Should I? There are no sword blades against me now. I start on the hippocras, so as to put off the question.

Fair Hair and Mush Face, I notice, are among those come to witness. They walk with a girl I don't know who wears yellow taffeta. As they near the coffin, I see Mush Face is wearing the same dress she did before.

The yellow-taffeta girl turns to the other two. 'I only went to her once when I overturned a candle and burned my wrist.' She looks to Mush Face. 'You saw her, didn't you, for your headaches?'

Mush Face nods.

'I heard she passed with blisters on her belly,' Yellow Taffeta whispers. 'Do you think she was a victim of the witch?'

Fair Hair shakes her blonde curls. 'Those ghastly poppets!'

'I know she was a murderess,' Mush Face answers, looking at the deer heart. Her eyes run over the other foods. She has a look as she does. It's a look I know but never would expect to see on one of the Queen's ladies: hunger. Suddenly Mush Face's head comes up. 'Poppets,' she stares at Fair Hair. 'You said poppets.'

Fair Hair looks blankly back at Mush Face.

'I thought only one had been found.'

But Fair Hair's eyes have gone to a figure darkening the doorway. Black Fingers. Who nearly killed me twice. Who tortured Ruth to death. The mustard seed catches in my throat, and I feel great thumps of blood under my stitches.

I catch a movement in front of the coffin. A kerchief flutters from Fair Hair's hand to the floor. Swift as a kite, Black Fingers cuts across the room to pick it up. He's only feet away from me.

If Black Fingers is startled to find me alive, he hides it well. *He can't hurt me in front of all these folk*, I remind the mustard seeds. Still, I measure in my mind how many steps it would take to reach the door, an old habit from my year at the Daffreys'.

Black Fingers offers the kerchief to Fair Hair. 'Milady.' Close as they are, I see Fair Hair pass him something small and square as she takes the kerchief from him. A slip of paper. All at once I recall seeing them leaving the same closet after Corliss's Eating. The herb dispensary, it was. Mayhap they're lovers. A dangerous game, to be sure, if he's the Queen's favourite.

A choked burble draws all of our attention. It's the Painted Pig, recovered from her faint the day before, and bobbing towards the coffin in a great ruff. Black Fingers leaves Fair Hair with a light nod and crosses to the Painted Pig, offering his arm.

I can see the Painted Pig hesitate before resting her arm upon his. I also see that while she may look recovered from afar, it's only with the help of much face paint. She's been weeping, which ought to soften me towards her but doesn't.

'Tilly was in the household of Lady Katryna when I was her lady of the privy chamber,' she says noisily to Black Fingers. Then, as if to answer why she should know the affairs of servants, 'It was a small household.' The Painted Pig steals a look at the Willow Tree. 'He looms like a hangman, does he not?'

Black Fingers dips his own ruff like a screen so he can nestle his lips to her ear. I can't catch what he whispers. Whatever he says, the Painted Pig tries to fit her face into a smooth mask, but it doesn't work. She steps away from him and smiles tightly. 'You are a comfort.'

Black Fingers catches her hand and brings it to his lips.

Suddenly there's a cry by the door and a rustle of skirts. I look up to see the Queen, her bosom puffing and cheeks reddening beneath her face paint.

I want to scream, *The ladies were poisoned! The hearts not recited! Your favourite is a murderer!*

My head's gone light and my stitches burn. I start to rise off my stool towards the Queen.

Black Fingers sees me from the side of his eye. His hand darts to his hip where his dagger, the one that ripped into my neck, sits brightly.

I drop back down onto my stool and take up the bread. But Black Fingers's hand stays at his dagger, his fingers around the handle. Three and a half paces to the door. I ready my feet to run.

But it's the Queen who moves first. She crosses direct to the Painted Pig and strikes her full across the face. It's such a blow the Painted Pig falls, great skirts and all, nearly taking Black Fingers with her. He pulls his arm away just before she can drag him down.

The Queen shakes where she stands, looking between Black Fingers and the Painted Pig, 'Would you betray me?'

The Painted Pig blocks her face and honks, 'Your Grace! I never!'

Black Fingers pulls at his ear again. 'You cannot think . . . Your Grace, you cannot believe—'

'I believe what I see,' the Queen interrupts. 'Your lips were on her hand.'

'If cordial affection towards a longtime friend brings you distemper,' says Black Fingers, 'then I shall leave you in peace.'

'You do not have my leave to go,' the Queen cries before he can take a step.

'I will not be leashed like a dog,' he whispers, sharp-like.

The Queen's shaking grows stronger, and I think for one terrible moment she, too, might have been poisoned.

'Your Grace.' The Willow Tree appears at her side.

His voice seems to break through the Queen's rage. Her shaking quiets. 'Help her up,' she orders. Several folk work to right the fallen Pig.

'Your Grace,' the Painted Pig says once standing again. 'I am an old candle next to your young light. Your sunlight! That you think I, who have been like an auntie to you, could presume . . .' She seems to grow wary of her own words and lets them fritter away.

The Queen looks past the Painted Pig to Black Fingers. She assays him. He lowers his head and raises his hand. After a heavy moment of held breath, the Queen takes it. They find seats before the coffin.

Black Fingers holds the Queen's hand, but his eyes are on the deer heart. I daren't not eat it. Not with him there watching. So for a second time, I do it. I eat a deer heart from a murdered woman's coffin.

It's only after I've eaten every bite that I recall the Queen didn't even startle at seeing the heart.

13. BARLEY GRAIN

*M*OTHERFUGGER, I CURSE to myself as I step carefully down the servants' stairs. It comes out unbidden, strange and filthy in my mouth. And right all the same. This is why we have cursing. I never understood what made folk do it. But now I know. All our dire feelings stain the heart, and the stains bloom into curses. I don't know how to sort this mess. The ways I've tried have only put me in danger.

The rain's finally come, and it's coming down hard. I sit on the bottom step of a set of stairs near the kitchen to wait for it to let up. It clinks like piss in the pot, but nicer because it's just rain.

A maid walks down the passage. I'm enough in the shadows that she doesn't notice me. Another maid, tall and pimpled, comes out of the kitchen, her cheeks pink with heat. This pimpled maid rolls her eyes. 'Cook's moaning about ladies requesting special dishes.'

'He's always moaning about making food,' says the first maid. 'Why'd he become cook?'

'It's the Queen's revels that's got him out of temper. Hasn't been a feast this grand since the old king. Best not have come with a request,' warns Pimples.

'But I have,' says the first maid. 'Calf liver. The lady gave me fourpence to give him for it,' she adds as if that should settle things.

'Is it for a certain fair-haired, young lady with a growing appetite?' Pimples smiles.

'Do you . . . What do you mean?' the first maid asks.

'She's the one got the cook moaning with her requests!' answers Pimples. 'One appetite gets another, as the old wives say.' Pimples says this last part like she means more than she says.

'She's with child?' mouths the first maid.

Pimples hushes her, then checks the passage. As she does, she catches sight of me in the shadows. 'Maker mine!' she starts.

The first maid follows Pimples's eyes to me. 'What the fug is she doing here?!' she hisses.

'Come for your girl who wants the calf liver, is what,' whispers Pimples. 'She's on with a certain man the Queen fancies. Queen had his wife pushed down a stair. Your girl's going to need the sin eater soon enough.' The first maid crosses herself.

At that moment the Painted Pig arrives noisily in the corridor. Pimples and the other maid press themselves against the wall. Pimples bumps a small tapestry with her bottom.

The Painted Pig's eyes work over the maids like they're meat that's turned at a market. 'Do you know where my maid is? She was meant to bring my correspondence last evening. I'm expecting a letter from my cousin.'

The two maids shake their heads.

The Painted Pig sees the tapestry behind Pimples askew. She tilts her head. 'That weaving is worth a goodly amount more than you. If I were the Queen, I should have your bottom sliced off for touching it.'

Pimples, flushing nape to brow, pulls away from the hanging, grazing the Painted Pig's silk skirt with her soiled apron as she does. 'Fat cow,' the Painted Pig snaps, and walks past the cringing maids.

I wait till she's about to pass me to stand up sharp. The Painted Pig pulls back like a donkey. Her hand reaches for her waist as if she were wearing old faith prayer beads, but none are there. She crosses herself instead and goes on.

I don't know why I did it, but it feels good to have folk mind me, even if it's a fearful sort of minding. It makes for a change.

—

Once the rain lets up, I go out of the scroll door and cross the courtyard. A gaggle of messenger boys plays marbles just outside the castle gate. The game knocks off when they see me, and they call out a whole list of names. But I just walk on towards home. The taste of the second deer heart is still on my breath, and I've remembered one thing that still might help with my muddle.

My door creaks threateningly in its poorly repaired frame. Inside my house, Paul, Brida, and Frederick are just waking. I find the Sin Eater's book and go to the foot of Frederick's stretching body.

'Why, she's in a fluster, now,' announces Brida, pushing herself up with her one good arm.

'And must we wait upon her fluster?' asks Frederick, unwilling to look my way.

Brida just says again, 'She's in a fluster.'

'Then we'll play at pantomimes to guess,' Paul mutters from under a cloak he's using as bedclothes.

'Tell her to leave us in peace,' Frederick directs Brida. I throw the book onto Frederick's chest. 'Oh-ho! Beware, we have been trained in broadsword and epée,' Frederick warns. 'At least the simulacrum.'

'Well enough to be the Queen's own players at her glorious festivities for the Norman envoy,' says Paul.

'Just read the book again, will you?' pushes Brida.

Frederick sighs. He pulls himself up to sitting and looks to Paul. 'Might I have a cup of ale to whet my stone?'

'Brida?' suggests Paul.

'Paul!' scolds Frederick.

Paul fetches the drink while Frederick opens the book. 'We were at the *D*'s, was it?'

It will take too long. I point to the book and pat my chest to indicate a heart.

'She wants to tell us something,' Brida interprets. Paul and Frederick keep their eyes on Brida. 'She's beating her breast.'

'Pantomime it is,' calls Frederick. 'Arms and fingers are marvellously expressive if you use them properly. Sweeping gests, please. No fiddling-at-your-hems mummery.' He's certainly mocking me.

'Is Frederick to read or not?' asks Paul.

'She's quite cross, as much as I can tell,' says Brida. Her gaze is fixed just to the side of my body. I pat my chest again and point to the book.

'Her chest,' Brida says.

'Love,' Paul guesses. 'She would like Frederick to read about the sins of love?'

'Passions,' sings Frederick. 'A sin of passion. Seduction. Adultery.'

'You've covered adultery. Dried raisins,' reminds Paul.

Brida asks, 'Is it a sin you wish him to read of?'

I shake my head.

'Yes? No?' Frederick looks to Brida.

'A food, then?' Paul asks.

Yes! I smile wide.

'I believe that's right,' Brida says. 'Oh, she's happier now.'

'And which food would that be?' asks Brida.

'A heart, it would seem,' says Frederick, finally grasping my meaning.

'I was going to guess a heart,' calls Paul.

Brida lowers herself onto her back before the fire.

'Are you unwell?' Paul looks her over closely.

'Time for a rest is all,' she sighs.

'We'll get you a bone broth,' says Paul. 'A nice, hot bone broth.'

'Sounds nice, that,' sighs Brida.

Frederick reads through the pages, his thumb marking each line of words as he searches for sins that warrant a heart. Paul joins him after a piece, reading over his shoulder. 'My, my. Should you, Brida, ever consider jarking, our rare-voiced patron will eat pickled turnips upon your grave.'

'Have you not found the heart?' Brida asks Frederick.

'I thought it would be found under "killing",' Frederick answers. 'But here we are entering the *L*'s. Very few sins starting with *L*.'

'Lust, of course,' reads Paul.

'Ah, here! The *M*'s,' says Frederick. 'Yes, of course.'

'What is it?' Brida asks.

'Murder,' Frederick answers.

'There are quite a few hearts to be eaten,' reads Paul over Frederick's shoulder. 'Bird, rabbit, lamb, even fish.'

Frederick runs his finger along the page. 'Bird heart is for murder without design.' He stops and looks up. 'Is it murder if it's without design? I take issue with the wording here. Paul, it should be killing, not murder, if it's unintended. Am I wrong?'

'I heartily agree,' Paul says back.

'Who claims authorship of this singular tome?' asks Frederick. He looks at the first pages. 'None.'

I suck my teeth.

Frederick turns back to the *M*'s. 'Rabbit for murder in

defence of one's life or as a soldier in battle. Again, I amend it to killing. Pig heart for wrathful murder. I grant the use of murder in this instance.'

'Hear, hear,' agrees Paul.

'Lamb heart for murder of a babe. Cock heart for murder of your father. Swan for murder of your mother. Bear for murder of royalty. Deer for murder of a royal babe. Goat for—' Frederick stops when my breath catches. 'Eureka, I surmise.'

Deer heart for the murder of a royal babe.

Maker mine, what have I stumbled upon? Corliss and Tilly Howe have both been poisoned and hearts placed on their coffins that claim they murdered a royal child. But I know from their Recitations they never did.

Questions come into my head so quick I can hardly sort them all. Why would somefolk slander Corliss and Tilly like this? To throw blame off themselves? To harm the women and their kin by ruining their names? That's all I come up with.

And what royal child or children were murdered? There surely must be those with a claim to the throne who died young, but apart from the babes Maris lost in her womb, I don't know of them.

Tilly said a heart would be on her coffin, so she knew something of the matter. What did she know?

The questions keep on, but the only one I can conceive an answer for is this: why might a royal child be murdered?

This one's easy to figure. Killing a royal babe changes who's next in line for the throne. Many folk might consider murder if it meant they could rule over all of Angland. I get a cold feeling when this thought comes, because it makes it seem like Queen Bethany could be the murderer – after all, she's ruling over all of Angland now. I close my mind against the thought. To think such a thing is treason. But it creeps back through like a draught under a door.

Who besides Bethany might kill a royal babe? The answer is anyfolk who profited when she became Queen.

Of course Black Fingers. He nearly killed me for speaking of it. Twice. And at Corliss's Eating it sounded as if he had ambitions for the throne.

The Willow Tree. With Bethany as Queen, he's one of the most important men in Angland.

The Queen's ladies too. They're Bethany's loyal friends.

Or was it not about Bethany at all, but her faith? The countess in the dungeon plotted to kill Bethany to put a Eucharistian on the throne. Mayhap others tried the same.

The questions swirl thick and muddy. I can't sort them all out. Somefolk is killing the Queen's women and then blaming them for a royal child's murder. That's what I know.

I climb up to the loft and lie down on the mattress, but my head's full of bees. My eyes settle on the wooden boxes lining the shelves up and down the wall. I wonder what's in the rest of them. I open the shutter to let in the moonlight and take a box from the lowest shelf.

A lock of brown hair tied with a silk ribbon
A seashell, pale and glimmering like it's wet
Three caraway seeds wrapped in a kerchief

That's what's inside. No rhyme or reason. I replace the box on the shelf and take out another.

> An old embroidery of a wren done poorly like
>   by a child
> A hazel twig to clean your teeth
> A nightshift
> Three straight pins, as you use for pinning clothes

In a third box, I hear clinking before I open it.

> A folded linen smock
> A head coif
> Bunches of soft blood moss
> Short blood breeches for the monthly courses

At the bottom of this box I find coins, a whole handful, but not Anglish. Two have square holes cut in them. And flat against the bottom is a parchment. I lift it out, but it crumbles between my fingers. As it falls away, I feel something inside. I brush away the pieces. A pressed violet.

Usually you keep one sort of thing in a box like blood moss or tools. But these boxes are all odd collections. I look over the shelves. Twelve's as high as I know how to count with surety, and there's more than that. What are they, and why are they on the wall of the Sin Eater's house?

I reach up to the top shelf and take a box from there. It's covered in a thick layer of dust that gets up my nose. I'll be sneezing out black snot tomorrow.

A hare's paw, like folk keep for good luck
A toadstone amulet
A wax portrait, cracked with age, of a girl in a
  hairstyle and dress far out of fashion

There's a kerchief too. It has two letters I know embroidered on it, an *E* and *W*. It's not Ruth's. Mayhap it's the girl in the portrait's. I look again at what's in the box. The hare's paw. The amulet. Could they also be the girl's? A superstitious girl from a long time ago . . .

And then I grasp it all at once. She was a sin eater too, this girl in the wax portrait. It's her box. Each box is from a different sin eater. It's their belongings. There's no folk to pass them on to when they die, so their leftovers stay here. I look again at how many boxes there are. They must go back so many years. Leading up to now. To me.

So many women slept in this loft. Mayhap on this same mattress. I curl back onto it, sniffing the ticking as if I might smell them in it. All I smell is old hay and mildew, but it sort of warms me, knowing there were others before me, even if they're not here now. It makes me feel like an *us* again.

As I fall into sleep, I wonder if any of them would know what to do with my muddle of poisonings and deer hearts.

14. CROW'S MEAT WITH PLUM

MERCHANTS' HOMES, I'VE come to find, are best on a cold day. Lattice windows, oak panelling, and hangings on the walls are all meant to fight the cold and damp. But when the day is warm and dying being done within, a wealthy home gets foul. I hate to think what Recitations might be like in high summer.

I'm let in by the maid, who steps aside for me to find my own way. By now I know to follow my nose to the burning herbs. But today there's a different smell. Old eggs.

Through a crack in the bedchamber door I see two old bodies, one abed, wrapped in rugs. He must be the one awaiting the Recitation. The other old body, I'm surprised to see, is the gnarled Willow Tree, the Queen's physician.

He's bent over the bed looking at something. Between the men is a parchment with circles and figures. I don't know whether to wait or go in, so I wait.

'An enema of Aurum potabile?' I hear the Willow Tree say.

'I never saw the need,' the dying man says back. 'My birth chart foretold longevity, robust health, and wealth.'

'Told by a rogue crystal gazer.'

'A scryer,' the dying man agrees. 'Came round two years ago in winter, offered to cast this birth chart.' The dying man farts. A moment later the smell of eggs comes strong through the door crack. 'The rogue claimed to have foretold the Virgin Queen. I believed him,' says the man.

'Don't we all when the stars augur what we wish to hear,' the Willow Tree says. 'But a virgin queen was foretold by many, ancients too.'

'A virgin queen who will usher in a lasting era of peace through the new faith.' The dying man nods. He looks up. 'Have you found the witch who made the poppet?'

'Do not fear, the Queen shall be protected,' answers the Willow Tree.

'You will protect her with a spell?' The dying man winces and farts again. 'The scryer promised me protection as well. He gave me a parchment with strange symbols upon it.' He reaches shakily into his robe and removes a folded paper.

The Willow Tree opens it and brings it near his face. 'These symbols are part of the language given to Adam by the angels. The language that spawned Hebrew and Greek. The symbols are imbued with divine power. If they have not protected you, it is you who are at fault, an unworthy vessel. Have you undertaken unworthy acts?' the Willow Tree asks. 'Did you pursue alchemy for gold?'

'Gold is a physical manifestation of the Maker's purity, a noble metal,' says the dying man.

'Again, you interpret what you desire, not what the ancients wrote. Did you offer a tribute to the Maker? Gold, perhaps?' says the Willow Tree like he knows the dying man's thoughts. 'A tribute must be of a kind. If you wish for life, you must offer life.'

The dying man startles. 'Your arms could be torn off, and worse, for uttering such witchcraft.'

'Your arms could be torn off, and worse, for trying to make gold,' the Willow Tree says back. 'My practice is rooted in mathematics, astrology, and the study of philosophers. It is an ancient art, and its mysteries have served the greatest kings and queens. It is categorically different from dark arts performed by ignorant women.'

The dying man says quietly, 'It is now you who interprets what you desire.'

The Willow Tree turns to leave. There's a flicker of gold at his chest like a fat slice of pie with a symbol in the centre. The symbol's the same one Mush Face was looking at in her book the day I went to Tilly Howe's Recitation.

'Am I to die today?' the dying man calls out.

The Willow Tree doesn't stop. 'We are all called to the Maker.'

'Have you nothing that might prolong my life?' says the man.

The Willow Tree sees me through the crack of the door. 'Perhaps it is time to think on your afterlife, sir.'

Up close, I see the dying man is sorely frightened to die. I feel sorry for him, so I say the words to begin kindly.

He's ready with his sins. 'Putting learning before the Maker, putting profit before the Maker, making a birth chart, the use of symbols to increase wealth and protect against ill.' His hand still clutches the parchment with the symbols on it.

I nod to the paper.

He looks at me sharp, then softens like an egg tart. 'Yes. Yes. Idolatry.' He goes on. 'And the common sins. Arrogance, parsimony, envy, greed. Tell me' – his eyes search mine – 'have you ever spoken with an angel? Is it the archangel Michael who shall balance my soul against a dove's feather?'

I don't know. I don't know at all what happens after we pass on, except what I was always told by the Makermen: if I was good, I would join the Maker in the sky. And now that I have every folk's sins heaped on me, I'll be Eve's handmaiden. Unless I obey the Maker's will in my every act, which I'm not sure I can do. And now this man's sins are getting heaped on me too. When I think on it, it makes me less sorry for him. Why should he be frightened when I'm taking up all his sins?

When I say the last bit to finish the Recitation, I don't say it kindly at all.

After my work, the road back towards Northside's oddly empty. Then I hear drums. Somefolk important has arrived in town. I hear trumpets too. It must be the emissary from the Norman prince, here to propose marriage to Queen Bethany. The one the great revels will celebrate.

I turn off the main road and head to the river, where folk will be gathering to see the emissary's barge. As I get nearer, the road begins to fill up. It gets fuller and fuller until I'm wending my way through a crowd, trying not to feel hurt when folk recoil at seeing me. I get myself a good view for the procession.

All the court has turned out. They've got good views too, on either side of the road down to the wharf. Across from me, a band of musicians wearing the Queen's badge sit atop a trestle. It's only after a good gawk that I recall I've seen some of them before. They're the strangers I spied at a newspanto. They play the same long lutes they carried then, but also flutes and viols. One man, young, dark-haired and taut-built, plays an instrument I've never seen. It's as big as a man and has brown curves like a horse's haunch. He bows it like a viol, but standing up. When he plays, its sound rumbles through my chest.

The highborn folk lining the road around the musicians all wear red and purple, silver and gold, not plain, woad-dyed blue like the rest of us. Behind them, grooms and maids try to keep costly hems out of the dirt and hold burning herbs to counter the stink from the river.

I look among the highborn. Finally I find him. The

Country Mouse's nose is pink with sun, and he's wearing a big ruff. His badge, I see, is a stag.

Next to him are two men who must be brothers, they look so alike. They're familiar, but I don't know from where. Mayhap my mother or I washed their laundry. One of the brothers says something, and the Country Mouse makes the nodding sort of face you do when you don't know what to say. It makes me laugh a little.

Another trumpet sounds, which must mean something's happening. Then a small man rides past on a tall horse. From the way everyfolk stares, this must be the emissary. The big horse makes him seem no more than a child. Near me, folk snicker and some even spit.

I look back to the Country Mouse. He's saying something to his groom. If I were the groom I could tell the Country Mouse my noticings, like that the emissary looks like a child. And that our country seems so big and our queen so mighty, but how little our country must be if the Norman prince can send a messenger to propose marriage. The Country Mouse would find me clever for saying this. A clever friend to help him sort his thoughts. He'd invite me for a walk along the river. Not the awful part in Dungsbrook, but the fine part, upstream. He'd say, *Why should either of us be lonely when we can pass the time together?*

One of the brothers next to the Country Mouse pulls out a small silver box. It catches the sunlight like the Country Mouse's ring did in the castle garden. The man opens the box, pulls something out with two fingers, and then, as if it were a perfectly usual thing to do, sniffs it up his nose. I've never seen the like. He offers the box to his brother and the Country Mouse. I look harder at the brothers.

All at once, I know them. Or one of them at least. And not because I did his laundry. It's the recorder, the man who sentenced me to be a sin eater. The one who was married to Ruth and made her a sin eater too. My neck burns hot, and even with the Country Mouse there and all, I don't have a mind to watch any more.

I turn down a small lane back towards home, but I'm stuck in a second crowd, clinging like a leech to the first one. It's a beggar crowd. The beggars all wait on the small lanes so folk must walk by them on their way to and from the procession. There's lame beggars, old beggars, beggars with babies wrapped round their middles, and poorer sorts of actors and jugglers. They all wear passports with the seal of the Queen's office on their rags that say they're deserving poor, permitted to beg by the Queen's mercy.

Not far down the lane I discover Paul. He's leaning against the front of a cordwainer's shop shaking a little wooden bowl I recognize from my home. He holds the bowl out to two guildsmen, one large, one small, who have stopped to buy a pie at a cart. Brida's nowhere to be seen.

Out in the daylight, Paul's face is a horror. His cheeks are stricken with white lumps like his skin blistered and then got stuck that way. He has no scarf today, the better to stir folk's pity. Under his scars, his jaw is strong and his nose straight. He might have been handsome once.

I notice his passport is pinned to his rags, but where

other passports have a seal in a circle that's regular and well-inked, Paul's passport has no circle and the figure is muddled. Circles are very hard to counterfeit. I learned that from my Daffrey uncles. Misgett Daffrey, my elder uncle, had an old sailor who worked as a jarkman counterfeiting begging passports. The sailor was accustomed to carving scrimshaw in bone. When he sold a false passport the seal was sound.

Why wouldn't Paul have a legitimate passport to beg, given his dreadful scars? Mayhap he didn't have chummage to bribe the Queen's office. Mayhap he was deemed corrupt for some reason or other.

If he sees me, Paul gives no sign. I walk past as if we are strangers, not homefellows.

Beyond Paul is a trio of scrawny actors preparing a panto. One of them barks to draw attention, promising a play called *The Queen's Verity*. I stop to watch.

'Maker save us from bad actors,' I hear Paul mutter.

One actor steps out to begin the show. It's the old Queen Maris he's dressed as. He swoons, complaining of the heat because he, Queen Maris, is with child. He pulls out prayer beads from the old faith and kisses them, praying to the Maker to protect the heir in his belly.

Two boys come on next dressed as Queen Bethany and the Queen's physician, the Willow Tree. They fawn over Queen Maris but then turn and begin to chant a witch's spell.

What comes next should be at a butcher's shop, never a panto. 'Where's the sacrifice?' calls the Queen Bethany actor.

The Willow Tree actor holds up a real pigeon, flapping in his hand. He cuts its throat and blood splatters all over their costumes. The pregnant Queen Maris grabs her belly and screams, 'Maker save me; these witches have killed my baby!'

Maker mine. I swallow. The guildsmen eating their pies are less calm. 'Call the constable!' the larger one urges the smaller. The boy playing Bethany sings a gleeful song:

> *Mistress Maris,*
> *Angland's heiress,*
> *How has your garden grown?*
> *I've stolen the bloom*
> *From out of your womb*
> *And now I can take the throne!*

The larger guildsman marches his well-fed bones to the singing actor and strikes him across the face. 'Foul-mouthed pig!'

Soon after, the constable barrels down the lane led by the smaller guildsman, and the actors break off their mummery to make a run for it. The constable catches one of the actors by the ear. Two strikes with his club and the boy is squealing, 'We were offered six shillings!'

'What's this?' asks the constable. It's more than a washerwoman makes in a season.

'To make a play that the Queen killed her sister Maris's babes by black magic—' The back of the constable's hand whacks the boy's mouth.

'Six shillings,' the boy says again as if the amount makes it less wrong.

'Who gave it to you?' asks the constable.

The answer is what you'd expect. 'Don't know.'

'Well, then it's the press for you, isn't it?' says the constable.

The press. The crowd of folk suddenly feels too close around me. I push hard against a goodwife to make way. She cries out but gets quiet again when she sees who I am. A friend pulls her out of my way with a low hiss. The hiss rankles. I lunge at the friend and give her a good hard shove too. She stumbles with a scream into a sweets vendor, smacking her head against his cart.

'Maker save us!' cries another woman. I turn back to the crowd. They've opened wide around me, their faces turned away. All of a sudden I want to run at them, make them all shriek and squeal. But it's not them who're nettling me. Not truly. It's the picture I see inside my head of Ruth the Sin Eater under the stones of the press.

I lurch to the side as if I might slip away from the picture. My head's hot and my chest aches. I walk faster as if to outpace my thoughts, but the picture dogs me down the street.

Ruth crushed. Ruth bleeding.

Soon I'm running, urging the picture to leave me alone.

Ruth, Ruth dying, the picture calls after me. *Bessie dying, Ruth—*

It takes a moment for me to catch what's happened. Bessie's name, fallen in with Ruth's. And suddenly the boy catches up with me, calling out his message. And like the sun's last light disappearing over the fields, quicker than you ever think it will, the picture of Ruth's death leaves my thoughts completely because the messenger's calling out my old neighbour's name.

Bessie's dying.

15. GRAPES

THE SMELL OF Bessie's house is so familiar, it's like I never went away. Broth smell from the pot always on the hearth. The mild, milky smell of Lee. The sharp tang of Tom.

'It's May,' Lee says when I come in the door. Her hand fiddles with the knot holding up her apron. She does it when she's nervous.

Through the leather bottom of my shoe, my right toes find the warp just inside the door. It's where a leak in the roof dripped rain until the board itself rose up.

'Well, she knows the way, doesn't she,' Tom says in his quick way. His hand goes out in habit to pat against my shoulder as he always did, but his fingers lift just before they touch me.

Bessie's in her bed, tucked up in the old blue-and-brown quilt Lee and I played fairies under. Her smell is strong here, the clean, old-body smell of hay with a little bit of must on the edge. Her right hand shakes without stop and one side of her face seems slack, like it's gone to sleep without the rest of her. But her hair is braided as it always was, combed smooth with a little grease. And there's her jaw, too broad to ever be pretty. It's all so familiar that a little knot like a plum stone lodges in my heart, and all of a sudden I want to cry.

'Clouds coming, are they?' Bessie says out of the side of her mouth. It's what she always said when Lee or Tom or I had a tumble or a trip. She'd say it right in that little breath before the wailing started. When she says it now, the stone in my heart rolls over, and I want to crawl up inside the quilt against her warm, familiar body, and never leave. The tears stream out of my eyes.

'Now, it's me meant to be crying, I should think.' Her words are slurred, but I hear them. And my tears won't stop; I know that. Whatever seeing her has opened up has a long way to go before it's emptied. I come to the edge of the bed and sit. Bessie looks at me, squinting in hard judgement with her right eye. 'You've put some size on you,' she assays. 'So you're managing.'

I shake my head through the tears. I'm not managing. I'm not.

But Bessie just looks back harder. 'You are, with your mother's blood in you.'

No, not her. Never a Daffrey. I am an Owens.

Bessie sighs back on the bed. 'I had hoped to last a little longer. At least long enough to witness the Queen's revels.

It'll be the talk of the age. My da fought the Normans in the last war. Oh, but I would have liked to spit on a Norman.' One corner of Bessie's mouth pinches into a smile. Her eyes flick over to me. 'Well, let's get on with it.'

I stutter through the words to start the Recitation. 'I haven't much to recite,' she begins. 'I've been a poor-tempered, miserly sort. Quarrelled near enough to take me to Eve's side. But I'm a good woman. Was good to my first husband, though he gave me no children.' Her right hand is like a moth, hovering and trembling above the blanket. 'And I was good to my second husband and our two babes, though Lee has the wit of a wood post, and many a day I'd like to trade Tom for a good milk cow.' Bessie's one working eye comes to rest on the far wall. 'Wish I had spoke more of my mind. Went into marriage with my first husband as green as grass. You've likely not been with a man, unless you went to whoring after your da passed.'

I gasp at the bluntness of it. Her eye weaves over to me.

'Thought not. You're a scrapping sort. So you won't know there's many men don't know which end's up on a woman. The first time, my first husband nearly stuck his prick in my arse. He had no idea there was two holes, and I was too timid to tell him.'

A laugh burbles up through my tears.

Bessie clucks. 'Always a laugh at a poor moment, you.'

I try to suck the laugh back in. But then she's laughing too, out of the side of her face. My tears keep coming down. They are mixed with laughing at her story, but also at the thought of where we've both come to.

Bessie shakes her head awkwardly. 'Wish I had done more of what I wanted and less of what's right. Might have more delicious bits to recite.' I'm startled into a hiccup. 'Oh, now, you're not still as starched up as you once were, are you?' Bessie says. 'With how you came into the world and what you've seen lately you should know, the more you live, the more the sinner and the sinless can't be pulled apart. All of us just getting by.'

How I came into the world? My face shows my muddlement.

'You must know by now your da wasn't your true da. Your mother had a man before. Supposed to be highborn, your sire. Rich. Your mother's folk, the Daffreys, went after him, as I recall. Tried to get coin to keep quiet about you.' She looks me over with her one eye. 'Oh, now, it surely can't come as a surprise. You're the very fruit of your mother's tree. Two of you, like peas in a peasecod.'

The picture comes. An old picture, faded from years deep in the corner of my heart, of a coffin lid in my very own house. Salt for pride. Mustard seed for white lies. Barley for curses. Crow's meat with plum. A loaf shaped like a bobbin. And ruby-red grapes.

Fresh grapes, for bearing a bastard.

It was right there in my heart all these years, but I never wanted to see it. And now my heart feels like it's coming unknit, like a thread's pulling out all the stitches. I'm a lie.

Two peas in a peasecod.

When I stole the bread, I told myself it was an honest crime. But what was honest about stealing?

When my mother had my uncles destroy the family altar, I took Da's side, telling myself how, had it been me, I would have stood by our beliefs. But somewhere buried in that memory is a girl secretly glad her mother's choice spared them the purgers.

And when I ate the deer hearts, I used my mother's words, *You're nothing if you're dead.* I told myself I needed to be alive to help the Sin Eater, but, really, it was my life, dressed up as hers, that I was saving.

Don't I know by now that folk see their sins in the way they choose? There's always a reason as to why selfishness is not really selfish and crimes are honest and waiting safely by while somefolk else is killed is really the more courageous choice. I've always had an answer for why I'm a goodly girl despite my sins. I thought I was an Owens. But mayhap I've always been a Daffrey.

I say the words to finish Bessie's Recitation. As I do, her arm that's not working rolls onto its side. I don't know if it's the shake of her illness, but her fingers brush mine. I look long into her eyes, trying to know more, to see myself from her view, but there's just her look, a little hard and a little soft all at the same time.

Tom is sitting at the kitchen table when I come from Bessie's room with the list of foods. Lee is turned towards the stove with a hand up to hide me from sight, but she's peeking through her fingers. When I leave, my feet find the warp by the door one more time.

I walk to the tumbledown cottage. It's been years, but my feet know the way, like Greta in the fairy story, finding her way home. A dirty boy with tufted black hair and a half-moon cleft in his cheek plays with a stick in the yard. I stand long enough that he runs inside.

My granddam steps out, shrivelled and shaking on a cane. 'Never called for you,' she says to the puddles. 'Get on now.' She makes the Maker's sign across her chest and hips.

I shake my hair and give a half smile, so she sees who I am. She hesitates. Steps from one foot to the other. 'Never called for you,' she says more quietly.

'What's this?' I hear a man's voice coming to the door. My uncle Misgett. His eyes narrow, then he sees the *S* and looks away. 'My sister's bastard come to mark us with Eve's eye. Drive her off.'

My cousin picks up the first stone, then my uncle. Then my granddam.

—

I walk without direction along the middle of the road, letting folk make way or not, numb to the cries of cart men and bustling goodwives. I make turns with no reason, lost as to where to go.

The lane I'm on widens into a little square I've never been to. It's got a stone fountain in the centre for folk to collect water from. My face is flushed and hot, so I take a scoop. It tastes poorly, like metal. As I step back something catches my eye. It's a marking on the fountain stone made in charcoal. Two straight lines with a wavy one between. Another witch's mark.

Am I followed by a witch? Is this why Bessie gave me such

news? Why my own kin threw stones? Why I'm dogged by the worst fortune a folk could have?

No, if I was cursed, it happened long before now. It began the day my mother bore me as a bastard. Her death, then Da's, then becoming a sin eater. Really, I've been fully fugged my whole life.

Two goodwives come chatting into the square with pails for water. One of them sees me dipping my hand into the fountain and pulls the other woman back the way they came.

My first thought is that they saw the witch's mark too. But of course that's not it. It's me. I'm what sent them running. *I'm worse than a witch's curse.*

A laugh comes up from my belly. Just like Bessie said, always at a poor moment. And then a thought comes. Say the mark on the fountain was a witch's curse. What harm could it do me? Is there anything worse than what's already been done? My laugh gets bigger. *What have I left to fear?* I ask the fountain.

It can't think of a thing.

I scoop up a long drink of water direct from the pool, fouling it again with my touch, good and proper. It still tastes wretched. That makes me laugh even more. After despairing for so many days, the laughter feels so good.

What if instead of fighting my nature, I gave in? I giggle at the foul water.

It says back just two words: *Join me.*

I strip off my shawl and my clothing. Goose pimples spread across my naked skin from shoulder to ankle. I step over the stone ledge, one leg and then the other, full into the fountain.

There's a certain comfort in rules. You know if you're good or if you're bad. And even if you're bad, you know where you fit. You belong. But I don't want other folk's rules to say if I belong any more. I want to say for myself.

I look round at the houses on the square and hear more than one shutter clap shut. Good, folk are watching and will spread the word of what they've seen.

I sit down slowly in the water, feeling its cool go up my legs, over my thighs, into my cunny and bottom. *I curse this fountain*, I think to the square. *I curse its water.* I gaze from shuttered window to shuttered window. *From this time forth, it will be known as the Sin Eater's Fountain. None shall drink from it or wash in it or touch it again.* Except me. Because I can't be cursed. I am a curse.

16. PICKLED CUCUMBER

THE SHAME AND grief that were in my chest are gone. And I feel an odd thing. I feel just a little bit free. I shan't be my father's daughter any more. What has it got me? I will look to my mother, the proper tutor for a sinner. The proper tutor for a curse.

A memory comes into my heart. One from a long time ago. We had gone to the market, my mother and me. Before buying anything, she had me pick up three rotten carrots that a vegetable vendor had thrown into a ditch because they couldn't be sold. She told me to wipe them clean and hide them in my apron. *Always be looking to your advantage*, she said. Then, when she bought some carrots, she took three and had me switch them subtle-like with the rotten ones in my apron.

'You've sold me rubbish, you cheat!' she cried to the carrot vendor, loud enough that folk turned to see who was selling poor goods. He looked at the mouldy carrots and offered to replace them. Mother accepted, and we walked away, three new carrots in her hand, the three good ones she'd bought earlier still hidden in my apron.

I remember Da was calm when I told him all about our clever trick. When he confronted my mother, she got rigid where Da was smooth. 'They're all cheats and swindlers. I cheat them before they do to me,' she said.

'Mayhap that's why they cheat,' Da said back.

I never wanted to be like the Daffreys, but I certainly know how.

I'm thirsty by the time I reach the tavern row in Northside, so I pull open the door to the worst-looking alehouse on the lane. It's barely lit, with dark corners where nasty things can happen. The kind of place I imagine my Daffrey uncles might go.

The alewife eyes me through the murk. When she sees me proper, she stands up straight. 'Sissy?! Sissy?! It's the sin eater come!'

There's the clatter of a pot in the kitchen, and a woman's voice calls out, urgent, 'What does she want? Give her what she wants!'

'You do it!' calls the alewife.

'I surely will not!' answers the kitchen voice.

The alewife lifts a whole cask of ale from a low shelf and places it on the floor in front of me. 'There we are,' she says like I'm an unbroken horse she means to calm.

'Has she gone?' calls the kitchen voice.

'Not yet!' shrills the alewife.

I just wanted a cupful, but a cask will do. I lift its weight and push open the door with my bum. There's a hiss from one of the black corners of the alehouse. I hiss back.

—

Paul and Frederick are asleep wrapped in their cloaks when I arrive home. Brida's tucked into my rug in front of the hearth. In the corner is a stranger woman atop my mattress brought down from the loft.

'Jane's with child,' Brida says aloud in explanation.

Again, I see. Beside the stranger is one sleeping babe. On her back is another, this one watching me with dark moon eyes. The firelight catches the stranger's features. Hair smooth like a still pool. Skin light-coloured like bread taken from the oven too soon. Her babes look less like strangers, but still with some strange in them. Most likely a whore, this one. No doubt come to town for the Queen's upcoming revels.

I place the ale cask down by the ewer.

'Jane's from the other side of the world,' Brida says with laboured brightness, mayhap to cover the awkwardness of having taken my mattress.

'Rest yourself, Brida,' says Jane, the sound of her words are as plain as if we grew up neighbours. The care in the words is also plain, though I see Jane keeps her distance.

I go to Paul's sleeping body and finger about his pockets. He starts up, waking Frederick too, but I've already pulled a thin blade from its leather sheath. Paul cries out and holds his hands to his face, but I'm back at the cask knocking out its keystone with the knife's handle. Once tapped, I pour the ewer full of ale.

Paul, Brida, Frederick, and Jane watch out of the sides of their eyes to see what I'll do next. Jane's children watch Jane. What I do is drink.

What would my mother do in a moment like this? I ask myself.

Get her mattress back.

So I turn to it and stare. Jane, still on top of the mattress, stiffens under my look, but says nothing. I keep my gaze locked on the mattress. By and by, Jane begins to fidget.

I am a curse, I think at her, then take another sip of ale.

Her fidgeting grows to a discomfort, and before I've even drained the ewer, she moves herself off the mattress and onto the floor. In reply, I remove my gaze. The whole room softens. I take my mattress and go up the ladder to the loft.

A straw pokes through the mattress into my back, and I scratch where it bites. As I do, I'm surprised to find flesh where there's always been just skin on bone. I look for Ruth's shape in the mattress to see if I've come closer to filling it, but there's only my shape now.

In the morning, my hearth is busy with a rare bubbling pot. The stranger woman, Jane, is making a pottage smelling of gurnards and onions. A smell that at one time would send me running for a bowl. Now, all I think on is tale bearing. My bones softened by a layer of fat; I leave the others to it.

Jane's children clamber over Frederick, lean limbs falling and rising like mill wheel spokes. They look a fair bit like him. Mayhap he's their father. The older child swats the younger, and the younger bawls. The older returns a smattering of abuse in not quite formed words. Jane adds her scoldings on top, but when I walk to the ale cask, she quiets them. I feel two ways about my squatters. They're a kind of company, filling the house with their pleasant chatter and a good, warm fug. But sometimes I fear they'd just as soon bury me in the garden and take the place for themselves. I swallow a mouthful of ale and look around. Brida and Paul sit quiet before the hearth, eyes averted. Frederick and the others are still. This morning they fall on the side of company.

———

A fine spring day. What would my mother do on such a day?

The market is just beginning to do custom when I arrive. There's a man selling codling apples with a girl that looks to be his daughter. My real da was a rich man, I think. How did my mother ever meet him?

In my head I see the Country Mouse with his pink nose from the day the Norman emissary arrived. Mayhap it was by the river that my parents met. *My sire comes to town on a barge. My mother's there along the banks collecting cockles. He calls to her, offers to buy her catch. She calls back that nothing she has is for sale, giving him a look that scolds.*

He reddens. 'No, I never meant anything untoward.'

The Country Mouse would say untoward, I think. My mother would offer up a handful of cockles for having an honest heart. He would ask if she would like to join him on his barge. The wharf is busy enough that she slips aboard without a nosy wherryman making hay about it, and she, no, I am alone on the barge with the Country Mouse. He wears the same slashed sleeves as the day I first saw him. He tells me how tedious he finds the ladies of the court, how they don't know simple country-folk things like how to wash a wool blanket without turning it to felt.

Then I tell him how court ladies bloody their short breeches just the same as country girls do, and he laughs. He has a cup of strong beer that we share, and I think how his lips are touching the same place as mine as we pass it back and forth. He looks at me, and I don't feel nerves because it's like he's always known me. His eyes crease when he asks if we can't just take the barge all the way past the town and on down the river until we find a wild place no folk knows about. We moor the barge by a green bank and play hide-and-catch in the long grasses. I run so quick he admires me for it. We part the branches of an old willow and find a shadowy little place where we can be ourselves alone.

I'm drawn out of my dreaming by two boys minding a butcher's stall nearby. The elder's swinging a bull penis around trying to swat the younger with it. Who knows how my mother and sire met? For all I know he cornered her in an alley.

Up ahead I spy the sweets man. He's got all sorts of jars with delicacies in them. When I was little I'd imagine which I'd choose if ever I had the money. Sugar-paste flowers. Candied grapes. Pearled comfits. So many sorts, but I always wanted the same thing. Today, I go right up and stick my hand into the jar of orange suckets. I pull out a handful, the sugar on them gritty, like sand.

'Hey now!' the vendor calls out, then sees my sin eater collar. He turns to the other stall keepers around him. 'Hey! Hey-o! What's this?' A man selling pickled vegetables shakes his head in startlement.

The orange suckets taste nothing like sand. The sugar grit on the outside melts on my tongue so sweet my ears tingle inside like when you eat honey, but even more so. And the orange! It's got a taste that's tart, but sweet, like you ate a bright marigold.

A stick of wood hits my forearm. The sweets man raises it up to strike me again. I slip behind a goodwife just as he lets it go, and it hits her in the belly. The goodwife cries out, and the sweets man curses. Then the pickle man yells for the constable, and I go off behind some other folk, a cackle coming out of my lips. It's nerves, not pleasure, the laugh. I get out of the marketplace before the constable comes round. I can still feel the sweet of the suckets in my ears.

And now I would like some shoes. Proper corked ones, so my feet don't bruise with every stone on the road. I make my way to the lane where I found Paul begging. I recall it had a cordwainer's shop on it.

Inside, there's a maid speaking with the master of the shop. 'A pair in white leather. And if you give her cowskin for calf's, you'll not get a groat from my lady,' the maid orders.

A journeyman at work carving a heel block is the first to take notice of me. He drops his knife to the floor with a clatter. I'll need to choose quick. I bustle past the maid to a shelf where they keep the finished shoes for delivery. I slip off my left shoe, since that foot's the longer, and hold the shoe against the finished ones to compare lengths. There's a beautiful pair of boots with upper leathers as soft as gloves, but they're far too long. Made for a giant. There's several velvet slippers, even a pair of a size with my own battered one, but the velvet would stain and tear on the walk back to Dungsbrook alone. The closest fit is a pair of black leather shoes with a rounded toe. They've a corked sole, just as I want, and a strap that buttons around the ankle. The woman they've been made for has a sturdier ankle than mine, but I pull them on nevertheless.

I look up to find the journeyman still in his seat, his hand in the air where it let go of the knife. The master shoemaker is staring fixedly at a knob of thread wax on the workbench. The maid has fled. As I leave the shop she's turning onto the lane with a giant of a man. Mayhap the one who ordered the great boots. She points the giant my way. I turn and hiss. The giant stops where he is. *I am a curse.*

I start to march off down the road, but I barely take a step before I fall. Corked shoes are nothing like flat slippers. The thick, raised soles mean I can't feel the road at all. It's like walking over a floorboard, but it's strapped to your foot. I wobble, step to step, trying to find the balance of it. The thick leather of the heel chafes, and my toes bump into the front part of the shoe. I try not to be disappointed. These are the shoes important folk wear, I remind myself.

What to do next? Where have I always wanted to go, but never dared? Once I would have said the castle or inside a rich merchant's home, but I've been to those. I've been up and down stairs. I've sat at the front of a Makerhall. I've even been in a jail. Where haven't I been? And then I think of a place.

My shoes get easier to manage on the walk back through Northside. By the time I get to Dungsbrook, I'm nearly walking at my customary pace. As I pass the lane to the woad yard, I hear the call of a hawk from a nearby tree. When I look, I see only a smaller bird by a nest. It must be a cuckoo. They mimic hawks to scare brooding birds from their nests. Then the cuckoo rolls the mother's eggs out and lays its own in the nest for the other bird to raise. Nasty birds, cuckoos.

The Domus Conversorum looms above the road a few houses from mine. It's the run-down dwelling where the old king made Jews live while they converted to the new faith. A place I've never been. I've never even seen any Jews. All I know about them are three things: they're the chosen folk in the Maker's book, they're strangers, and that, kind of like fairies, there aren't any left in Angland.

A window gapes open and black like a toothless mouth on the ground floor. A collapsed chimney slumps on the dwelling's roof, and, all over, sandy bricks crumble like cottage cheese. It's as if Brida were a building, wasting away from the outside. Still, the building must have been fine once. Stone is for manor houses or Makerhalls. What a thing, to live in a stone house.

The door has been repaired and repaired again and not with good wood. It pushes open with a touch, which bodes poorly. My uncle Misgett would say: lots of bars and bolts on a door is a sign that folk inside have got more to lose than you. That's the place you go for the take. But when folk don't bar their door, it means they have less to lose than you, and you're the one who might get taken. I think on that for a good moment. Then I step inside. I have no lock on my door either.

I expect the smell of Brida, foul air to match the rotting building. Instead, despite the darkness I'm met with the comforting, gamey smell of tallow candles.

Through the shadows I make out a large sitting room with only the stout legs of a table left. Behind the legs are the innards of the toppled chimney I saw from outside. A carpet of dust tells me no folk've passed this way in a fair while. But deeper in I find a narrow path of footsteps cutting through the dust to a set of stairs. Folk have been here lately.

And then I hear a lute.

My guts drop. The music is coming from up the stairs. Somefolk is here.

It's music of a kind I've never heard. Both sweet and sad. A flute joins with the lute. There's more than one folk. How could such a thing be coming from the ruins of the Domus Conversorum? Mayhap Jews are like fairies, and it's magic. They were the Maker's chosen folk, after all.

The flute plays a different song, but one that still belongs with what the lute's playing. It's like when you sing in a round at May Day, but more intricate. The song makes my heart squeeze up like I'm grieving. I want to weep but also smile. It's not fairy music, it's music of the heavenly plains. But played by angels or demons? I gird myself, and step towards the stairs. Whatever lies beyond, I tell myself, I am more fearsome.

Beyond the fourth step is blackness, so I follow the music, feeling my way with my shoes, until I reach the landing. To one side is more blackness, but the other wavers with the faintest flickering light through a poorly hung door. The music's so strong I feel it all the way down in my guts. I go on to the door with no notion of what I might find behind it.

It's as if a conjuror has made another world appear. Inside the ruined Domus Conversorum are the Queen's musicians, the strangers I heard play at the emissary's arrival. They wear her badge. Six or seven of them. All sitting atop stools in a circle, playing lutes, flutes, and viols. As I step in, the wiry, dark-haired man I saw before brings his bow up to his giant viol and suddenly its sound is rumbling again through my chest.

Behind them, against the walls, are rugs and blankets and other bedding. Sacks and trunks are strewn about as if the musicians came from afar. A window lets in feeble light and tallow candles burn from ledges and tables.

An old body with hair on his ears, but not his crown, stands. The music stops awkward-like. The musicians get still. 'This is our place, if it please you,' Hairy Ears says. His accent is like the strangers that come in summer by wagon to perform comedies in the town square.

I wait for them to notice my *S* and skitter-scatter with alarum. I'm sorry for it. I would like to hear more of their sweet and sad music.

But they don't scatter. 'Please leave us,' Hairy Ears says again, not angry or scared, more like a child who has a piece of cake and hopes to hold on to it.

I bring my hand to my collar to show him who I am, but he keeps speaking. 'This is our place. The Queen, she give us the invitation to come bring our music. But no inn will take us. No folk lets us the rooms. So we come to here, where our kin before us come for to be safe.' The whole while he speaks, Hairy Ears looks me dead in the eyes. So do the other musicians. There's a dripping feeling on the back of my neck. Something's deeply wrong.

I assay whether the tallow candlelight passes through the musicians' bodies. It doesn't. At least they aren't spirits. They're real, solid folk.

I grab the *S* on my collar and hold it up for them all to see. *I am a curse.*

Hairy Ears takes a step back and speaks to the wiry man playing the chest rumbler in a stranger tongue.

I stamp my foot hard against the floor. The musicians murmur at one another, but they don't take their eyes from me. I feel naked and weak. Why don't they fear me? Choler heats my heart. I huff like a bull. And then, without thought, I run through the room knocking the candles from their holders, spraying burning tallow everywhere. Stools scrape hard against the floor as the shrieking musicians scramble into the corners of the room.

At last, I tell the Domus walls. *This is how a sin eater should be greeted.*

—

I walk to my fountain. *The musicians must not have seen the collar properly in the low light*, the fountain tells me. I want its words to make me feel better, but I'm not sure it's telling the truth.

I let my bare feet dangle in the fountain's water. The new shoes have rubbed them raw. My toes move back and forth, cool and light, but I'm not feeling the freedom I thought I might after a day as a curse.

The nails of my toes are filthy. I jiggle my toes so I can't see the dirt through the water. The flesh on my calf moves back and forth. That's new. Mayhap my monthly courses will come back with all this new plump on me. I stopped getting them when food got scarce. I'll need to get blood moss and sew up blood breeches to hold them in place.

I remind myself again that I'm free. Beholden to none. I jiggle my leg again to see the flesh wiggle. But it's no good. My mother was skilled at this sort of thing, at doing as she pleased. But not me. I run my tongue over my back teeth where there's still the faint taste of orange. Eating sweets is nice. Having new shoes is, too. But what would please me more?

To live in my old home.

To have my old life.

To see Da again.

I can't get these things. But I do think of one thing I can get.

I leave the fountain and make my way back through town. It doesn't take long to find what I want in the back of a wagon. And none see me lift it.

When I arrive home there's no messengers waiting. Off looking for me, mayhap. My squatters are gone too. I go up to my loft with what I took from the wagon. It's not a particu-larly valuable thing. Just a wooden box. I place it on the bottom shelf alongside Ruth's, alongside the boxes of all the sin eaters before me. I don't have anything to put in it yet. But in time I might. It feels good to see it next to the others.

I haven't more than sat down on my mattress when a rapping comes at the door. I wonder if there's ever a day that passes on this earth without death. A whole day of only life, living and thriving. There's another rapping at the door. Not this day.

The messenger's well dressed and wears a badge I don't know. A Recitation, he tells me, for a condemned prisoner in the Queen's dungeon. I feel the little plum stone in my chest again, grating against my heart. I'm going back to the place Ruth died.

17. HIPPOCRAS

IN MY OLD life, I never purposely walked the town at night. What girl would when there's hog boons and goblins and worse trolling the darkened alleys looking for a choice bit? A howl from the lane to the woad yard scares me and the messenger right proper. I remind myself, *I am the hog boon. Brida's the goblin.* And the worse? They're all tucked away in the castle poisoning and setting poppets at one another. *Safer out here.*

Crossing the town square, I wonder if the condemned prisoner is the Eucharistian countess I once saw in the dungeon. The one put there for plotting against the Queen.

A constable comes into the square and raises a lantern towards me and the messenger. I open my shawl to show my

S, and he leaves us to our business. My nerves fade. There's a sort of peace in the night-time. Figures melt into shadows, eyes watch from the dark, but like putting my own box on the shelf, I feel a sort of belonging. Mayhap my place isn't a house or a family, mayhap it's my trade, sin eating.

———

At the castle, I'm led across the quiet courtyard. The plum stone in my heart seems to swell, my breath coming harder around it.

I climb down the ten mouldy steps into the dungeon. The countess's cell was one of the nearest to the entrance, I remember. But it's not hers I'm taken to.

A man waits outside the cell, wearing the same badge as the messenger. Mouldy Beard, the young guard from my last visit, unlocks the door. Inside is an old body, sitting as if waiting. There's candles and a writing table and his chair has a cushion. He offers me the chair. Then he kneels on the stone floor. It's the Eucharistian way to give your Recitation.

He hasn't much to recite. He doesn't even recite being Eucharistian. I think it's because he doesn't believe it's a sin. It feels odd for me to know he has a sin, but for him not to recite it. I keep wanting him to say it. I even say it in my own heart. But then he finishes, and there's nothing for it. I say the words to end and give the scant list of foods to the man with the badge waiting outside the cell.

I've done my duty, but I can't quite leave. It's Ruth. I feel like part of her is still here, farther down the passage, in the cell where she died. A part of her that's unsettled. Waiting.

She's with the Maker now, not in a cold, stone cell, I remind myself.

But then my feet start down the passage, and soon I'm in the dark curve that takes me to the nethermost part of the dungeon.

I stand outside Ruth's old cell door, suddenly afraid to look in. Afraid her bloodstains will still be there. I remember the promise I made to her on Da's grave that I would sort out this mess of deer hearts for her. I haven't done it. I've just been biding my time, hoping it would happen on its own. I think that's what she's waiting for. For me to act.

There's a soft cough inside the cell. My heart leaps. *Ruth.* I scramble to the door's hole to see if it's her, knowing that it can't be, and hoping all the same.

But of course it's not. I know the gnarled figure inside even from the back. The Willow Tree, a candle at his side, leaning over a body.

'Are you there?' he calls. I step back from the peephole before he sees me. 'You may unlock the door, I've finished.'

When there's no answer he calls louder, 'Hello?!' Footsteps echo down the passage. I move into a shadow as Mouldy Beard comes around the curve. He peeps into Ruth's old cell.

'Found the witch this time, did you?' Mouldy Beard asks.

'Lamentably, no,' the Willow Tree says back. 'Maker help us.'

Mouldy Beard unlocks the door, and the Willow Tree comes out wiping his hands on a dark cloth. As he passes Mouldy Beard he says, 'You can remove the body.'

It takes a good while for Mouldy Beard to drag the woman

out. She smells of burnt meat. I keep my eyes in the shadows so I won't see what the Willow Tree did to her. After Mouldy Beard's gone, I finally make my way out of the dungeon.

It's deep night, and a full moon lights the courtyard. I don't know if it's the Willow Tree's work or the witching hour, but my guts are all wobbly. *I belong in the night*, I remind myself, and start to make my way home.

I haven't gone far across the courtyard when something curious catches my eye. From the shadow of a doorway, a small light flickers twice and then disappears. A moment later it comes again, like a candle flame, flashing twice, and then gone.

I'm trying to fathom what it might be when I catch the sound of a door opening on the other side of the courtyard. I keep still as a rabbit as a hooded figure walks sure and direct through the moonlight towards the flashing.

The light appears again, this time steady. Steady enough that I can see it's a candle held by a man. The hooded figure joins him. If they speak, it's too low to hear. All at once the hooded figure reaches into the hood and tugs. He offers what he's plucked to the candle man. The candle man wraps the hairs in a kerchief.

Hairs plucked under moonlight. I hear my mother's voice recounting how witches wait till the full moon to pluck hairs for their blackest magic. As if hearing my thoughts, a guard suddenly calls, 'Who's there!' One hand on his sword and the other holding a lantern, the guard trots towards the two figures.

The candle man doesn't even startle. Instead, he and the hooded figure wait, calm as anything, for the guard to approach. The guard raises the lantern to the candle man's face. It's the Willow Tree.

Then the other man pulls off his hood. The guard starts back. Then hastily bows his head. It's not a man. It's the Queen.

She directs the guard to join her. He follows at her side like a dog, lighting the way to the scroll door that leads to her quarters. The Willow Tree watches them go, then pinches out his candle and shuffles across the stone courtyard with only moonlight to guide him.

My arms and legs get light like I might swoon. The witch finder is collecting hairs for witchcraft and the Queen is a part of his treachery. And I witnessed it. Had I returned home direct after the prisoner's Recitation, I'd never have seen a thing.

Ruth. Mayhap this is why I was drawn to her cell. Mayhap it's time to sort out this mess.

I hear Bessie's voice, *You've your mother's blood in you.* My mother never sat back waiting for something to happen. She was wary like a fox, but a hunter still.

But what can I do? I ask my Daffrey blood. There are guards all about the castle, and, worse still, Black Fingers.

Follow the Willow Tree, my blood says. *Softly, nimbly, find out his game.*

The Willow Tree's shadowed figure is growing harder to see. My whole body's alight with nerves as I begin to trail him.

I follow him across the courtyard, beyond the scroll door. He passes through an archway where the stones are crumbly beneath our feet. I get a sudden inkling where he's headed. I've been here once before. He finally stops before two ancient, wooden doors. The Queen's private Makerhall. Then he disappears inside.

And I follow.

I step as quiet as my new shoes allow into the Queen's Makerhall. The Willow Tree's vanished. Just then, there's a small scrape up by the altar. I duck down behind a pew as the Willow Tree appears from the vestment room, holding a long beeswax candle. A woman I don't know follows after, carrying a cloth bundle. The Willow Tree begins to chant softly.

He's saying stranger words mixed with Anglish. It's not a new faith prayer. It's witchcraft, I know it.

The woman is nearly as tall as the Willow Tree and much thicker. She places her bundle at the foot of the altar and opens a book. She joins the chant.

> *Ho ktistais,*
> *Ho ktistais,*
> *Thou art powerful and eternal, Maker.*

They say the words over and over again, and then some more. I get dizzy with the sound. Mayhap I'm falling under whatever spell they mean to cast. I shake my head, and my collar clinks. The Willow Tree raises his hand, and the woman gets quiet.

I hold myself still, barely daring to breathe. The Willow Tree surveys the pews. He pauses for a moment on the bench in front of me. I hold my breath until it hurts. Then he takes up the chant again. When the woman joins him, I finally let my breath go in a long, quiet rush.

They chant until the beeswax candle burns down the width of three fingers. Then all at once they stop. The quiet pricks at my nerves.

The Willow Tree speaks softly. 'Maker, we come here to your temple. We speak words more ancient than the Makermen's. Your devoted servants, we seek protection for our mistress. We place her substance and her likeness before you.' The Willow Tree takes his kerchief with the Queen's hairs and puts it on the altar. Then the woman brings out a miniature portrait and lays it beside the hairs.

The Willow Tree bows. 'Protect her, Maker, against the forces now at work to savage her. Protect her as you protect your champions.' It's some sort of black magic mixed with the Maker faith. I didn't know there was such a thing.

The Willow Tree goes on. 'We beg you to take our offering. A tribute given in exchange for your safeguard. A sacrifice. A life for life.' It's then that I hear a muffled shriek from the bundle at the base of the altar. The terrified cry of a baby.

18. SHORTBREAD

ALL AT ONCE I'm not a curse. I'm a girl alone in a terrible predicament. I try to quiet my breath, but it just comes all the louder. These two mean to murder a babe in a Makerhall not ten paces from me.

'Silence it!' the Willow Tree hisses. The woman drops to her knees and grabs at the squealing bundle. She raises it to the altar.

I feel a warm stickiness on my hands. I've squeezed my nails into my palms so hard, they've begun to bleed.

'Do it presently!' the woman whispers hard.

The Willow Tree reaches into his robe and takes out a short, thick knife. He chants again:

Ho ktistais,
Ho ktistais . . .

The bundle begins to kick, but the woman holds it tight, muffling the sound.

My knees are leaden, but I will them to rise.

The Willow Tree steps towards the altar. The bundle twists under the woman's grasp.

I'm standing now, but I've done it so suddenly that my head's full of stars, and for a moment I can barely see. I stumble forward anyway, for there's no time.

Ho ktistais
Ho ktistais . . .

The Willow Tree raises the dagger in the air. I'm only halfway there. A glint of candlelight from the knife blade hits my eyes. I won't make it in time. The woman pulls the cloth from the tiny, squealing body, and I see a flash of pink skin as the knife comes down. There's one last squeal.

I cry aloud as I fall hard onto my knees.

The Willow Tree's head whips towards where I've fallen, but I'm back behind a pew. 'Block the door!' he whispers.

The woman's already running for the entrance. If they'll kill a babe in a Makerhall, what will they do to me if I'm caught? I squeeze my jaw shut to stop my teeth from shaking. I need another way out.

Behind the altar is the vestment room. Mayhap there's a passage in and out for the Makermen. I scramble along the cold, stone floor beneath the pew towards the side of the hall. When I get to the end I listen. I only hear one set of footfalls: the fast pat of the woman near the entrance. I hazard a look. The Willow Tree is only paces away, and he's still got his knife.

'There!' he hisses.

I dash out and make for the front of the hall. I hear the woman's feet on the stone floor pursuing me. She's faster than I am. I don't know that I'll make it.

Look to your advantage.

I don't have any. But then I remember the Willow Tree's voice. He's kept it low and quiet. They don't want any folk to hear what they're doing. I cannot speak, but I can surely scream.

I open my mouth and hurl my voice wordlessly into the hall. The stones echo my scream back again and again. The woman freezes, her eyes widening. I don't stop to see what she does next. I stumble into the vestment room. There's a small door to my right. I race to it. I don't know where I'm going, but in I go. The door swings closed behind me.

The passageway is narrow and completely dark. I keep my hands along the walls to feel my way. I make a turn and then another. I listen for the woman or the Willow Tree, but they must have fled when I screamed.

At long last, my fingers find a door. I open it as quiet as I can and come out in a hall dimly lit by moonlight. A table sits centre, and the Queen's badge, a falcon above a rose, hangs on the wall over the head chair. Along the other walls are the banners of the most loyal families. Black Fingers's lion hangs to the side of the Queen's banner. Beside the lion is the family banner of Katryna, the Queen's stepmother, the fair-haired maiden rising from a flower. Beyond that is a banner with a stag. The Country Mouse's family.

In my head I see the dark pool of blood on the altar. I didn't stop them. I crawl under the table and hug myself into a ball. I breathe in and out, in and out, for a long, long time.

———

Dawn light's just creeping in the window when I'm startled awake by voices passing outside the hall.

'It was witches?' a woman's voice asks.

'Don't know,' a second woman answers. 'But the Queen's likeness was on the altar. And the blood . . .' I see the altar again in my mind. 'Hope you've plenty of rags in that basket.'

'Oh, I've seen how the little ones bleed out,' says the first voice. 'You'd think all they had in them is blood!' My heart lurches in my chest. She says it so easy, as if it's nothing to have seen a babe murdered.

What black place have I come to? What hope do folk have in a world such as this? I bury my head in my knees, so I only barely hear her when she finishes. 'Slaughtering a piglet on the Maker's altar, the sin eater will feast on that one day.'

It takes a moment for her words to settle in. When they do, my bark of laughter is so loud, I fear the women will hear it from the corridor.

A piglet, not a baby.

It's the first good news I've had in I can't remember how long. Whatever the Willow Tree is about, it's not murdering folk. I shove my skirt into my mouth, because after all the misery of this night, my heart wants to laugh. Never did I guess I'd count a pig slaughtered in a Makerhall as good fortune. Which just makes me laugh all the more. Which is how they hear me.

19. KIDNEY PIE

I'M HELD IN a chamber on the ground floor of the castle. Through the window I can see the dungeon entrance across the courtyard. The window's glass is old and has thickened near the bottom so the dungeon door seems to be sinking down towards the earth.

The Willow Tree refolds his hands at his waist. The thick, silver needle on his finger catches the light from the misshapen window.

Black Fingers stands across from him, his eyes dark from rim to centre. 'The sin eater was not summoned,' he says low and hard to the Willow Tree.

'Her arrival is surely a portent,' says the Willow Tree back. 'Where was she found?' He seems calm and settled, not at

231

all like I saw him last night. It makes him all the more terrifying.

'She was found in the banner room,' Black Fingers says. 'Near the Makerhall.'

The Willow Tree gets very still. If he didn't know it was me who saw him in the Makerhall, he must surely guess it now. The air in the room feels too close and smells of smoke like the chimney's not been swept.

Black Fingers tugs at his ear. 'Is she responsible for the bloody horror found this morn in our Queen's Makerhall? Is she our witch?'

The Willow Tree lifts his head. A square of sunlight falls on half his face, 'If she was near the place . . .'

Oh, Maker mine. He's going to blame me for his sorcery. My teeth start shaking again.

Black Fingers's voice gets low. 'I will question her. And I will make this one speak.' The shaking moves from my teeth to my guts.

'No,' the Willow Tree says quick. 'I will take her and perform a witch's trial instead.' He doesn't want me to tell Black Fingers what I saw.

'The Queen's protection is my purview, not yours,' Black Fingers snaps.

'And witches are my purview,' the Willow Tree says back.

I don't know which is worse: to be crushed by stones by Black Fingers or bled and burned by the Willow Tree. The smell of smoke gets stronger. I must be swooning.

'The Queen is threatened on all sides,' spits Black Fingers. 'Witches, Eucharistian spies, and two of her own ladies shown to be murderesses of royalty by the deer hearts on their coffins! Other sovereigns will not waste time in taking advantage of a Queen so weakened by scandal. If this creature' – he nods towards me – 'can offer any intelligence on the matter, I will discover it!'

The Willow Tree gives a barking sort of laugh. 'The Norman king doesn't believe Queen Bethany is complicit in her ladies' sins. Neither does the Lowland king, nor her Eucharistian cousin in the North. No, sir, they hear of deer hearts on coffins and see our Queen surrounded by traitors and spies, just as they fear they themselves are. The deer hearts are no threat to her.'

'And the witches?! The Eucharistians?!'

'I will protect her!' The Willow Tree's voice gets too loud for the room. 'The ancients foretold a virgin queen who would unify the world under one faith. I do the Maker's work! And you, sir?' His voice gets even louder still. 'Your statecraft is to kill and scheme and plot like a common rogue!'

Suddenly there's a scream from deep in the castle. More cries follow, coming from the courtyard. 'Find the doctor!' I hear.

All at once there's banging at the chamber door.

'How now?' cries Black Fingers.

A guard steps into the room, 'Fire!' He nods to the Willow Tree. 'The doctor is needed urgently.' Then he sees me. 'The sin eater as well.'

The Willow Tree's voice booms. 'There it is! She's not our witch.'

'What?!' Black Fingers cries. 'Moments ago you wished to perform a witch's trial!'

'Yes, when I believed her to have come to the castle without purpose. But now I see the Maker's work in this. He drew her here with the prospect of death!' The Willow Tree goes on. 'Like a maggot to rotting flesh. This is why she came.'

'Not good enough!' says Black Fingers.

'Then I shall perform a trial here, now. Will you act as witness?'

Black Fingers's eyes narrow.

The Willow Tree raises up his hand, his witch pricker catching the light. It's half the length of a finger and as thick as a coffin nail. Quicker than you'd ever guess he could, he thrusts the needle deep into the meat of my shoulder. A howl rips from my guts out of my mouth. The guard who announced the fire begins the Maker's Prayer. The Willow Tree pulls the needle out, and I clutch at my shoulder to stop the blood.

The Willow Tree looks at Black Fingers with wide, bright eyes. 'I am certain, my lord, you have heard enough cries of true pain to recognize that as honest. She is not our witch.'

I don't know what Black Fingers believes, but he doesn't want to let me go.

The Willow Tree keeps speaking. 'The sin eater is the Maker's servant. I believe you once said yourself that to interfere with the Maker's will is' – the Willow Tree clears his throat – 'treason.'

A vein bulges from Black Fingers's brow. Finally, finally he gestures to the guards to allow me to pass.

As we walk down the passage, the Willow Tree speaks aloud. There's no folk but me to hear. 'I do believe the Maker gives signs to his most trusted servants. This fire is his sign to me that you are necessary, and, therefore, I should show you mercy.' His flat-backed head sways side to side as he goes, his words light and easy. 'But should you prove a danger, I will use you on the altar. A sin eater's blood would no doubt prove a most potent offering.'

He starts up a set of stairs. I follow. My shoulder throbs where the needle stuck me, but little giggles break into my breaths.

No curse can harm me. *I am a curse.*

———

The chamber smells of meat and sage. Two bodies lie on couches. A slender apothecary in a dark robe is already at work over one body covering the burns with salve. The uncovered parts of the body are black with ash and mottled white and red like a skinned rabbit.

Meg, Tilly Howe's friend, leans over a second body, placing linen bandages on one shoulder. I take up a bandage from her stack and press it to my own shoulder.

The Willow Tree holds a kerchief to his nose and assays the room. Just standing so near to him makes my guts feel loose. 'What's happened?' he asks.

The apothecary doesn't answer, intent as he is on his work. Meg does instead. 'One of the ladies heard a cry from the bedchamber next to hers and called for help. Took four guards to open the door. The lady inside was saved, but the fire spread to the chamber above. Young lords,' she nods at the bodies, for it's difficult to tell who they are. 'I helped Tilly Howe, Maker keep her soul, with enough births, I'm not bothered by the blood and the . . . the smell.' A soft moan comes from the man Meg tends.

'Poppy oil,' directs the Willow Tree. 'And snails. Their phlegm pulls heat from the body.'

The apothecary sits back. 'They've had their dose of poppy oil. More's like to kill them.' He says nothing about the snails.

I stay as far from the Willow Tree as I can manage in the close space, but my eyes keep finding their way back to him. He may not have killed a babe, but he's still a witch. I wonder if he made the poppet.

The apothecary stands.

'Your work is not done,' says the Willow Tree.

'There is a third patient, sir,' the apothecary says back.

'Oh?' asks the Willow Tree. 'Where is he?'

'She,' answers the apothecary. 'The lady whose room caught fire. She was brought to a private chamber for her comfort.'

'I shall go to her myself,' announces the Willow Tree. The apothecary wants to argue, but gives in, bowing his head.

Once the Willow Tree's gone, I let go of a breath. I take a moment to wrap my shoulder tightly in the bandage. It's sore and throbbing.

'Meg, fetch a bowl of water, would you?' the apothecary asks. As she's leaving, the apothecary goes on. 'I hope the sin eater will allow us to stay and soothe the injured during her work.'

I find a stool and set it out of the apothecary's way, which I hope is answer enough. The man with the piebald flesh has red stockings under a layer of soot. It's the Rooster. His eyes are partly open, though he seems to be asleep. I say the words, but he doesn't stir. The apothecary clears his throat and moves a small jar on the table. Poppy oil.

I hear a voice behind me. 'Would you hear my Recitation?'

My heart gets too big for my ribs. I know the voice even though I only heard it once. It's the Country Mouse. 'Tell me,' he asks slow and thick, 'is my arm woolly like a sheep?'

I tuck a laugh inside a cough. The burns cover his whole shoulder. I hope the poppy oil is strong.

'You may speak your sins to me,' I say. I expect my words to be crusty and hard, like bread left out too long, but they come out right.

Meg arrives carrying a full ewer of water. She sees me with the Country Mouse and makes herself useful squeezing drops of water into the Rooster's mouth.

'It's you, isn't it.' The Country Mouse takes a few slow breaths. 'The one who found my ring.' His eyes stay on the ceiling like it hurts to turn his head. 'My burns are not deep, not the worst of burns. Not like . . . him.' He must mean the Rooster. 'The apothecary says the great risk is corruption, but the pain might do me.' His face almost smiles and, in spite of my weariness, or mayhap because of it, it makes me smile too. The room's warm, so I unwrap my shawl and place it to the side. 'So, I recite everything I've done wrong now?' he asks.

'Yes,' I say as gentle as I can. 'And I'll tell you the foods I'll eat.'

'What if I don't want to burden you with my sins, seeing as we're old friends?' This time I do laugh. It's what he said when I first met him.

I look to Meg and the apothecary, but they pay me no mind. 'You could give me your virtues instead,' I tell him.

'Why there's a thing! How is it no folk has ever thought of that? Reciting our virtues before we die instead of our sins. How brilliant.'

In my mind I hear, *you're brilliant*. I start to laugh a little again, but tears come out too, like I'm too worn out to know which is which. I wipe my eyes on my sleeve. 'Speak.'

'Well, now I can't recall any virtues, only sins. Not praying enough. Thinking poorly of my father for sending me here to seek the Queen's hand. Who am I to marry a queen?'

'Loyalty,' I interrupt. 'That's a virtue.'

'What makes you say that?'

'The ring. Your gold ring.'

'Of course, my ring.' His bandages rustle with his breath. 'I remember that day, you know, the day I met you. Your face was so different from everyfolk else's. Open, if you will.'

My tears come a little harder, but so does my smiling. It's my daydream of how a lord and a common girl might meet come to life. Come to my life.

'Kind,' I say. 'Another virtue.'

'Charitable,' he answers. 'That's one for you.'

'Not always,' I say.

He coughs or laughs; I can't tell which. 'Good, I don't want to look poorly by comparison. I've thought of another sin.'

'Honesty,' I say back. 'Another virtue.'

'Mmm,' he warns. 'I'm a thief. I've stolen a cat.'

'A cat?'

'A kitten,' he amends. 'This town, it's a hard sort of place.'

'I've always lived here.'

'I can tell you, there are other places. Winter's still winter. Plague still comes. But folk wish each other well, if you know what I mean. Here it's not like that.'

'So you stole a cat?'

'Kitten.' He shifts his head and breathes hard for a moment. 'I imagine I'll return home now. I'm surely not fit for a queen now, if I ever was.' I look at his shoulder. At the very least he'll be deeply scarred, worse than Paul's face. 'What'll become of the kitten when I go? Or if I die?'

He says it easily like he doesn't really believe it might happen. I want to tell him death does happen. Every day, I see it. More regular than rain. Into my head comes a picture of what his coffin lid would look like. I think another thought to get away from the picture. 'The kitten survived the fire?'

'She did at that. I tucked her into my shirt. Is she about?'

I look over the couch, but there's no kitten. But then there she is, underneath, asleep on the floor rushes.

'Did you find her?' the Country Mouse asks. 'She would be a comfort.'

I scoop her up. She has grey fur and grey eyes. She sniffs about my clothes, pulling at them with needle claws.

'Wait.' His breath catches. 'Have you touched her?' There's fear in his voice.

Drops of water fall into the basin behind me. My daydream fades away.

'My touch won't curse her,' I say quiet.

'Are you certain?'

'I am.'

'Oh . . . fine, then,' he says, but his voice falters. It says this moment is made of paste, like the jewel in the necklace my da mended. But I don't want the Country Mouse to be false.

'Faith,' I say hotly. 'Another virtue.'

There's a moment before he speaks again. 'Do you ever think we're living the wrong life? Like if we could choose for ourselves, we'd choose better than the one we've got?'

'I'd choose my da back,' I say before I can stop myself. I have to remind myself my da wasn't really my da.

'I'd trade places with my younger brother,' he says, and the finger with the gold ring twitches. 'But there's no use in wishing is there?'

'We can make little choices,' I think aloud to him. 'Like how we go about the day. And who we want to be like.'

'I suppose we can.' He gives a shuddering sigh, and his breathing gets rougher. The poppy oil must be waning. Behind me the apothecary gives a small cough.

I want to talk a little more, even just to prove the moment isn't paste. Instead, I place the kitten on the stool and say the words, 'When the food is et, your sins will be mine.' My hand is a little bird, my fingers like feathers, as I touch him shoulder to hip and shoulder to hip again. 'I will bear your sins in silence to my grave.' Then I whisper so low and quick he'll never hear it, 'I'd choose you.'

'May it be,' he says back. My heart catches, wondering if he heard me.

Even if he didn't, it's a good ending. Me touching him. Him saying my name. I know how he would say it, if I could choose for myself. I take the empty bottle of poppy oil and put it in my sleeve for my sin eater box. A token of him.

20. DRIED RAISINS

OUTSIDE IN THE passage, grooms carry away burnt wood and cloth. Maids kneel with brushes, scrubbing at the ashes.

'Her lock was stuck with pitch so the door wouldn't open,' a skinny maid with a few hairs on her lip tells a plumper one. 'Took four guards.'

'Another poppet was found,' is what the plump one says back.

The skinny one gets pale. 'It made the fire in the lady's room?'

The plump one shrugs. 'Poppet was found in the Queen's bedchamber. Made of beeswax and dressed like the Queen herself.'

'The castle's full of witches!' hisses the skinny one.

An old body who looks like a steward steps over, and the maids drop their shoulders into cleaning the blackened stones. 'I'll have no more mouth-running from you two,' the steward says. 'A heretic traitor's trying to frighten the Queen and her suitors is what's about. The fire, the poppet, the blood – the Queen's secretary told us himself, and he isn't a man to be wrong.' The steward steps in front of me, and moves his arm like I should follow.

He leads me down a set of stairs and along a corridor. Just as he turns a corner, he stops short. He looks to the wall and clears his throat. Beyond him I see a man and woman pulling out of an embrace in an alcove. The man is Black Fingers.

'My lord,' the steward calls. 'I'm bringing the sin eater to . . .' His voice falters.

'Then do it!' Black Fingers says, sharp-like.

'Yes, my lord.' The steward nods and skirts around Black Fingers, eyes direct on the corridor ahead of him. Black Fingers remains where he stands, masking the woman he's with, still in the alcove behind him. I see only her pale pink skirts as we pass.

We arrive at the door of the third fire victim. Mush Face stands against the wall in her plain wool dress, a basket in her hands.

'Has the Queen's physician gone, milady?' the steward asks her.

Mush Face nods. 'But none came to the door when I knocked.'

The steward steps up to the door and gives a loud rap. 'Sin eater's come!'

'I've been waiting,' Mush Face calls out. But it's not the steward she's speaking to. Behind us down the corridor comes Fair Hair. In a bright pink stomacher and pale pink kirtle. She was the one embracing Black Fingers.

'I was looking for something to bring her comfort,' Fair Hair says to Mush Face, raising a small basket of her own. She joins Mush Face by the door. Fair Hair's stomacher, I notice, is too tight and her breasts are like rising dough pushing out of the open partlet at the top. She's plumped up. I'm not the only one who seems to notice. Fair Hair wriggles under Mush Face's gaze. 'May we see her?' She nods towards the door.

The steward coughs. 'The sin eater's been requested, milady.'

Fair Hair sighs. 'Perhaps we should return later.'

'Let's wait,' Mush Face says back, placing her basket against the wall outside the chamber.

The steward knocks again.

'Is lavender or sage better for headaches?' I hear Fair Hair ask Mush Face.

'How would I know?'

'You spent so much time with the old midwife,' Fair Hair answers. 'Or were you contemplating joining a trade so you could afford some new sleeves?'

A maid finally opens the chamber door. The steward gives a small nod and leaves down the passage. While the maid's announcing me, I see Mush Face's hands disappear into her wide sleeves, the only ones I've seen her wear. 'Are you certain it's your head that pains you?' she says low to Fair Hair. 'I heard it was your belly.'

Fair Hair hisses right back, 'Perhaps you should watch what you say, lest you wind up with a witch's pin in your cunny.' I don't let my step show my startlement, but I steal another small look at the two ladies as I go in. Fair Hair's cheeks are as pink as her stomacher. Mush Face stares back at her with an odd look. Almost like respect.

—

The woman inside's face is bare, but I still recognize the Painted Pig. Her eyes are ringed with red, and her unpainted cheeks have a faint mottle that reminds me of Paul's skin. Her hand flutters to cover it under my look. 'White lead paint poisons the skin,' she says. 'The more one uses, the more one must use.'

I find a stool. The Painted Pig's left foot is bandaged. The rest of her seems untouched. 'I may not die from my burns,' she says once we're alone. 'But somefolk meant to kill me. I fear greatly for my life. I wish to recite my sins now, lest my opportunity be lost.'

I say the words to begin the Recitation. Like the last chamber, this one's warm. It makes me want to sleep.

'Covetousness, arrogance, vanity,' she begins. She's prepared for this. Her sins shoot off like arrows from her soul to mine. 'Fault-finding, meanness . . .' My eyes get heavy, and it's my own head jerking up that wakes me. She's quiet, as if she's done.

'Any last words—' I start.

'Did Corliss recite a sin that warranted a deer heart?' All at once I'm very much awake. 'Did Tilly Howe?' The Painted Pig looks to the door, but we're alone. 'Well, I will not recite something I did not do, no matter the consequence.'

She knows something about the deer hearts.

Please say more. Please say more. Please say more.

I remember my uncle Uric. He knew how to get folk to talk. I saw it more than once in the Daffrey kitchen. What he'd do is this: sit opposite them and say nothing. It seemed too easy, but a few minutes with quiet, terrifying Uric staring at them, folk'd rush in to fill up the silence with words.

I look the Painted Pig direct in her red-rimmed eyes and count my breaths in silence. It takes only until eight for her to speak. 'It was Corliss and that frumpy little midwife, in all events.' She says it sharp-like, then stops like her body's at war with her thoughts. 'I shouldn't blame Corliss. All of us were living in Katryna and Baron Seymaur's household – Corliss and the other ladies, their tutors, Katryna and Bethany's physicians . . . Maris was still queen and desperate to produce an heir so Angland would remain Eucharistian.' She worries a ring on her finger. 'We all saw what Bethany was involved with. None of us protected her well enough. Katryna, her stepmother, should have done, but she was with child and doing poorly. Bethany was a rash, choleric, un-tethered girl, just like her father. And Bethany's own mother was killed for witchcraft, incest, fornication! We knew well what might happen.'

She gazes up like her thoughts are strung across the ceiling.

'Then Katryna died leaving little baby Miranda and Bethany alone with the baron. And only a few years later the baron was executed for treason. I remember the day he died. His badge, those golden wings, burned on the castle gates. Took two blows to sever his head.'

She sits for a moment, then her voice gets soft. 'We helped Bethany, but not in the way she wanted. We swore on the Maker's name never to reveal what we did.'

All at once, she looks direct at me. 'I am not so thick as they all think. The secretary believes a Eucharistian is trying to dethrone our Queen, but I am sure the threat is closer to home.' She's got begging eyes, but I don't know what she wants. All she's told me is a jumble of old stories, and none that explains the deer hearts.

The Painted Pig clutches at her hands. 'The truth should have died fifteen years ago. It was Corliss's folly. She wove the secret into a tapestry so one day Queen Bethany would know what we did. And now its meaning has been discovered, but not by the Queen. By whom, I don't know. All I know is this: we're being murdered so the crime will be revealed to the world on our coffins. But we didn't kill a babe. Not Corliss and not Tilly and not me.' She sinks back slow and loose, like a wrung-out rag.

I think she's finished, but then she says one more thing. 'If I die, will judgement come down upon my killer?' She looks at me as if I have the answer. I know what the Makermen say, but that's not what she's asking. She's asking *me*, will I bring judgement on her killer.

My lips say the words. 'When the food is et, your sins

will be mine.' My fingers touch her shoulder to hip and back again in the Maker's sign. And my head nods one nod.

I will find your killer.

She seems to breathe easier. But it's not for her I'll do it. I'll do it for Ruth.

21. GARLIC

WHEN I OPEN the door to the Painted Pig's room, Fair Hair and Mush Face are gone. A shudder runs up my back at the sight of the Willow Tree, not two paces away. Was he listening at the door?

'I've come to take the list of foods,' he says as if to the Painted Pig, but I know it's meant for me. I stand before him and tell him the foods, smelling the same musty smell I did when he took the list of foods after Corliss's Recitation. I wonder that he doesn't let a steward or maid bring the list to the kitchen clerk.

Once he's gone, I lean against the wood-panelled wall to have a think. I still smell smoke in the air, and there's tracks of ash along the floor.

Let it tell you, comes Da's voice.

I let what I already know come back to me. Corliss and Tilly Howe were poisoned and hearts placed on their coffins, saying they murdered a royal babe, even though they never confessed such a thing.

The Painted Pig's door was stuck with pitch and a fire set in her room. She was meant to die next. Her words echo in my head. *We're being murdered so the crime will be revealed to the world by our coffins.*

It's like the fairy tale of Mr Fox where Clever Mary kills him and, in so doing, shows the town his crimes. If the Painted Pig's right, the killer isn't blaming them for another folk's crime. The killer truly believes they killed a babe. But they didn't.

So who did? And what babe? And who placed the hearts on their coffins?

It's like thinking through honey. What would my mother say?

Look to your advantage.

Knowing something others don't is an advantage. That's the root of every rogue's play, know more than your mark. The Painted Pig's given me something most others don't know: a tapestry with a secret. Mayhap that's where I'll find my advantage. And I have a mind which tapestry she means. Diana of the Wood, the one from the Queen's sitting room that Fair Hair said Corliss gave to Bethany.

I daren't go back to the Queen's quarters to look at it with Black Fingers so eager to torture me. But I don't need to. The tapestry's stuck in me like porridge in the gullet.

I slide down the wall until I'm crouched on the floor. In my head I go around each part of the tapestry.

The naked Queen under a full moon. Easy to remember, that.

Her hand against the trunk of a tree, a winged fairy in its branch, coming out of a flower.

The Queen's other hand on her belly. Something about the belly, I remember, felt wrong.

A blue boar curled like a dog at her feet. A lion too, and a stag.

Each small bit I recall helps me remember more, like the links of a chain necklace bringing me round to the pendant.

There was a word too, woven into the tapestry's leafy border. The word had letters from my name: two little *N*'s and between them was a curved line with a dot next to it like a tree leaning over one apple. Under the apple tree was a little gallows. Under the second *N* was a little worm. Would the word help unravel the riddle? It doesn't seem very secret to have a word in plain sight. Then again, I don't know what reading's like. Mayhap it's a very rare word or a word only some folk can read.

I think about what I've got from the tapestry, and I know what I need. It's waiting for me at home. I go to wrap my shawl around me, but it's not there. I took it off in the Country Mouse's room. I chide myself for forgetting. *At least it's near him*, I can't help thinking.

———

Passing through the town square I come upon a newspanto touting the upcoming revels to mark the end of the Norman emissary's visit. A feast in the field beyond the castle. The crowd's larger than usual, packed with folk already come to town for the festivities. It's just a few days away. I used to love feast days, not that everyday folk were invited. It was only highborn folk, but older girls and boys could get work scrubbing pots or carrying dishes to and fro. There were lots of scraps to eat.

Cakes and comfits, I think. *Roast potatoes*. My belly rumbles. Mayhap it's thinking on the feast, or that I've become accustomed to regular feedings, but I'm dreadfully hungry.

I walk on into Northside smelling the stink get stronger and stronger until I reach Dungsbrook. Almost home. My belly rumbles again. *Rich gravy atop a chop*.

A laugh barks out of me with the horridness of my own thought. A chop is for betrayal. How could I wish for such a thing?

I turn onto my lane. There are two messengers outside my door. 'Was a fire in the castle,' the first announces. He's got the Queen's badge on his arm. He must have been sent before they discovered I was already at the castle.

The second boy straightens up. 'Fever at the jail.'

I try not to be grateful.

———

It's the same jail cell where I waited what seems a life ago for a sentence that didn't come. Or, rather, came different. Ten prisoners and two turnkeys have been buried in a common grave. Six Simple Eatings are laid out in the cell. The families who brought them remain outside on the road where the air passes freely and no infection is like to touch them.

The loaves are small, but I know now why the Sin Eater had a slow way about her. Six loaves in one sitting is a great lot. I squat on my haunches since there's no stool. As I eat the first loaf, the recorder comes to my mind. Grey Beard in the dungeon said the recorder made his own wife a sin eater. So why did he choose me?

The recorder sentenced me in more than this life, I think. A true curse. When it's his turn to pass, I'll be sure to thank him in kind.

I chew the second loaf of bread. It's good. I look for a baker's mark, but it's homemade. The others still left to eat don't look nearly so nice.

The day passes to evening. Some of the families go. The air cools, and finally it's me in the jail cell, blue like a rock cave, licking cream from a bowl. I haven't slept in a good long while. It's in the noticing that I get weary.

My belly is heavy above my hips as I walk home. Rounding the corner onto my lane in Dungsbrook, I see shadows idling outside my door. I get taut as a bow, readying to run. But then the shadows step out into moonlight. Old bodies, bent and cracked, not cut-throats. No fight in them at all.

'Who's that come?' says one shadow as I near them. He carries a long staff, his hand over its top.

'Frederick's doxy,' says the other. At first he looks to be a hunchback, but it's just a sack hung over his shoulder.

The first shadow gives me a good look, then raps the other shadow on the arm, 'It's not! It's verily not! 'Tis a sin eater.' He turns and covers his eyes.

'Hardly fat enough for a sin eater,' says the second shadow, his eyes on the dirt lane. Then: ''Tis a poor idea, a sin eater's place as a stalling ken. A poor idea.' He spits and shifts the sack.

'Don't offend her now.' The first shadow doffs his dark cap in my direction, then pulls the second shadow's cap from his head.

'What's that for?' the second shadow says, but he follows the other, taking a step away from the door so I can go in.

My home has become an inn. Brida is seated in a corner, sipping from a bowl. Frederick lounges by the fire with Jane's children, chatting with Paul, who has his rags wrapped carefully about his face despite the warmth. An inn and an ordinary house as well, since Jane is also about, stirring a pot over the hearth. Then the door opens behind me, and the two shadows come in too, caps still in their hands. The first shadow places his staff by the door.

'Coins in the basin,' calls Frederick from the fireside. 'For the feed pot. We take no profit from it.' His eyes walk past me. 'Our benefactress has returned!'

I thought I had made myself mistress of my own house, but now I see they've been creeping up on me. They're like the slow rot that overtakes roof thatch. *I'm on top of it*, you think each day. *Not so bad*, you tell yourself. Until the one day you wake in a pile of rotten thatch and nothing over your head but white sky. If my mother were here she'd chase them all out, but first I need something from them.

I go direct to the hearth, where there's a bed of grey ash. Jane scoots out of the way, taking a platter of oysters with her. I kneel and draw the letters I remember from the tapestry in the ash. Jane's children dart forward to see what I'm doing. Jane gives the older boy a hard slap across the hand that makes him howl.

'What is it?' asks Frederick, gathering the boy into his arms and nuzzling his belly until giggles take over. Frederick looks at the ashes and shakes his head. 'Don't know that one.'

One of the shadows speaks up hesitantly. 'You talking to a sin eater? That's bad truck.'

'I'm talking to the room at large,' Frederick says. 'A soliloquy, not a dialogue. If she overhears, so be it.'

The first shadow looks at Frederick doubtfully. 'Lot of words there.'

'What's her catch?' asks the second shadow, taking an eyeful of the room but nodding towards me. 'She's not a rogue, is she? I'm not paying duties to angle in these parts.'

'She has her mysteries,' says Paul from the hearth. ''Tis the price of sanctuary.'

'Is it sanctuary?' says the first shadow. 'The door was marked so, but I've never been at sanctuary like this. It smells of death and it's got a sin eater and a leper.' He glances at Brida, who eyes him back. 'What's next? Egypsies and Eucharistians up there?' He looks up the ladder.

'You are free to leave!' says Paul, hard.

The first shadow shifts, taking the measure of Paul. Paul is young and strong, despite his scars. The shadows have had many a lean year.

The first shadow raises his hands for peace. 'We're just here a short time. Do our business while the Queen's revels are on, then be on our way.' He pokes his thumb back to his staff. I see the hole that his hand had covered around its top. That's where he puts a hook for angling. Anglers look for unshuttered windows and hook out linen and clothes to sell. It's a not very clever or dangerous sort of dodge, usually done by folk who're not very clever or dangerous.

The second shadow takes a step back and says, eyes to the floor, 'We thank ye for your hospitality.'

'Fine,' says Paul.

I turn back to the ash letters, tracing my finger over them a second time.

Frederick leans over to look. He points to the little *N* with the dot next to it. 'This is the mark for a constable, no?'

'Wouldn't know,' the first shadow says, puffing himself up. 'Upright rogues never use beggar's marks.'

'You found the sanctuary sign on the door well enough,' says Frederick, sharp-like.

The shadow's silent.

Brida squints. 'Constable mark has a dot under, not beside it.'

Beggar's marks. Sanctuary sign on the door. My mind chases after their words. Is that what the messenger took for a witch's mark? A picture language for beggars and vagabonds. It explains why all sorts of folk keep coming in.

Jane looks up from her oysters and wipes her brow with the back of her hand. 'What she's drawn in the ash isn't marks, it's reading.' Her voice is flat and tired.

'Your doxy's spoken,' says one of the shadows to Frederick.

Frederick takes a closer look at what I've drawn. He shakes his head. 'I read Anglish, French, and some Latin' – he looks to Jane – 'and this is not a word.'

Paul looks more closely. 'The old tongues have different letters.'

Jane dumps the oysters into the pot. 'Must ask a physician or a Jew.'

I click my teeth. How the fug am I to do that? The only physician I've met is a pig-slaughtering witch, and all the Jews were converted or driven away by the old king. Then I recall the musicians in the Domus Conversorum. The ones I threw burning wax at to scare.

'Not happy, this one,' says the first shadow, waving his hand at me like I'm giving off a smell. 'Not happy at all.'

I hiss and run at him like a goose. He steps back, nearly tripping over Brida's stump of a foot, and grabs the second shadow's arm. 'Oh, fug! What's she doing?!'

I keep at them. The first shadow grabs his angling staff. With his head turned to the side, he waves it blindly in my direction like a sword. 'Stay back.'

I herd them towards the door until both shadows stumble out of my house. Then I pick up the ewer and a rag.

The bang of the door startles the shadows who are hurrying away down the lane. I look over the mark on my door, two eyes astride a woman shape. I squeeze the water from the rag and scrub. This house is my sanctuary. It will be home for who I choose only. A reeking leper, a peevish cripple, a gabby-goose actor, a pregnant whore, and her bastards. My folk.

22. BRANDY POSSET

I SLEEP SO SOUNDLY, it's midday before the knocking pulls me out of bed. Hearing the messenger say Bessie's name is sort of like an exhale I've been holding in. I didn't want her to die, but there's relief in no more waiting.

Lee and Tom are at the Eating, of course, and other faces I know. And yet they seem different. It's like my old memories were all looking through one window into a house and now I'm looking in through a different window. It's the same room inside, but the light hits it different. Tom's a grown man, with hair coming out of his ears. Gracie Manners, who always knew everything there was to know, has three children pulling at her skirts and the look of an old daffodil. Even the house seems different from Bessie's Recitation. Smaller.

Before I leave, I pass through the kitchen. Sitting on a shelf is the old salt bowl painted with bluebells. I take it with me to add to my sin eater box. A token of Bessie.

—

My feet look mottled under the surface of the water in my fountain. Like the Painted Pig and Paul's skin. I go to pull my shawl around my shoulders and remember again I left it at the castle.

A few folk come through the square. They see me and go about their business direct, not dallying about. Two children timidly cross to an alley, and I hear the beginnings of a bat-the-stone game.

The sun sets through great, pink clouds. I pull my feet from my fountain and dry them on my skirt. As I do, I see the picture I thought was a witch's mark. A picture language for beggars. I recall the pictures in Corliss's tapestry. Mayhap the secret's in them. Once I think on it, the animals at the Queen's feet aren't difficult to figure. Family badges are often animals. The lion could mean Black Fingers. The stag would be the Country Mouse's family. The boar, another loyal family. But what the tapestry means beyond that, I don't know.

As I walk home through Northside, it comes to me that it's not just Bessie's place and my old neighbours that seem different. The whores lining the tavern row drop their eyes before I pass. And no boys push each other at me for sport. They keep out of sight. I walk down the middle of the road and folk move out of the way, just like they did for the old Sin Eater. Like the ruby sea in the Maker's story.

I pass the apothecary lane. *A physician or a Jew*, Jane said might know the word in the tapestry. Would an apothecary have enough learning? I remember how the apothecaries fled from me after my throat was cut. I hawk a good bit of spittle into the dirt of their lane, hoping I'm watched.

I stand again before the Domus Conversorum. There's no music coming from within this evening, just cool darkness. The last time I was here I stirred up fear. Now I need the musicians' help. I listen for any sign of them, but there's nothing. Mayhap I dreamed them up.

Just then I hear the deep music of the chest rumbler, the stringed instrument as big as a man. It moves through me again, making me feel wistful, but I don't know for what. Music's like a spell that way, you feel things you don't mean to. Even though I'm a curse, I say a little prayer for protection.

The stairs are as dark as before, and at the landing there's just one flicker of light, this time coming from a door at the other end of the passage. I knock gentle, then push it open.

My mouth widens in delight. It's a workshop as fine as any I've seen. All along the walls stand curved, wooden bodies of lutes and viols. The dark-haired, wiry man who played the chest rumbler sits with it between his legs fixing a string. Next to him is a worktable with joinery tools and other bits of wood that look to be pieces of instruments. On the table and floor are curls of wood like thick ribbons. It's the workshop of an instrument maker.

The Instrument Maker lays the chest rumbler down as gentle as a babe, then rises back up to face me, a pincher tool clenched in his fist.

I hold out my hands to say I mean no harm, but the Instrument Maker only tightens his grip on the pincher.

'Is mine place,' he says. It's like what Hairy Ears said before. 'What you want?'

I wave his gaze away. He closes his eyes halfway like he's laughing. Mayhap he's poor-sighted. I pick up a tallow candle from the worktable to light my *S* collar. He cries out and ducks behind his bench. He remembers the hurled candles from my last visit.

I wait. When he's sure I'm not throwing things, he stands back up. I show him the *S* again.

'Sin eater, yes,' he says. 'I see it. What you want?'

My guts drop. What creature looks into the eye of a curse outside the protection of a Recitation? Mayhap the musicians truly are spirits.

The Instrument Maker's eyes keep their crease but lose their warmth. 'I have not this belief,' he says as if sin eaters are unicorns or elephants that some folk believe in and some folk don't.

And then, as if he truly is a spirit, he asks the very question sitting on my own tongue: 'Why you not have fear?' He goes on. 'The vagabondi who come, they have fear because all the lies your folk tell of Jews. They leave us in our peace. Why you not have fear? Why you come molest us?'

Molest them? I laugh before I know it.

The Instrument Maker roars at me in anger.

I stumble, dropping the candle. He's a fiend. Or mad.

He runs at me, and I scramble for the door. But it's the candle he's gone to, stamping out the flame just as it's catching the wood curls strewn on the floor. 'Leave!' he screams.

I'm backed against the door, my heart thudding against my rib bones.

'Leave!' he screams again.

But I won't. I squeeze my eyes shut, and hush my pattering heart. *I am a curse. I have Daffrey blood.*

I hear the Instrument Maker's angry breathing.

I live with lepers and actors, I tell myself. *I survived Black Fingers. And Black Fingers's cut-throats. I am here to mend my muddle.* As I say these things to my heart, it gets steadier. My guts get stiller.

The Instrument Maker is still breathing hard, his body ready to fight. Nevertheless, I summon my blood and do what I've come for. I walk slow and steady to the worktable and trace the letters from the tapestry in the wood dust.

$$\text{חַוָּה}$$

The first letter like a little *N*.

The leaning apple tree with the gallows under it.

The second little *N* with a worm below.

The Instrument Maker's breath settles, and his head tilts as he looks over the letters.

'I do not know your words well,' he says.

I smooth out the wood dust and try the tapestry letters once more.

The Instrument Maker comes in closer. His body loosens. 'Ah, is Hebrew, yes?'

I don't know. I point to the letters.

'*Chav-vah*,' he sounds out, as if hawking up spittle. He traces the letters with a brown finger, its nail pared short. 'Chavah,' he repeats. 'Why you want know this word?' he asks quiet.

I need him to tell me what it means. I point at it again.

'You come here for this?'

I nod.

Suddenly his eyes crease into a smile, and his mouth opens into a laugh. He's like a spring day this man, thunder one moment, sun the next. 'Why for this?' he says easily. 'Why you come and the candles throwing? Why?' He looks into my eyes like he's truly searching for the reason, but there's something else too. Something different. He's looking at me like I'm folk. Like there's nothing about me that's cursed or vile. I haven't been looked at like this since I became a sin eater. Not even by the Country Mouse.

I move my hand like Frederick does when he talks, urging the Instrument Maker to say more, to tell me what the word means.

'Chavah, yes? You know this name?'

I shake my head.

'Is from the holy book we share.' His eyes crease again. 'Chavah: Eve.'

It catches me in the guts. But his face is open, and his eyes don't blink. He's speaking the truth.

'Eve,' he says again, seeing the question on my face.

The word above the tapestry's picture of the naked Queen is *Eve*? It's not possible. Or if it is, it's blasphemy. Eve was the foulest sinner in all Makerdom, the original rebel who fell from grace.

A noticing flutters up from my heart. The Queen's belly in the tapestry was wrong somehow. It was all one smooth belly. Why did I find this odd?

Because there should be a hollow in the centre. A navel. It's the sign we all carry that we're woman-born. Only one woman in the world wouldn't have it because she was made direct by the Maker himself. Eve.

The Instrument Maker is right. The picture shows the Queen as Eve. But why ever would the Queen's dear friend Corliss make such a terrible tapestry?

'You have surprise it is Eve's name.' The Instrument Maker tilts his head. 'Well, one of her names. She has two, yes?' He sees my confusion. 'Chavah, but also Isha. The mother and the woman . . . no, the mother and the virgin, yes?'

I choke back a giggle. There's no sense in his words.

His head jerks back like he's going to become angry again. I cover my lips and look down in apology. After a moment, he seems to accept it and continues, 'Chavah and Isha, the mother and virgin. The Eve who has the baby, and the Eve who has not yet had the baby. Two different names.'

Livestock have different names, like how cattle are called heifers before they've gone to the bull and are called cows after they bear a calf. Mayhap the old tongue does too.

He points again to the letters in the wood dust, 'This is one name for Eve.'

The riddle is that our Queen is the virgin Eve?

'Chavah,' he repeats. 'The Eve who has the baby.'

The floor swivels away from my feet, and I clutch for the table. Queen Bethany had a baby. The Instrument Maker darts forward and takes my arm to steady me. The warmth is startling. When was the last time I was touched? Paul closing the wound in my neck? Paul's touch was a bird scratching. This is like finding something I didn't know I had lost. The missing of it is there now, niggling at the little plum stone in my heart. Before I can help it, I'm clutching him back.

The thoughts swell up in my head, crashing like water down a mill wheel. Queen Bethany had a baby, and Corliss wove the secret into a tapestry in a language none but the most learned would know. Paul and Frederick didn't even see the shapes as letters. I only took them for Anglish because I know so little.

Notions push like key bits against the wards in my jammed lock. The lock isn't open yet, the wards are still jammed, but I'm starting to get the shape of the jam.

The murdered babe I ate two hearts for, it belonged to Queen Bethany. No, she wasn't Queen yet. She was of an age with me, as Tilly said, but in line to the throne, unmarried and living with her stepmother Katryna. What would she and her dearest friends have undertaken to save her from ruin? Corliss, her governess; Tilly, a midwife – would they have killed her royal bastard?

If this news were to come out, Bethany'd be ruined, even after all this time. The Norman prince and the other suitors would refuse her. She would most like lose her throne. A woman who beds out of wedlock is a whore. And a whore who kills her own child is worse than that. What folk would accept such a woman as their ruler?

An enemy of the Queen is killing the women so the world will see their coffins and know the truth like Mr Fox in the fairy tale.

But there's a second secret. The babe didn't die. Hearts were placed on the coffins to make it look like it did. The key knocks against the wards in my lock again. The more I think on it, the less sense it makes.

All I know is the Queen had a baby. The ladies who knew are dying. And the Queen's bastard may be alive.

23. SALT

I STUMBLE HOME AFTER dark and crawl onto my mattress. In my dream, Ruth's placing stones on my chest, one for each sin I've eaten. Fornicating, gossiping, not praying as one ought. A whole pailful for greediness and lust. Incest. Killing a royal baby.

The Sin Eater wears a badge like nobles do: a face with the lips sewn shut. Behind her the countess I saw in the castle dungeon is singing a song about cuckoo birds laying eggs in other birds' nests. But then the dream changes, and it's my own sins that are piled on: stealing, thinking ill of the dead, betraying the Sin Eater.

Then it shifts again, and it's my mother, not the Sin Eater placing the stones. Stones for sins that make no sense, like giving birth to a fairy with wings and burning rich, yellow beeswax candles down to nubs. My mother wears a badge of a fox with grapes in its mouth, dripping juice. Then my granddam comes, adding more stones. I wake choking for breath, but there's nothing on my chest.

I lie back on the mattress. My dream was like a narrow well that's too dark to see down into, but something's floating up, bobbing and breaking at the water's surface. Something I'm meant to see in the murk. Candles. What was it? No, beeswax. The poppets were made of beeswax, not tallow. Only a rich folk could have made them.

I climb downstairs to use the piss pot. Brida's on my-now-her rug. Jane's children are there too, all in a snoring heap though it must be midday. Jane herself is awake. At first I think I must still be dreaming, because Jane's standing before a large panel of wood painting a picture. But I'm not dreaming. She's got a brush and pots of paint, and her picture looks just like a big house, but in a stranger style. I can't fathom why she's doing it. A pregnant whore painting a picture inside a sin eater's house. A rapping at the door pulls me from my wonderings.

It's just one messenger outside. He's a little taller than me, black hair circling his head like wool. He's older than the usual boys. Must be from a poor family without a penny to send word by messenger. He's harder than the usual boys too. Something in the eyes that looks right through your clothes to your naked skin. His eyes flick to my face then to the roof of my house, a tight little curve cutting into his cheek as one side of his lips rises in a smile. The name blooms in my mind as he says it. 'Daffrey. Recitation for the old woman.' He's changed since I last saw him, but now I make out the face I once knew. My cousin tucks his fingers into his waist as if out for a stroll, as if it's an idle morning and not the one when our granddam is dying.

—

The wind comes cool off the river and pulls at my skirt hem. The house is the same, slouching into the river's edge, its roof thatch thick with waving weeds that seem to match the eddies of the river water. A scuff in the road behind makes me turn. I catch my cousin, hands still tucked, just looking away. His forearms are bare where he's rolled his sleeves. Black hairs curl round them. I can still feel his hands grabbing at my legs from when he and his brother held me down in the kitchen so long ago.

I don't want to go inside.

I am a curse, I say silently to the doorway.

I am a nightmare, I chant in my heart as I cross under the door beam.

I chant them both as I step on the uneven floorboards. I chant them as I hear my cousin's footfalls behind me, not two paces away.

Out of habit, I go to the kitchen. The roof is lower than I remember, or it's sunk. The old stove sits in the corner, cold. I turn and find my cousin doubled. One stands on either side of the doorframe, leaning their lankiness against its posts. They avoid my gaze, playing at idleness, but I can feel their thoughts on me.

I hear a thud from the ceiling and nearly jump. One cousin's cheek cracks into the half-moon Daffrey smile. My granddam must be up the stairs, through the door my cousins flank.

I stir my blood, lift my head and walk towards them, praying they will move. They fold out of the way just before I reach them. Their nearness curls in my guts like filth spreading, going up to where my hair begins and down between my legs to where my other hair begins. I want to scratch and scrub the filth away and wash myself clean.

Instead, I walk the floorboards to the stairs, feeling their gaze behind me, chanting my chant:

> *I am the curse.*
> *I am more frightful than them.*

In an entire year living in this house I never once mounted the stairs. The old roof is too low for me to properly stand except where the house beams prop it up, and it all stinks of mildew. There are only two chambers on the second level, one shut tight, the other ajar. The mildew smell grows as I push the door open.

It's not the roof thatch that's made the rotting smell. It's her.

White tallow candles are lit by the wall. She's below a faded blanket atop a rope-strung bed. Old straw mattress ticking pokes out of a linen cover, embroidered with flowers. The bedcover is velvet and was once red, now the brown of an old bloodstain. The rogue dowager queen.

Her eyes are milky in the candlelight, like eggs half boiled. 'Who is it come?'

My voice is not as full as I would wish. It comes out more as a bark. 'The Unseen is now seen.'

'Oh,' she says, sharp-like. Then 'Oh,' again, this time as if a bit lost. She shifts in the bed, her papery skin rustling against the sheets. 'Are my sons here?' She turns her head as if looking about the room. 'I would have them witness.'

'Speak your sins,' I say, taking a stool.

She girds herself up, as if readying for a great speech. 'I've done it all, all the worst and worse than that,' she says with a sort of pride. 'Must send a cook from the Orient to prepare some of my worser sins. You won't fit the foods on the coffin lid.' She waits for the words to land. The room is silent but for the whispers of her skin. 'Can you call to my sons? I would have them witness.' She's prepared her Recitation, a celebration of her rogue life. But it's the sort of thing that wants an audience, and none has come to hear. A blade of pity pokes in between my rib bones. I sit up straighter, to throw it off.

She coughs sharp, mildewy phlegm, and reaches out a shaky arm for a cup. Her arm's thin as a bird's. In my mind I feel her hand's back on my face, her knuckles striking my cheekbone. I feel the edge of a thrown ewer hitting my hip, leaving a half-moon scar to match my half-moon Daffrey smile. I remember a broom handle in her papery hands crashing against my ear. If I took her wrists in my hands now, I could snap them. Against the stool, I feel the breadth of my thighs. Pressing into my sides, I feel the heft of my arms.

My breath drops deep and low into my belly and comes out as a laugh. She will never hurt me again.

'What is it?' she asks, nervous as a horse at my laugh.

'None have come for you,' I say. 'Name your sins, old woman.'

Her eyes try to make me out. 'You're the bastard.'

'Your blood. Your daughter's daughter.'

'She never would deny you. Couldn't resist the fruit of her own body. More fool her. Wise girls have the midwife kill the bastard before it makes its first cry. I offered to do it for her. Once it's out and living, you never can deny it.'

She wants to hurt me. I lean in. 'I'm the only kin who would come. They know, your sons. They know you're crossing to the Maker. They'd rather drink or game than sit by your stinking flesh and smell the piss on the sheets.' The words roll out. She holds herself hard against them. 'I am a curse,' I say. 'I am your curse. The one you made. I will eat a Simple Eating on your grave. You can go to Eve bearing the rest of your worst of the worst.'

'You cannot,' she cracks. 'The Maker forgives all if it is recited.' Her voice is thick and phlegmy. 'Eat cream and mustard seed,' she says with urgency. *Jealousy and lies.* 'Drink sack . . .' *Mockery.* 'Black pudding, garlic.' *Revenge, miserliness.* 'Pork snout, duck tongue, roast pigeon.' *Smuggling, usury, thieving.* She knows all the foods. 'Eat a lamb's heart.' *Killing a babe.* 'Tell me you will. Tell me you will eat the foods from my coffin.'

She's not my granddam any more, just an old, scared woman close to death. The plum stone in my heart grates against my rib bones. I want to dig it out with my thumb and force it down her throat.

'I will eat your sins,' I whisper around the plum stone. 'I will carry them to my grave.'

She sinks back against the bed, quiet.

I leave the house. I walk down the lane lined with its thin grass blades. Daffrey or Owens. Why must these be the choices? What if I could be something new, like the green shoots coming up out of plain earth. Something all to myself.

I go to Northside's tavern row. I look in tavern after tavern until I find them. Misgett's deep in a card game with a table full of other rogues. He puts down a card bearing a queen and a black flower. Uric's perched, silent as a carrion eater, on a stool nearby. The table chatter hushes. I stare first at Misgett, then at Uric. 'I give you the foods for your mother's Eating.' Both men get still.

I list the foods, then let the moment get heavy. When the weaker rogues begin to fidget in the silence, I say, 'Fail in her Eating, and the food will rot atop your own coffins, for never will I touch it.' I reach across the table. The other rogues hiss and jerk away, one uttering the Maker's Prayer under his breath. Misgett doesn't move and doesn't stop me either. I take the queen with a black flower. A token of the Daffreys.

24. GINGERBREAD

I EXPECT THE PLUM stone in my chest to be gone. It's still there, stuck hard. In the stink of Dungsbrook, a few lanes from home, I find home is not where I'm going.

My fingers follow along the wall for balance in the indoor dark. I can smell the tallow candles burning.

The Instrument Maker looks at me uncertainly from his workbench, the unfinished wooden body of a lute in his arms. When I walk towards him, he stands up quick, overturning the bench. I step over it to clutch him, wrap my arms around him, press my face into his chest. There's a short questioning bark on his lips as he tries to guess what I'm after. His breath pushes against me, and he twists to find his balance against the fallen bench.

I grasp him tighter, a shaking sob coming from deep in my guts. He gets still, his heart thumping through his skin. I press all of me against him. His body is taut, resisting, yet to me it's the soft protection of my father. He tries to turn from me, but he's the breathing warmth of the Country Mouse. He doesn't embrace me back, but he's my mother. He is all the folk no longer with me and all the folk I cannot have.

My sobs are hard and awkward, and snot and saliva smear across his shirt. The sobs come faster and faster, then slower and slower, till I'm left with hiccups. My fingers loosen around him, but he doesn't pull away. He lays the lute, still clutched in his hand, down on the floor. Then he takes my hand.

He pulls the bench up and sits me on his lap. A callus on his thumb brushes my palm. Short, dark hairs skim my wrist. I forgot all the ways you can feel another person. I push my cheek against his jaw to feel his beard. I leave my brow in front of his lips to feel his breath. I want to get inside him. I want him to hold every part of me. It's like when I was so hungry for food, and I could think of nothing else. I am the same hungry for touch, warmth, skin, breath.

I pull the neck of his shirt open and push my face in, his curly hairs going up my nose. I pull, pull, pull at the shirt until his whole chest is bare. He lets me do it. Even helps pull the shirt over his head, then holds me close against him.

My legs find their way around his hips until I am buried in his arms. My breath matches his, the hiccups catching me only now and again. I open my hands against his back, soaking in his warmth like sunshine.

Skin has a smell I had forgotten. A small smell. It's different from the big smells like Paul's farts or Brida's rot. Skin smell you have to be up close for. His smells like raw wood and sharp varnish and the gamey smoke of tallow candles. I breathe into him, and he breathes into me. It is the closest I have ever been to another body since I was a child.

When I am done, when I have swallowed up all his touch, I pull my breath apart from his, his body from mine. We sit looking at each other, his eyes filling me full up.

Gentle-like, his fingers rise towards my face, but they stop just before they get there. At my collar. He touches the *S*. He touches the heavy brass it hangs from. His fingertips crawl around the collar like a spider until they reach the back. They tug and pry gently, hunting for something. I watch the Instrument Maker's eyes open in surprise when he finds no latch. I watch his surprise grow to a shuddering anger when he discovers the lock. Then, suddenly, he's at his worktable, scrabbling for tools.

He stands behind me working at the lock. He stops twice to light fresh candles. He's a fool, I think, as he works. The Maker sealed this lock. But it feels good just to have him there tending to me, his arms bumping warmly against my shoulders, like when my mother would plait my hair.

And then all at once, there's a click. It's quiet, but I hear it like firewood splitting under the axe. The warmth of his body leaves me as he steps back.

For a moment I can't even breathe. I don't dare. Then I bring my hands to my neck. The circlet gives under them, hinging open. I pull off my collar.

My chest bone floats up, like a brush bobbing in a tub. I feel so light. Bare.

The Instrument Maker speaks. At first I think he's said a stranger word, but then I hear it.

'Free,' he says.

25. BLACK PUDDING

IN MY LOFT I lie on one side of the mattress. The collar lies on the other.

Free. I don't know what that means.

I thought I did. I thought it was stealing orange suckets at the market. Or being a curse. But now I don't know.

I touch the place where the collar sat. Grey skin peels off like cobwebs. The inside of the collar itself is scaled with the stuff. And crumbs too. I don't know how they got in there.

Without a collar to mark me, I could run away. Is that what free means? To brave the roads to another town where no folk know me? I still wouldn't be able to speak. I'd need to hide my marked tongue. But I could find the other unseen, whores and lepers. Beg them to take me in. Hide in the dark corners of the town, stealing food, shivering through winter, praying the constables don't whip me and burn my ear through as a vagrant. It sounds worse and worse the more I think on it. Is this what free means?

Mayhap I could go elsewhere. Farther away. Slip onto a barge headed downriver, and then onto a bigger boat. One going to a stranger land, like where the Instrument Maker comes from. A land where they don't believe in sin eaters. I could just be a girl again. A girl with no kin. Unable to understand the land's tongue. Among heretics and heathens. Is that free?

I hear Jane down the ladder scolding her children. They're playing hide-your-head with the ewer. I get a twist of sad, right in my heart, thinking about running away to another place. I grouse about Brida and Paul, Jane and Frederick, but they've come to be solidly on the side of company. They're my folk.

The twist turns to an ache. This town is home. Da's buried here. All my memories are stuck here, in these roads and houses, these folk. This earth and sky. I feel like a wherry that's come untied in heavy rains, spinning off in swift, dark water.

Is this what free feels like? I ask the collar. But it doesn't know what free means either.

A rapping sounds at the front door.

My heart seizes up. *Not now.* I tell the collar. *Not before I've sorted this out.*

But the rapping comes again, hard. Must be a Recitation. A soul that can't wait.

You are the only one who can unburden it, says the collar. *They could make another sin eater*, I say back.

284

Would you have the recorder do that? the collar asks. *Curse another girl like you? Would you be free then?*

And in this moment I know that running away will never make me free. My soul carries the sins of this town. I'll carry them with me until I die. I can't shed them any more than I can shed the memories of my da or my Daffrey blood.

I look at the collar softly gleaming in the afternoon light. It seems to take up as much space as me.

Another rap comes at the door. I still don't know the answer, but there's a soul that can't wait. I place the collar back around my neck, securing it in place with a pin bent through the hinge where the lock sat. I go to meet the messenger.

———

Walking down the road, the collar bumps against my neck. It's too loose. I worry that the pin will slip out, it'll clatter to the ground, and the Makermen will come and lock the collar up again. But the pin holds. I arrive at an alehouse.

The Recitation's for a girl not much older than me called Jenny Brown. Jenny's abed with a cut foot that's festered. She's fevered, coming in and out of waking, and there's red streaks running up her leg. Her mother sits close by with a wet cloth to cool her. She wears the apron of an alewife. Jenny's da prays in the corner. They're plain folk, like mine were. I wonder if my life might have been like this if things had gone another way.

It takes a moment for Jenny's eyes to find mine and then another to grasp what they see. When they do, a little well of tears springs up and out of her eyes, down her cheeks. She clutches her mother's hand. 'I don't want to leave,' she whispers. 'I don't want to go without you.'

I know the fear of losing your ma and da. 'You won't be alone,' I tell her. 'So many folks have passed on to the Maker before you. They'll be waiting.'

'Auntie Rose,' her mother says soft. 'Grandpapa Saul.'

Jenny nods a little nod. A thought catches her. 'I'll be judged for my sins?' Her mother squeezes her hand, but she can't give her daughter comfort.

'I'll take your sins for you,' I say.

There's a break in Jenny's fear, a little relief that pulls at her lips until they almost smile. 'Will you?' she asks.

I nod until she nods along with me, until her mother's nodding too. Until Jenny's smile breaks into a little choked laugh.

'I haven't done anything,' she says. I think she's talking about her sins, but then she keeps on going. 'I haven't done anything yet. In my life. I wanted to . . . I always hoped that when I passed, I would have done something. Something of substance. Been a mother. Or a midwife. Or even just made ale that folk wanted to tell their neighbours about.' She laughs at this, but then it turns to crying. 'All I've done is alehouse dishes.'

'You've been a daughter,' I tell her.

'Did my life matter?' her voice cracks.

I grasp for words to reassure her, but I don't know the right ones. So I nod, strong and sure. I say, 'You'll be remembered.'

Back on my mattress, I lie again side by side with the collar. It's like a bedfellow. Like if I had a sister. But this sister is a sin eater. And me, lying across the mattress looking at her, I'm just May. Da's girl. My mother's daughter. Me.

Mayhap freedom is being able to be more than one thing. Like, I could be May right now, here lying in bed. And if I get up and put on the collar, then I'm choosing to be a sin eater. When I take the collar off, I can go back to just being May. Mayhap freedom is choosing for yourself. Even if the choices are piss-poor.

As sleep comes over me, a stray thought bobs to the surface of the well in my mind. It's the banner of Katryna, the Queen's stepmother: a fair-haired maiden coming out of a flower. The fair hair reminds me of another fair-haired maiden. There's a little click in the wards of the lock. It seems plain once the notion's in my mind.

I thought that Black Fingers might be the killer behind the muddle, but he can't be. The killer is trying to ruin the Queen by uncovering her bastard. Black Fingers doesn't want the Queen harmed. He wants to get an heir on her.

And the Willow Tree wants the Queen to stay on the throne too. His gruesome witchcraft in the Makerhall was all to protect her.

The killer isn't either of them. The killer is somefolk in a desperate predicament. One with piss-poor choices.

Fair Hair, the lock whispers. I saw her embracing Black Fingers. And plumped up like she's with child. If she is pregnant by Black Fingers, who wants to marry the Queen, she might be desperate enough to hurt the Queen however she can. Particularly if she fears the Queen had Black Fingers's first wife thrown down a set of stairs. If the Queen were dethroned for killing a bastard, for instance, Black Fingers wouldn't want her any more. Fair Hair would be free to marry him. Free.

Could Fair Hair have understood the secret message in the tapestry? I remember Mush Face reading a stranger book with drawings in it. Mayhap Fair Hair knows stranger tongues too. I once saw Fair Hair coming out of the herb dispensary. Herb dispensaries are where some poisons can be got.

I look up at the sin eater boxes. The one with the seashell. The one with the badly done embroidery. The one with a lock of hair. What will be in mine when I pass on? What markers are there of me and what I've lived? That I've mattered?

An empty bottle of poppy oil
A salt cellar
A playing card

This living is so hard. I want a marker of it. A marker of Ruth dying. Of Black Fingers nearly killing me. Of the Willow Tree's black magic. Of all the fright and confusion the folk at the castle have caused me. I want to catch Fair Hair. I want to catch her and make her feel all the grief she's caused me. And when I do, I will cut a golden curl from her head and put it in my box as a token.

26. HONEY CAKE

THE THING ABOUT piss pots is that they're in your chamber. So if you've got one, you don't need to find a jakes. To catch Fair Hair, I'm going to need a jakes.

I lie abed in the slats of dawn light. Sometimes in the morning, the shiny, cunning notions you have in the night come back grey and small. I give mine a good think over. They're still shiny.

Here's what I reason: I need to get Fair Hair alone, and I don't fancy searching for her chamber in the castle, picking the lock, avoiding her maid, mayhap getting stabbed again by Black Fingers, and all that. But folk who're pregnant have to piss all the time. So I need a moment when she's got to use a jakes and not a piss pot. And I know a moment that will do. Two nights from now are the Queen's revels to mark the Norman emissary's departure. The revels are taking place in a great tent in the field outside the castle. Not a piss pot around. But folk will need to piss, so there'll be jakes dug. That's where Fair Hair'll go.

I hear Jane's children below me knocking about with each other. Brida's soft voice bubbles up the ladder.

A sin eater might pull too much notice near the festivities. But there are surely other sorts of folk whose presence won't be questioned, especially in the bustle of getting everything ready. My uncles kept men in their company who used disguises. Abraham-men who feigned they were mad, lame folk that pretended to be heroes from past wars, dinder-danders who dressed up as highborns so as to make folk trust them before they fleeced them. I could do the same.

The best folk to counterfeit are the kind other folk want to forget. It takes some thinking to contrive a good disguise. It's my squatters, finally, who spark the notion. I climb down the ladder with a handful of coins. Before I do, I put on my collar, securing it again with a pin. I daren't let anyfolk see I can take it off. The punishment for removing it is surely dire. At the least, it'd be locked back on.

Outside, the messengers are ready with their words, but I've errands to do first. I need a new shawl, a bit of chalk, a tallow candle, and some hay. And a pail of old piss.

—

At the market, the vendors are wary, but when I put my coins down, they give me space to take what I need.

Shopping done, I make my way to the old earthen jail with an empty pail.

A new turnkey guards the cell. He jumps up at my arrival, looking side to side as if he might find the whys and wherefores there. I wait until he catches my meaning and unlocks the door.

I expect the women and girls inside all to scamper off to the four corners, but instead they do something astonishing. They crowd in.

A thick woman who smells like old hops comes right up to my shoulder. 'Hear my Recitation, would you? I'm to hang at tomorrow's dawn.'

'I haven't any coin,' says a girl who can't be more than twelve but has eyes much older. 'But I'll tell you where to scrump strawberries if you hear mine. There's a goodwife never locks her garden gate.'

'Elders first.' An old body pushes through. 'I've got the most sins, as I'm the longest lived. I should be first.'

In truth I've come for the pail of piss, but hearing their voices I can't help but think how unjust it is that folk in jail aren't allowed a Recitation. Once I would have said they weren't goodly women and so didn't deserve one. But what sense does that make? A Recitation is to cast off your sins, and who needs that more than jail folk?

There's a skinny girl at the back of the crowd. Her brow is creased with worry, but she's not pushing forward. I move towards her, the women giving way so as not to touch me.

'The Unseen is now seen,' I say to the skinny girl. 'The

Unheard is now heard. The sins of your flesh become the sins of mine to be borne to my grave in silence. Speak.'

Her voice won't come at first. It starts and stops like a wheel stuck in a rut. But when it does come, it rolls out strong, stronger than you'd ever guess a skinny girl's voice could. 'I've such fury in my blood. I get enraged. And I do things I wish I didn't.'

As she speaks, the other women settle in. There's nowhere for them to go, so they listen. The skinny girl goes on. 'Most times I keep my anger in and hold myself against it. I know a girl's meant to be meek and kind. I've been told enough.' The thick woman who spoke first gives a murmur like she's been told the same. 'I worked as a maid in a fine house. You know the two-storey house in merchants' row that's got yellow-painted shutters and red tiles on its roof?'

'I know it,' says another girl. 'Next to the one with blue glass in the window.'

'That's the one,' says the skinny girl. 'I've been there three years now, keeping the house as tidy as you'd ever want. Brushing cinders every day from the hearth. Scrubbing out the closestools. Caring for the goodwife when she's poorly. I do it the best I can. But then last Makersday, she comes to tell me her husband is moving them to his family's estate for the summer months, and they won't be bringing me because there are maids in the countryside.' A couple of women suck their teeth. 'I told her I haven't any other work. Where am I to live? How am I to eat? She said it's none of her concern and I shouldn't speak so boldly to my betters.' A girl takes the skinny girl's hand, but the skinny girl throws it off. 'The goodwife never even learned my name. Three years I work there, and she still calls me "girl"! I told her she wasn't my betters, she was my worse because she was leaving me with no work. She slapped me for that. Then she said she'd tell all the other goodwives that I was of so choleric a temper that none would take me on as a maid.'

All the folk, even the turnkey, suck their teeth at such a thing.

'She said she'd take my good name! How would I find a place after that?' cries the skinny girl. 'And that's when the rage came up all over me. When it comes on, I get deaf, like I can't hear my own thoughts. I regret it sorely now. Maker forgive me, but I slapped and scratched at her as hard as I could.' Some suck their teeth again, some harrumph like they'd have done the same. The skinny girl's voice gets smaller. 'I put out her eye. And so I'm set to hang.' She tells me a few other small sins, lying and forgetting her prayers and the like. I tell her the foods I'll eat after she hangs.

'But I've none to make the food,' the skinny girl says once I'm done. 'Not even for a Simple Eating.'

I wish there was something I could do or say, but there's nothing except to make the Maker's sign across her body. May it bring her comfort. I turn to the next woman.

I hear the Recitations of all the women set to die. It comes to me that they've not done much worse than some of the folk I've heard outside the jail cell, they just had the bad luck to be caught. Most don't have kin to bring the foods to their graves so the Recitations become a heavy sort of thing, not the relief they should be. Many, like the skinny girl, sinned out of anger because folk were cruel or things unfair. Anger seems to make folk feel strong, but not in a way that sticks.

At the end, I go to the piss pot and fill my empty pail. The day's done when I come out onto the road. Still, I can see folk moving about in the field beside the castle. They've already begun preparing for the revels.

In two days, I tell the field, *I'm going to catch Fair Hair.*

Once I'm tucked up in the loft, I remove my collar and place it on the mattress next to me. I idly rub at the skin on my neck, delighting in just being May, until sleep comes.

———

The next morning, the day before the revels, it's not just me readying myself at dawn. The whole household is abuzz. I pin on my collar. Frederick sings a song. Paul wraps a clean cloth about his face. Jane ties her smaller child across her back, while the larger child jumps around in everyfolk's way. Brida watches from the hearth.

We all end up starting out of the door at the same time, the gaggle of them just ahead of me on the road. They must be going to the field to see about work. For my part, today I'm going to assay where the jakes are and where the tent is. Get acquainted with the place, like my uncle Misgett would do. Before a dodge, he'd watch folk. He'd watch the place. Note things like if the door opened in or opened out. One makes a swift exit. The other might get you caught. I haven't dressed in my disguise. I'll save that for the revels themselves tomorrow evening.

'Paul, you could be taken for a Saracen with your face wrapped so,' says Frederick as we leave the stink of Dungsbrook.

'It's better than folk hissing at my scars as if I'm no better than a filthy sin eater,' Paul says, nasty-like, as if he doesn't know I'm just a few paces behind them.

'Imagine,' Frederick says. 'At one time all you needed to assure your soul's passage to the heavenly plains was to kill a dozen Saracens in the Maker's name. Now we must all live a good and dutiful life or join Eve in eternal torment.'

'Not all of us,' comes Jane's voice. 'Where I'm from folk don't believe in Eve.'

'Ah, there's a question for the Makermen!' laughs Frederick. 'Do sinless heathens go to Eve? What about the goodliest pagan grandmamas? The sweetest of heretic babes?' Frederick tickles Jane's eldest. 'Surely their souls are not forfeit. Tell us, Jane, what do your folk believe happens when we pass on to the ghostly realm?'

'I was sold young,' says Jane back. 'But I remember an altar in my home for kin who had passed on. For the grandpapas and grandmamas and the ones before them.'

———

At the edge of the field I feel a right fool. There isn't going to be one tent. There's going to be at least four, each as big as a house. No, two houses. One of the tents is already raised, but the others are just being laid out.

A richly dressed man oversees the folk already at work. A clerk stands beside him holding open a large scroll with drawings and figures on it. They venture a glance towards me, and I see them stiffen. Frederick's approach pulls their attention away.

Frederick bows to the overseer and clerk. I can't hear them talk, but Frederick points back to Jane and Paul. The men look askance at Paul's rags and Jane's stranger face. Frederick's arm gestures get bigger. A few moments later he comes back. 'They'll take us all on. Paul, I told him we were rakers by trade and that you had been badly burned as an apprentice. It seemed ill-advised to spell out our association with the play performing tomorrow as they seemed rather pious.' Frederick looks to Jane. 'The painters are working on the adjacent tent, my love. Makerspeed.'

Jane and her children disappear behind the bulk of the one raised tent. Frederick and Paul join several men working at raising another. The centre tentpole is as tall as a two-storey house and topped with a big, wooden bird. It's meant to be a crowned falcon, like from Queen Bethany's badge, I think. The men pull the pole to standing using three long ropes.

While they work, I notice that the canvas for the tent roof is still on the ground. Canvas is as heavy as velvet, and the roof canvas as wide as a Makerhall. Just by looking you can see it's far too heavy for Frederick, Paul, and the others to lift. I don't know how they'll get it up to the roof. And then the sorcery begins.

Frederick and a man with a crooked nose take hold of a small rope running up the tentpole. Together, they pull on it. Just the two of them. As they do, up goes the roof canvas, drawn by smaller ropes. There's no reason in it. Only two men are pulling, but the enormous, heavy canvas is going up all around them. A porter and two boys stop to watch, as struck by it all as I am. The porter calls out to ask how they've done it. Frederick calls between heaves, 'Pulleys!' As if that answers anything.

The porter's question brings the tent raisers' attention my way. Their looks don't linger, but I feel the men mark me. After that, like nervous horses, they glance towards me every now and then to see if I'm still there.

Paul, Frederick, and the other men continue to raise tent-poles and canvas. As they go along, the crooked-nosed man uses a measuring string to show the others where to stake down the ropes and plant other poles. Before I know it, the sun's high in the sky, and an entire canvas chamber has been conjured in the field before me.

Some of the men pause to drink some small beer. Crooked Nose steals a look at me, then says low to the others, 'Why's she still about?' He picks up a fist-sized stone, and glances around. Some of the others pick up stones too. Their meaning's plain. I look over the men threatening to stone me. Paul's among them.

Right at this moment I take a decision. Once I've sorted out this mess, I will cast Paul from my home. He's not company. He doesn't deserve sanctuary. Brida and the others can stay, but he's no longer welcome.

I go on my way. Farther into the field, I see that the large tents are all getting joined together like the wings of a great manor house. There's small tents too, that seem to grow off the larger ones. I don't know what the small tents are for.

I pass Jane and several others painting the canvas wall of the largest tent. They're making a great picture together. They've already finished some trees heavy with fruit and a grassy meadow. I remember the painting I saw her doing in my house. Was it for the revels? Now Jane is doing a deer with a fawn. She's skilled at it. Her deer doesn't look like a goat at all.

Beyond the tents, there's a whole other band of folk at work building a field kitchen. There's reason in it, I suppose. If you're to have a feast out-of-doors, you need a place to cook. There's fire pits already dug, and folk are setting spits above them for roasting meat. A wagon full of cauldrons, grates, and flesh-hooks sits nearby for when the kitchen's done, and stacks of noisy crates hold ducks, rabbits, chickens, and pigeons to be slaughtered. A bit farther off, a herdsman shows off his sheep to one of the castle butchers. One sheep has already been hung up to bleed out. The kitchen builders and tent raisers need to eat too.

Much farther off in the field I see the lone back of a man. Pissing. Looks as if the jakes haven't yet been dug. I'll have to wait until tomorrow to finish my assay.

—

One messenger sits with his back against my house snoring in the sun when I get home. His foot jiggles along with his dream. I kick a small stone at the dreamer, but he doesn't rouse. I come close and stand so my shadow covers his face. He starts. 'Never did! Never did!' It takes a moment for him to recollect where he is and why he's come. 'Eating for Sorrel Beckworth on the Foundry Lane by the river,' he finally says.

Foundries must need water if they're by the river, but entering Foundry Lane, it seems all heat and fire.

Two benches have been moved outside the shop where the man died. Inside, three men stand along a wall, leather aprons across their fronts. A body covered by another apron is laid out on the earthen floor. One muscled arm is uncovered, its skin reflecting the yellow flames of the forge.

'Coffin's coming,' says a great bull of a man when I step in. 'Isn't it?'

A younger man, most like an apprentice, nods his head. 'Bart said he'd be by with it shortly.'

'Don't we have nothing to put him up on?' the bull man says suddenly. 'Get the trestle.' He waves at the apprentice.

''S gone, Fitz,' says the third man. 'Won't mean nothing to Sorrel now.'

The Bull wipes his brow leaving a line of dark soot across his skin. 'We're too small a workshop to be making cannon. Told the Queen's man we were too small.'

There's no food I can see, let alone a stool.

The Bull seems to think the same thought. 'Where's the . . . ? Get the . . . !' the Bull cries at the apprentice. The young man hurries to a bundle on top of a sack of sand. He unwraps bread, cream, salt, garlic, and a skinny leek. He turns with them, then pauses, not knowing where to put them down.

'You dumb fug,' says the Bull, yanking off his own apron

and laying it down gentle-like in front of me. 'Wait, wait,' he says, and goes to a great cannon mould. He pushes its bulk towards me and offers it as a seat.

As I eat, other founders join the three witnesses, fitting their bulk into the cramped workspace.

'Where's the coffin?' asks a man no taller than me, but broad as he is high.

The Bull swells up for a quarrel, but the apprentice answers quick. 'Bart's bringing it by shortly.'

The Bull sinks back into himself. 'Why're we all set to making cannon? Too small for cannon here. Thought it was peacetime.'

The broad man nods. 'What's the Queen marrying a stranger prince for, if not peace?'

An older man says, 'She'll not marry him. She's the Virgin Queen! What would she be if she married him? The king's wife, is what.'

'Bart's here,' says somefolk by the door, and the men make way for a newly planked pine coffin. Despite their bulk, the men are nimble. Must be, I think, to work in such close quarters.

There's quiet while I finish the Eating and say the closing words. Walking out of the door, I see the Bull and the broad man have come out to smoke their pipes. 'Bet the cannons're for the bloody Eucharistians in the North,' the broad man says softly to the Bull. 'Northern folk believe the Queen and her ladies used witchcraft on Maris to murder her babes and take the throne. Fighting words, those are.'

The Bull nods. 'Baron Seymaur was killed for that, wasn't he?'

'Nah, he was killed for trying to get on the throne himself. Got the axe. Fortune and title both forfeit. Burned his golden wings outside the castle.' The broad man checks his pipe, then looks back inside the foundry door. 'Was it the cannon mould that did for Sorrell?'

'Fell and crushed him like a press.' The Bull spits on the ground. 'We're too small for cannon.'

———

I walk back under a sky spotted with plump clouds like wool batting. I think about what Jane said on the way to the field this morning, that where she comes from folk don't believe in Eve. I think on how the Instrument Maker doesn't believe in sin eaters. The thoughts make me unsettled, like they had said the earth wasn't firm or the sky could crack and fall. I'm like the untethered river wherry again, spinning in dark waters.

Up in my loft, I take off my new shawl and shoes. I unpin my brass collar. I turn the collar around, peering close at the thing that so recently bound me. It was to remain locked forever by the Maker's will. But it's unlocked now, and the earth hasn't split, the sky hasn't fallen. I don't believe Jane and the Instrument Maker are right. But mayhap they're not wrong, either.

You're just a thing, I tell the collar, trying out the words.

It looks right back at me, hard. It wants to be as big as a Makerman. It wants to be as weighty as the Maker's word. It wants to lock me up with no breadth for choices. But it can't any more.

You're just a bit of metal now, I say. Then I add, a little tremble in my guts, *a bit of metal that I own.*

I listen, all nerves, fearing what it'll say back. But it says nothing. It's quiet.

So I go on. *You're like a smithy's tongs or a washerwoman's apron. Tomorrow I'll wear you because I need you for my work.* Then I place the collar in my box on the shelf, where it will sit until I need it again.

It feels good to do it. I'm still unsure about Jane and the Instrument Maker's words, but I'm on firm ground again. Like I'm no longer an apprentice. As if in putting the collar where it belongs, I've become the master.

27. COCK BRAIN TART

THE MORNING OF the revels, the household wakes early again. I remove my collar from my box and pin it in place. Then I wrap my new shawl with care over it so it can't be seen until I'm ready. I put on a head coif from one of the old sin eater boxes. It's part of my disguise.

I promise I'll return it, I swear to the box.

I pull on my new corked shoes. In my sleeve I place the tallow, hay, and chalk I bought at the market. Then I pick up my pail of two-day-old piss.

—

I stand in wonderment, taking in the sight of the field. It's like a fairy kingdom. The tentpoles are all topped with crowned falcons, and along the eaves where the tent roof meets its walls, there's a cloth of gold fringe.

But the true marvel is the paintings. A midsummer night with a sky of stars above blooming moonflowers and evening primroses frames the tent entrance, so it looks like you could walk right into the painting. My chin drops with staring.

'Move it along!' shouts a man hauling a fountain with two others. They place the fountain just in front of the tent opening.

'What's this?' asks a folk behind me. 'A water feature?' It's Frederick's voice. He and Paul are both gandering like me. The sight of Paul gives me a star-shaped flush of anger between my rib bones.

I'll deal with him after, I tell the great tent. *I've a killer to catch first.*

'Fountain of wine,' the fountain carrier tells Frederick.

'Why, the festivities will be Roman in their decadence!' Frederick sings out.

'We got another one coming; can you move it along?' the fountain carrier says back.

I make my way to the side of the tents close on Frederick's and Paul's heels. We come upon Jane and the other painters still at work. Jane's children run to Frederick when they see him. He gives them a nuzzle, then sends them back to Jane. The elder wants to stay. 'Shall you be the tiniest mechanical and help us build the stage?' Frederick tells him. 'Come round later to the tiring room, and Paul will dress you up as a bear.'

Frederick and Paul continue to one of the small tents

attached to the bigger ones. There's men already at work ferrying trunks and clothing racks into it.

'We were meant to start at dawn,' says a clean-shaven man with hair as long as a woman's.

'I brought reinforcements,' Frederick answers.

'Is that Paul, now?' says a tall man with a trim, grey beard and booming voice. 'Haven't seen you in an age.' Paul embraces the tall man, then he and Frederick join in the work.

I keep going on to the very back of all the tents, where the field kitchen is. As I walk, I see the richly dressed man who was overseeing things yesterday. He's got guards with him today.

The pit fires of the field kitchen are already smoking. The boys turning the spits have shed their shirts even though the morning's still cool. A line of scullions runs between a wagon and a second small tent ferrying linen cloths, plates, and dishes inside. This small tent must be where they'll plate and dress the food for the feast.

Beyond the field kitchen, I finally find the jakes. They've been dug far enough away that the sight and stink won't bother any of the highborn folk. Far enough away, I hope, that a cry might not be heard in them, especially over the music of a play.

The outsides of the jakes have been hung with cloth to make them seem grander than the quick-made huts they are. Still, they're large enough for a woman in a farthingale to get into and out of, which means there'll be enough room for my plan.

Now I need to find a good spot to wait. To the side of the field is a small hill, not much more than a mound, really. It's got a few large stones good for sitting and should afford a view onto not only the jakes, but the whole path from the tent entrance back to them. With luck I'll be able to see anyfolk who goes for a piss. But it's too open a place for me to sit now in full daylight. I'll need to find somewhere to wait for sunset where none will question me.

Still carrying my pail of piss, I cross through a cloth flap into the main tent. It doesn't take long to find Frederick, Paul, and the other actors atop the largest table I've ever seen. It must be their stage. The small tent with their trunks and clothing racks is just behind it.

Frederick is fitting the back of the stage with a long wooden groove. The clean-shaven, long-haired man is walking about singing a song. The tall man with the booming voice is jabbing his arm forward and back as if he's fighting with a sword, but he's alone and there's nothing in his hand. It's such an odd scene, folk won't notice a common girl in among the others sitting quiet.

As I watch, the actors all gather together to place a tall archway over the top of the stage. Not long after, I see something I recognize. Two actors carry in Jane's painting of a stranger house on the flat wooden panel. They slide it into the groove Frederick built. The painted panel stands up and makes the stage look like it's the road in front of a stranger house. There's a second wooden panel too. It's painted to look like a deep, dark wood.

Paul, Frederick, and the others tie ropes to the top of the

panels, attach them to the archway above, and then use the ropes to lift the panels up and down. It's like when they were raising the tent roof. I don't know how they can lift something so heavy with such ease. They must be strong as oxen.

My thoughts wander to the few plays I've seen. Not newspantos, but proper plays up on a stage with grown actors playing them. It was always summer, and the company of actors would come to town dressed in festive robes and singing songs from the back of a wagon. As a child, you knew you weren't supposed to talk to them, since actors are vagabonds. They don't belong to any one place and have no kin ties. Gracie Manners said some of the actors whore themselves out in the towns they visit too.

Whoring: *dried plum.*

The play I most remember was a comedy about a master and his servant. The actors were strangers, with accents like the Instrument Maker has. In the play, the master didn't want to marry a woman he had got with child, so he made his servant change places with him. There was lots of play with juggling and tumbling, but also lots of play with words. The servant made one joke about the apples on his master's tree, which could mean either the bastard the master made or his bollocks. It made all the folk listening laugh.

The actors were all men, even the one playing the woman with child. That actor was clean-shaven and painted his face with white lead, like the Painted Pig. I remember she said the paint poisoned her skin. That's what happened to Paul. If he started playing women when he was my age, he might have passed ten years wearing white lead on his face and hands. But the Painted Pig's face wasn't nearly so spoiled as Paul's. Mayhap it's different for different folk.

The afternoon wears on. The tent walls all get staked down, and rich fabrics are hung on their insides to cover the plain canvas. Tables are set for the feast with centrepieces on them, mostly green branches tied with violets or large feathers. In the centre of the branches are little towers with the banners of Queen Bethany and the Norman prince. Other folk hang giant candle sconces that look like deer antlers from the tentpoles. It's pretty and an awful lot of work.

Musicians arrive with lutes, viols, and even a trumpet. I wonder if they're the musicians from the Domus Conversorum. I look for the Instrument Maker and his chest rumbler, but he's not with them.

Frederick and the other actors greet the musicians. Then the actors walk around the stage and call out words to indicate when the musicians are meant to make music during the play. Paul, I notice, has gone. It must be getting towards evening.

Suddenly I hear a strong voice. It's the richly dressed overseer with not just one but a whole gaggle of clerks. The overseer barks something and the clerks spread out, looking over all the tables and chairs and centrepieces, straightening this and fixing that and making sure everything is in its place. I pick up my piss pail and go before they reach me.

I nip along the edge of the main tent to the back, where there's a curtained doorway into the small tent for plating up food. It leads out-of-doors to the field kitchen and the jakes beyond.

Inside the little food tent, there's a miniature castle made entirely of spun sugar with windows and gates and everything. I can't help but take a moment to look it over. Another table is stacked with plate upon plate of stuffed fowl dressed in different fashions, one cooked swan even covered back up with its own snow-white feathers to make it look alive. There's also a thick quarter of venison dripping with honey and roasted apples. It brings the taste of deer heart to my lips.

Tonight, my heart thumps. *Tonight, I'm opening the jammed lock.*

Oddly there aren't any scullions or cooks about. The tent is empty of folk. As I wonder on it, I step out of the tent into the late-afternoon light. Direct into Black Fingers and his guards.

28. SACK POSSET

THE GUARDS HAVE rounded up all the kitchen folk. I'm at the very back of the gathering with the half-dressed turnspit boys. While Black Fingers looks on from the side, the guards are reviewing each and every folk to be sure they belong. Which I surely don't.

I turn back towards the little tent. I'll retrace my steps and slip out another way. But before I can duck inside, a guard spies me.

'No you don't, girlie,' he says. 'Back with the others you go.'

I'm stuck. Three or four guards seem to be doing all the checking. Black Fingers looks impatient, but he's still watching the goings-on. My heart leaps into my throat. Even with my collar covered by my shawl and a coif covering my hair, Black Fingers might recognize my face. I can't get caught.

I move to the side of the group farthest from Black Fingers. A lower cook ahead of me stamps with waiting. 'I've got salmon to dress.'

Another lower cook blows out his cheeks and mutters, 'They had me leave my wine sauce on the fire. Guess if it's spoiled.'

My eyes keep going back to Black Fingers to see if he's seen me. *There's three guards all checking folk at the same time*, I tell myself. *There's plenty else to take his attention.* But my arms are light and tingly. I recall Ruth the Sin Eater, her steady quiet, and try to settle my nerves.

The two lower cooks get waved up to the guards to be checked. It's mostly scullions and spitboys left now. They seem not to mind the pause. The one direct in front of me digs in his ear with a little twig.

I belong, I chant. *I belong.* But my heart patters like a rabbit's.

'Come on.' A guard waves me forward. He looks me square in the face. *I've covered my collar*, I remind myself. I still feel naked under his eyes. It amazes me that I was ever at ease with folk looking at me direct.

'What do you do here?' the guard asks looking me over.

Maker knows I can't speak, not least because he'd see the *S* tattoo across my tongue. So I bow my head as if I'm shy and raise my pail of piss. The pail's movement sends a waft of old piss stink right towards the guard.

'Maker above, that smells like a jakes,' he swears.

I nod, letting the pail rock back and forth.

'Lower the pail, girlie, and move off a bit,' he directs. 'They won't be soaking table linens until after the feast.'

I point towards the field kitchen, making sure to swing the pail widely as I do, so the smell comes stronger. It's the key to my ruse. I smell so foul, he'll want to move me along as quick as he can.

Then, from the side of my eyes, I see Black Fingers look over to see what's taking so long. 'How now?' he calls.

The guard's deciding what to say. I cannot be caught. Black Fingers will kill me. I rock to the side so my feet wobble in my raised, corked shoes. I let the wobble pass up my arm and tip the pail forward so a little wave of piss swells over the side and onto the grass just in front of the guard's boots.

'Hey now!' cries the guard, stirred to decision. 'Just a laundress,' he calls back to Black Fingers. The guard covers his nose and mouth. He waves me on. 'Go on, then. Give your piss to the scullions or what have you. They'll give you your penny.'

I take a peek towards Black Fingers. His eyes are following as I walk on to the field kitchen.

———

The smoke of the pit fires burns my eyes. The sun hasn't quite set, but it's low enough that I dare to sneak over to the little bluff I found earlier. I climb up. From its top, I can see all along the side of the tents. At one end is the main tent's entrance where all the highborn folk will go in and out. At the other end is the small tent I just left for plating up food, the field kitchen, and the jakes.

I find a nice flat stone for sitting and place my piss pail a ways off. My disguise worked. Mayhap my plan will succeed, and by evening's end, I'll have made good on my vow to Ruth. A wish comes to me, a little wish that's been creeping towards my heart for days like a vine coming in between the tiles of a roof.

If I catch the killer, mayhap the Maker will forgive me my other sins and I can go to the heavenly plains when I die, instead of suffering at Eve's side.

The sky is wide tonight, filled with pink and gold clouds standing tall and thick, like great white bears. The bears float across the sky, away from the setting sun, towards the blue night. The bears seem like good luck. Like I might get my wish.

From my spot I can also see the little costume tent just behind the actors' stage. The company has come out-of-doors. Some actors are standing in the grass making humming noises like singing, but without words. The clean-shaven, long-haired man is jabbering on to Frederick about something. Jane's reappeared and is pinning a hat in the shape of a pigeon onto one actor's head. Mayhap it's meant to be a dove.

When the sun finally disappears and darkness comes, the actors go back inside. Linkboys light their lanterns, ready to guide folk coming and going. The Queen's guests begin to arrive.

—

The lights inside the main tent throw shadows of the high-born folks within onto its walls. The shadows get larger and smaller when the wind moves the canvas. Music comes through the tent walls too. It's odd that the wind and music are both things you can't see, but one moves the cloth and the other doesn't.

The music's the same kind as I heard at the Domus Conversorum. Both sweet and sad. Even though I didn't see him, I hear the Instrument Maker's chest rumbler. He must be inside. I don't know why, but the thought gives me courage.

All at once the music changes. There are trumpets like somefolk's arriving. I look to the entrance and see a line of folk bowing. The Queen and the Norman emissary must be going in.

Not long after, the play begins. I know because the music changes again, and I hear Frederick's strong voice even all the way up on the mound where I'm sitting.

I sit and wait. I wait so long that a cricket starts singing near my left foot. Hopefully Fair Hair is drinking lots of wine so she'll have to piss all the sooner, and I can get off this stone. I shift my legs, and the cricket gets quiet.

Finally somefolk comes by. The crescent moon is bright, so I see the face of the highborn man as he walks alongside the tent. He's well into his cups. He waves to a linkboy, ready with his lantern. The boy guides him on towards the jakes in my plain view.

As the man approaches the jakes he takes the lantern from the boy and goes on alone. Then, if you'd believe it, he doesn't go inside. After all that way, he pisses right on the jakes' wall as if it's too much work to open the door. Folk are odd.

The night wears on. I can see the flickers of the pit fires

now and again all the way over at the field kitchen. There's less bustle there, which I take to mean folk are giving their attention to the play more than the food. Not many folk are going to the jakes. I worry that my plan won't work. Mayhap Fair Hair won't need to piss. Mayhap she'll find somewhere else to do it. More crickets join the first.

Just then, two wide skirts sway into view. Young ladies from the way they walk. One waves at a linkboy, and his lantern bobs as they start on their way to the jakes. I can't yet see if it's Fair Hair. They're talking, though the voices don't carry the way Frederick's does. No, only one of them's talking. As they come past I see it's the girl who wore yellow taffeta to Tilly's Eating, walking with Mush Face. They go on by. It takes a moment for me to remember to breathe again.

I am a curse, I remind myself. *I am the terror of the night.* But when I recall the poppets and the dead women, my breath gets stopped up again. My courage begins to wane. Catching a killer alone in the tight quarters of a jakes suddenly seems like a poor plan.

Before I can think on it more, two gentlemen leave the tent. They catch up with Yellow Taffeta and Mush Face. One of the gentlemen bows, and the ladies stop. He says something to make Yellow Taffeta laugh. The other gentleman turns away as if bored. He reaches into his coat and brings out a small box. Even before he opens it, I know him. The recorder. Like the day of the emissary's arrival, he pulls out a small pinch of something and sniffs it up his nose. Yellow Taffeta asks him a question, and the recorder gives her a pinch from the box. She sniffs it and coughs heavily. The other man laughs with his head tilted up, and I see his face. The recorder's brother, same as the other day. His brows are heavy, and the shadows dip in and out across his cheeks. Then I see a third dip: a thin cleft in the middle of his chin. My finger goes to my own cleft. There's a cold dripping under the skin of my neck. *Not two folk in twenty have such a thing*, Da said.

I see this man in my mind embracing my mother. It's not a memory, just a notion turning over. He could be my father. Pieces slide into place. The recorder made me, his brother's bastard, a sin eater the same way he did his barren wife. Clearing the family of its stained women. Choler burns a hot, white star in my chest, getting larger and larger. It wants to fight. It wants my arms to be strong enough to run across the field and dig my nails into the recorder's flesh. I grab at my arms and squeeze them. Why can't I be Black Fingers, who can press folk beneath stones, or the Queen, who can command armies?!

I'm so enraged I almost don't see Fair Hair come out of the tent and give a coin to a linkboy to lead her to the jakes with his lantern. The recorder and his brother must wait. I may not be strong enough to hurt them, but, Maker help me, I'll give Fair Hair what she deserves.

I slip off my stone and walk silent through the grass. Fair Hair pauses to greet the recorder and the other ladies, so I have a moment to trot ahead through the dark and get into place around the side of the jakes.

Fair Hair leaves the linkboy by the back of the tent, takes his lantern, and walks the last twenty paces to the jakes alone, most like because ladies don't like boys listening to them piss. He's just as happy. The moment she leaves him, he's peering in the tent to see the play.

When I hear Fair Hair open the door to the jakes, I dart around and catch the door before it shuts. In I go, dropping the bar in the lock behind me.

Fair Hair startles, then raises the lantern to see better. 'I need no aid, miss, and haven't a coin for you anyhow. Take your leave.' She waves me away and waits.

I stand my ground and unwrap my shawl to reveal my collar. And this is where my plan begins. It's not a fancy plan, like my uncles' complicated games of confidence. It's not an educated plan like the Willow Tree's midnight ritual. It's a simple plan for a cursed girl, and I pray it will work.

I take the chalk from my sleeve and begin to draw along the wood walls of the jakes. What I draw is the letters from the tapestry right out of my memory. Before I even finish them, Fair Hair's eyes widen, and a cry leaves her mouth. Then I draw more. I draw the mark for sanctuary from my door and the mark from my fountain. I draw all the Anglish letters I know, like M and A. I draw them all over the raw, wooden walls. Even I think, taken together, they look like witch's marks. And it seems Fair Hair does too.

She shrieks the Maker's Prayer for protection against evil. I say my own prayer that the music of the play is loud enough to cover her noise. Then I reach into my sleeve and remove the poppet I fashioned this morning. The white of the tallow almost glows in the jakes' gloom. The poppet's female shape is plain, as is the hay on its head, yellow to match Fair Hair's blonde curls. I lift the tail of the brass *S* hanging from my collar, as good as any pin, and hold it above the poppet's heart, as if I would slide it into the soft fat.

Fair Hair looks like she might puke. 'Please don't harm me! I never meant for them to die. Please.'

She is either more artful than I thought or terribly simple. She never meant for them to die? How could poison not kill? I raise the pin again.

'Please! Please, don't! I had no recourse but this. The Queen will kill me if she discovers I'm with child!'

That I believe.

She goes on. 'She's done so before. She had my love's wife pushed down a stair.' Her voice drops to barely more than breath. 'I had to try to kill the Queen. I never dreamed the poppets would kill the others in her place, I swear to you. Corliss was a good woman. And the midwife. I did not know my witchcraft was so powerful.' Why isn't she speaking of the poison or the deer hearts?

Fair Hair drops her head. 'He said you knew. He said the sin eater told him there had been a killing. He had just discovered that I was the one making the poppets. He tried to cut your throat to keep you from telling anyfolk.' She begins to wail. 'I am sorry, so very, very sorry.' She looks at the poppet in my hand. 'Please don't kill me and my child.'

She's been truthful, I can tell. She confessed her crime. But it's not the right one. She planted the poppets, but not the deer hearts. She knows nothing about the poisonings. So who is the killer? My plan worked, and yet not at all.

She shrieks once more when I cut a lock from her hair. I still want my token.

There are voices outside the jakes. Men's voices, in alarum. I open the door. The linkboy and three guards are coming across the grass from the tent. The linkboy points at me, and a guard raises his lantern. When the light hits the guard in front, I see it's not a guard at all. It's Black Fingers.

I race out and around the jakes. Up against its wooden back, I go over my choices. The field is wide and open, a poor place to hide. To one side is the field kitchen and the small tent for plating up food. To the other is the actors' costume tent. I peek around the corner. They've nearly reached me. I squeeze my hands together for luck and dash out across the grass towards the costume tent.

Black Fingers's voice booms across the night. 'Turn her going!' I can hear the thumping of the guards' boots on the earth behind me. My own corked shoes wobble beneath my feet. I daren't stop. If they catch me, I will not escape this time. I think of a sword slicing down between my head and my shoulder and run harder. With a sudden jolt, my ankle rolls out to the side. I keen in pain but keep going, hobble-running towards the tent. I hear heavy, male breath steps away. Just a few more paces. With a last burst, I push into the tent, just before the guards reach me.

29. MUSTARD SEED

IT'S DARK INSIDE, but I make out the shadows of the trunks and costume racks. I also take in two folk, one helping the other to dress or undress – I don't know which – by a lantern on the floor, papered over to keep the light low. The only other exit is the flap leading into the main tent. I step behind one of the racks hung with coats and robes, disappearing into the velvets and brocades just as a rush of air behind me signals the guard's arrival. With care, I sink to the ground. I can see the actors' feet on one side of the tent and the guard's feet – no, two sets of guards' feet – near the entrance. Then another set comes in. Black Fingers.

'Where's the girl?' he bellows.

'There's a play on now!' one of the actors whispers. 'Just

on the other side of that canvas.' A flute song and sweet singing come from inside the main tent, as if in proof.

'This is the Queen's business,' answers Black Fingers, only a bit quieter. 'A girl came in here. And you will help me find her.'

His voice is enough threat that the actor answers quick and tight, 'The only place is with the costumes.'

'Then search in the costumes,' says Black Fingers impatiently. Through the clothes I see a guard spear a pile of clothes in a trunk.

'Don't stand there like asses!' Black Fingers calls. The actors' feet begin to move too. One of them comes to the far end of the rack I'm behind.

'It took the elder sin eater two hours to die under the press,' comes Black Fingers's voice. Maker mine, he knows it's me. Fair Hair must have told him. 'First her blood was pushed into her head and limbs. Her fingers and toes turned purple and swelled like potatoes.' The air gets thick in my chest. I try the tent wall behind to see if I might slip under it, but it's staked down tight. 'Then the veins of her eyes popped and wept blood. That was in the first minutes.' I feel the clothes swaying as the actor makes his way along the rack, looking between garments. I slide until I'm at the rack's end, hiding behind the very last robe. Beyond is just open ground between me and the guard stabbing at clothes in trunks. 'Mmm.' Black Fingers goes on. 'Her rib bones broke through her flesh, and all her juices dribbled out, like a goose on the spit.' The actor's fingers appear above me. I close my eyes tight as a sob rises in my throat. But no, I'll face my end like my mother would. I open my eyes and from deep in my throat summon a mouthful of spittle. Before he rats me out, I'll spit in his face. The actor pulls the robes apart.

It's Paul.

The moment lasts a lifetime. Me taking him in. Him seeing it's me. A faint sound as he catches his breath. Paul, who if not for Brida, would have left me to die in the apothecary lane. Who nearly stoned me. Who called me pollution and filth. Who has armed guards and the Queen's secretary at his back ordering him to find me. I already know he'll give me up. I should hawk my spittle smack in his eye now before he does it.

But I don't. Suddenly I don't want to face my end like my mother, tussling like a fox. I want to face it the way I imagine Ruth did, strong. I swallow the spit. I look him dead in the eye, not hard, not shaky, just steady.

Paul looks at me back. Not hard, not shaky. Soberly.

'There's no folk here,' Paul calls to Black Fingers, letting the robe fall back around me.

I choke back a giggle, nearly giving myself away.

'She came in here!' Black Fingers hisses. I hear the slap of a hand hitting Paul's face, and the thud as he lands hard on the ground.

'You, man,' Black Fingers says to a guard. 'Search the rack again.' A pair of boots leaves the trunks and walks direct to where I'm hidden. A sword blade slices into the robe next to mine. In a moment I'll be spitted like a rabbit.

'Sir!' Paul calls out sharply. I see his feet go to the outer door of the tent.

'What now?' says Black Fingers, turning towards him.

'Look. Look just here,' he pulls at the bottom of the tent cloth. 'Perhaps there was a loose stake.' The guards kneel down to check. In a moment they'll know there's no loose stake.

Then I catch Paul's game. He's pulled their attention away from my side of the tent. Black Fingers and the guards are all facing away. He's giving me a chance to escape through the flap leading to the stage. Where hundreds of folk, including the Queen, are hearing a play at this very moment. But what choice do I have?

With Black Fingers and the guards still turned towards Paul, I hobble on my hurt ankle over to the stage entrance. I look back once. Black Fingers is watching as his guards pull at the tent canvas. Paul's face is turned towards them, but like a cat, his eyes move to mine. They're as sullen as they've ever been, but they look direct at me. Quick as lightning, I nod in thanks, then slip through the canvas.

30. BEEFSTEAK

I EXPECT A HUNDRED eyes on me. I expect all the mighty folk of the country to shout, 'Look there!' I expect I'll have to run. But when I come through the tent flap it's not like that at all.

On top of the stage stands one of the flat wooden panels, rising up before me, taller than the tallest man. I can't see any folk at all. But they're close. I hear Frederick speaking on the other side of the panel. I'm just behind the stage.

My ankle throbs. Its flesh is swelling. Suddenly a trumpet sounds, and I hear a soft whir. I look up to see the other wooden panel lowering rapidly. It slides into its groove. There's another whir, and the first panel begins to rise. One of the actors stands to the side of the stage working the ropes.

All at once, the long-haired actor comes round the side of the panel back behind the stage where I am. He's dressed like a lady. He whips off his coif and outer skirt to reveal what looks like women's nightclothes beneath. He's working so quick, at first he doesn't see me. But then, suddenly, he cries out in alarum. I hear Frederick on the stage side of the panel say, 'My love?'

Another trumpet sounds. Long Hair waves his hands wildly for me to go. Frederick calls again from the stage, 'My love, why do you tarry?' Before I can breathe, Long Hair darts round the panel again, back to the play.

I need to get away. At the far side of the stage is the actor pulling the panel ropes. Beyond him are the musicians. And beyond them, thank the Maker, I spy a groom walking with an empty dish. The small tent for plating up food is not far, and from there I can escape into the field.

I creep to the edge of the scenery panel. But then I stop. There's still five paces between me and the actor pulling the panel ropes. Five paces of open stage where I'll be seen by everyfolk in the audience.

There's nothing for it. I snatch up the clothes Long Hair left on the ground and put them on. They're too large, which is a fine thing, because my face gets shadowed by the large coif. As I'm dressing, I spy a club like constables carry at night tucked behind the scenery to be used in the play. My ankle can hardly bear my weight, so I take it as a cane. I can hear Frederick and Long Hair exchanging oaths of love before the audience. With luck, folk will be so gripped by their playacting that they won't pay me any mind as I cross behind them on the stage. I say a silent prayer and limp into the light.

Just as I step out from behind the panel, Long Hair dashes round it for another quick exit. We smack direct into each other, falling in a heap. If I hoped to avoid notice, I failed utterly. All eyes in the entire tent whip to me. I've been starved of folk's gaze for months, and now there are more faces turned on me than I've seen in all my life. I cannot breathe. I cannot move. I'm startled still.

'My love . . . what's this?!' comes Frederick's voice.

Long Hair's pulling himself up. There's a trickle of blood coming from his nose where my head must have struck him.

'Oh, my love, you have been injured by this . . . unexpected arrival.' Frederick's talking loud, like he's still playacting for the audience.

Long Hair presses his hand to his nose. 'Who is this creature who has happened upon our lovers' tryst?' he says back, also for the crowd.

Frederick peers at me from above. 'It appears to be – oh, Maker mine,' he utters this last bit under his breath. He recognizes me.

'Is she insensible?' asks Long Hair urgently.

'Merely stunned, I believe,' answers Frederick. He leans down and wraps my shawl around my neck. He's hiding my collar.

'Who is it, and why has she come upon us so unexpectedly?!' presses Long Hair.

'Can you not see, my love?' Frederick answers. 'It is my grandmama.' Frederick nudges me with his foot. I want to move, but hundreds of eyes seem to pin me to the floor.

'Your grandmama!' says Long Hair. 'Here in our most secret grove. What strange fortune follows you.'

'Help me, my love,' Frederick directs. He and Long Hair each take one of my arms. Together they lift me to standing. My turned ankle falters beneath me.

'Why, your grandmama is lame,' speaks Long Hair, helping me catch my balance. I look for the constable club.

'Yes, and mute,' adds Frederick.

Long Hair spies the club on the ground. 'Lame, mute, and carrying a truncheon. A rare woman, indeed.'

'My grandmama descends from the great Boudica, warrior queen of the Celts. She is my most fervent protector,' Frederick invents. 'She came, no doubt, to warn us of the villainous rogues that populate these woods. Dear grandmama, we thank you for your vigilance.'

My breath has returned. I venture a step.

'Ah, she is going!' says Long Hair. I hobble towards the side of the stage. 'No, no, the wood is behind us, dear lady,' Long Hair urges.

'She ever went her own way,' calls Frederick. 'I doubt we shall see her again. Ever.'

He says this a little hard.

I step off the stage, past the startled rope man and a batch of staring scullions. The musicians come next, seated on stools. I go by a flute player and a man playing a long lute. In among the musicians I spy the Instrument Maker bowing the chest rumbler. He glances my way. When he sees it's me, he starts as if he's been bitten.

The entrance to the food tent is just ahead. It opens to

the field. Hoping that folk's eyes have returned to Frederick and Long Hair, I limp into the food tent.

I'm nearly free. After I cross the field I won't even stop at my house. I'll go over the river, take to the road, and go, go, go.

The tables inside the food tent are now stacked with dirty dishes, scullions moving them to baskets and hauling them out to be washed. Only one small table still holds food. There's several marchpanes, bowls of comfits, and other sweeties. A head cook's ordering about two lower cooks who are moving the sweets around on the plates. There's a woman working at the table, too, wearing a coif like mine so I can't see her face.

All at once the head cook's ordering stops. 'What're you doing here?' he says loud. I ready myself to hobble-run, but he's not talking to me. He's talking to the other coiffed woman.

'The Queen requested this,' the woman answers, holding a polished dish of whipped syllabub in her gloved hands.

'All the Queen's requests come through the kitchen clerk, milady,' says the cook. 'For the Queen's safety.' He gives her a good look over. 'What's your name, milady?'

The woman turns so her coif blocks her face. 'You would make the Queen wait upon you? She'll have your head.' Her words are strong, but they smell like rot.

The cook hesitates, and the woman goes hastily towards the main tent – and the Queen – the syllabub dish still in her hands. With one painful step, I reach out as she passes and knock the dish from her hands onto the floor.

She drops to her knees as if she can salvage the custard. I still haven't seen her face, but the cook must have done because he says, 'You're Lady Katryna's daughter, Maker keep her soul, aren't you? Lady Miranda!'

The woman's coif whips up at her name. She leaves the syllabub and makes for the door to the field. A moment later she's gone.

The daughter of Lady Katryna and Baron Seymaur. The Painted Pig spoke of her. Katryna died in childbirth and Seymaur was executed as a traitor. Their daughter would have had her title and inheritance seized by the throne. It comes to me that this Lady Miranda has a very good reason to hate the Queen.

The head cook squats over the syllabub and spoons a bit into his mouth. He spits it out.

'What is it?' asks one of the lower cooks.

'Tastes off. Could be poison,' he answers with hard in his voice. 'Get the Queen's secretary.' Black Fingers.

That's when I follow Lady Miranda out of the tent at a run.

31. GRISTLE

MIRANDA'S BODY IS dark against the low light of the field kitchen pit fires. She's running, but not very well. It's dark, and the field's uneven. And she's no doubt accustomed to flagged stone beneath her slippered feet.

I veer away from her. I'm not running well either. My ankle keeps me stumbling. But the jakes aren't far. They'll give me some cover, and from there I'll make my way across the field and towards town. All I know is, I want to stay away from Miranda. With luck, Black Fingers'll go towards her first.

It's as I'm rounding the corner of the jakes that I hear his voice. 'Milady? How now? What's happened?' I look back to the field kitchen. His arm is still wrapped in a cloth. The Country Mouse.

I should keep going. I should break for the edge of the field before Black Fingers and his guards swarm out of the tent. But he's alone with a killer. My breath comes fast and hard. Grass tickles against my swelling ankle.

'What – why are you here?' Miranda says.

'The tent was too warm, I came out to take some air. It's Lady Miranda, isn't it? Are you unwell? You were running.'

'I am unwell, yes. And turned around. Tell me, which way is the road?'

'The road? I'll call somefolk to help you. There must be a linkboy about.' The Country Mouse turns towards the main tent. 'Hello?' he cries. 'Hello?!'

Quick as a fox, Miranda pulls a long, iron flesh-hook from its place near a pit fire with a gloved hand. 'Keep quiet!' Miranda says, jabbing the hook at the Country Mouse. 'Do as I say, and take me to the road or I'll gut you.' Her body's bent like she's been cornered by dogs. Before I know it I'm running towards them.

She sees me out of the side of her eye and steps back without thinking. Good, she's off her balance. But she's still got the hook. Its tapered prongs glisten with meat fat as she turns on me. It's the first time I see her fully. A forgettable face in a simple wool dress and wide sleeves. A small gold brooch her only adornment for the revels. Lady Miranda is Mush Face. The girl who went hungry in Bethany's castle even though her mother had been a queen.

With my lame ankle, I haven't got much hope in a fight, so I use what I've got. I hold the S on my collar up to catch the firelight.

But Mush Face doesn't falter like Fair Hair did. Her breathing doesn't even change. This should be a warning to me. She's desperate or mad. Indeed, before I can think what to do, she jumps forward and slashes at me with the hook. My ankle rolls as I jerk out of the way. I fall hard on the ground, nearly landing in a pit fire. Wavering heat flushes my face. I roll away from the fire only to find myself looking direct at the prongs of Mush Face's flesh-hook.

There's a thud as the Country Mouse charges into her, knocking the hook away. She scuttles after and rises up with it clutched in her two hands like a broadsword. 'I'll kill you both.'

The Country Mouse is on the ground, holding his burnt arm and breathing fast. Knocking Mush Face was too much. She rushes him, raising the hook like she's going to strike.

I scream the only words left to me, 'Tell me your sins!'

My voice startles her to stillness, the flesh-hook still raised to strike. 'Are you the Maker's revenge?' she breathes.

'Your sins,' I say again. I don't have any other plan.

Mush Face keeps the hook aimed at the Country Mouse. 'If you have followed me, then you know my sins.'

'Recite them,' I call.

Her face suddenly loses its dullness. 'I killed them.' She speaks hard and direct, as if she's got no shame to say the words aloud. 'My father fornicated with the Queen when she was fourteen. Did you know that?' She searches me for surprise and finds none. She says harder, 'Corliss and the other tutors taught me to read Latin, Greek, Hebrew. It was the one benefaction I received. And what did it buy me? I discovered a tapestry with the Queen's shame woven into it. The Queen got with child by her own stepfather, my dear papa.' The hook's still aimed at the Country Mouse. 'That gabby-goose Tilly Howe confirmed it once I gave her enough wine. Tilly delivered the child. The Queen made Corliss and the rest swear to kill it. And now I'm killing them. For my half sibling who was murdered. For my mother, who was betrayed by her husband and stepdaughter. For the fortune that was stolen from me.' She looks at my collar. 'You know the truth. You heard their Recitations. There were hearts on Corliss's and Tilly's coffins.'

I do know the truth. No hearts were recited. But Mush Face thinks there were. She doesn't know the bastard wasn't killed. Tilly Howe kept that from her.

'Those are my sins,' she says with a sort of pride. 'I killed two. The fire was a mishap.' She nods at the Country Mouse. 'It's more difficult to control than poison, but the old lady wouldn't take my wine. She'll die soon anyhow. Her burns have turned black, and she's fevered with the corruption. She'll not last two days. And, now that the Queen is as alone as I am, I will kill her too.' A blackness comes into her eyes, and her fingers tighten on the hook. She's going to try to kill us.

She pulls back to strike, so I go straight for her, grabbing at the hook's shaft. We wrestle it between us. Years of scrubbing and rinsing bedclothes builds you up different than years of books and embroidery; still, she holds fast, pulling me around in a circle. I feel sudden heat against my legs. She's turned me up against a pit fire. Clever as a fox, she is. I push back against her hard, but my ankle gives and slips down into the pit, my heel burning in the embers. One more push from her, and I'll fall fully into the fire.

I grab behind me. Metal burns into the palm of my hand as I catch the handle of a cauldron hanging from the spit. I shriek like a crow and swing it as hard as I can into her face. It catches her jawbone, throwing her head back with a crack. She lands on the trampled grass, moaning like an animal.

I fall to the grass too, breathing hard. But something sharp sticks me in the chest. It's a golden brooch, the one Mush Face was wearing. It must have fallen in the fight. I pull it out of my skin. A pair of golden wings. It's Baron Seymaur's badge. It must be her only token of her family. I recall I saw the wings that awful night in the castle's banner room beside Katryna's badge of a girl coming out of a rose.

No, the golden wings weren't in the banner room. But I feel as if I saw the two badges together. A girl coming from a flower and golden wings. Where was it?

Then it comes to me. I saw them in Corliss's tapestry. In the tree, there was a girl coming out of a flower with golden wings. The two badges, joined into one.

The whole picture comes into my mind, the Queen touching her belly with one hand and touching the tree with the other. The joined badges are the fruit of the tree. The fruit of the Queen's tree.

All at once wards slide into place, and the lock opens.

I stagger to standing. Across the grass, Mush Face has raised herself up to hands and knees. 'I haven't told you the list of foods,' I call to her.

Mush Face raises her head. Her jaw hangs at a sickening angle.

'When you die a traitor's death,' I say, 'I'll eat pig hearts for each of the women you murdered.' Mush Face pushes herself to kneeling. 'There's no punishment for being born a bastard,' I tell her. Her head swings towards me, her eyes confused. 'But if you succeed in killing the Queen,' I go on, 'I'll eat swan heart on your coffin. For killing your own mother.'

She looks at me, not believing. But I'm right. *The belly knows*. Mush Face read the stranger word, *Chavah*, on the tapestry and believed it was the only message, as folk who know their letters would. But common folk see meaning in pictures, like beggar's marks.

The tapestry says that Queen Bethany's bastard is the child of Baron Seymaur and Katryna. At least, the child *thought* to be Baron Seymaur and Katryna's. Mush Face is the Queen's bastard.

'That's a lie,' Mush Face cries through her broken jaw.

The Eucharistian countess in the dungeon served Katryna as a lady-in-waiting. She spoke about a cuckoo bird, and I thought at the time she was talking nonsense, but she wasn't. She must have known, or at least suspected, the truth.

Bethany wanted to kill her bastard. She asked Corliss, Tilly, and the Painted Pig to do it. They swore they would. But then they deceived her. They helped Bethany, but not in the way she asked.

When Katryna's labouring went poorly, it wasn't just Katryna who passed. The babe died too. Fragile things, babes.

Corliss and the others replaced it with Bethany's bastard. They made a bastard into a changeling.

'There were hearts on the coffins!' Mush Face screeches with gritted teeth.

'They were placed there wrongfully,' I finally say aloud. 'I don't know who put them there, but they never were recited.'

I let that sit for a breath. Then I say one last thing. 'You killed the only folk who wanted you alive.' Corliss, Tilly, the Painted Pig. 'All the rest, if they find out who you are, will want you dead.'

She's a clever woman, Mush Face, and I see the wards in her own heart clicking into place. Her eyes spark bright and then get dull. She knows it's true.

From the direction of the main tent come men's cries. Black Fingers and the guards. Mush Face scrambles to her feet and stumbles away into the field. I need to run too.

I look for the Country Mouse. He's pulling himself up. The guards will be here shortly. He'll be safe with them. Blood's seeping into his linen bandages. No, not linens. His shoulder's wrapped in a shawl. The one I left behind.

For just a moment he looks over at me. Then he turns and calls out to the guards coming from the main tent. 'She ran off that way,' and he points them away from us, in pursuit of Mush Face.

Whispering a thank-you with my heart, I stagger off into the dark field.

32. FRUMENTY

I LIE AGAIN ON the grave of my da. It seems the safest place to wait out Black Fingers and his guards. And I know I won't be back again for a good long time. Black Fingers. The Willow Tree. Mush Face. I need a fresh place where no folk want me dead.

Looking up at the gravestone from where I lie, the *O*, *N*, and *S* in OWENS look the same even though they are upside down. It seems a kind of magic that they can do this. The *W*, on the other hand, turns into an *M* for May. And the *E* becomes something I don't recognize. Kind of like where I am now. Some of the things about me are the same. Some are new. And some have lost all sense.

I say three prayers on the grave. Two to the Maker, first

in thanks for guiding me safely out of the field, even though my ankle's a swollen wreck and my hand badly burnt. And, second, a prayer for safe passage out of town. The third prayer is to my mother for teaching me all the things I thought I didn't want to know. I see now I needed my Daffrey blood to come this far. To make good on my promise to Ruth. And I'll need my Daffrey blood again in the coming months. I finish the prayers as always, *May it be. May it be. May it be.*

—

In the darkest part of the night, I return to Dungsbrook. Brida is sitting on my-now-her rug. Jane and her children are asleep on the other side of the hearth. I take off the skirt I took from the actor behind the stage and place it next to Brida. A gift. I wish I had something for Paul.

Brida sees my burnt hand and takes a noisy breath through her nose hole. She points to the drippings jar by the cook pot. Grease. I put a good dollop on my hand and slip the jar into my apron pocket for later.

Up in the loft I return the coif I took. Then I open Ruth's box one more time. I touch her ring and the charms made for her babes who didn't live. I know now why the women were poisoned. Whether Mush Face will be caught and who placed deer hearts on the coffins are still mysteries. But I did my best by Ruth. I know it.

All at once the door below opens. My whole body tightens, sure it's Black Fingers and his guards. But there's no voice, just soft footsteps. Must be Paul or Frederick returning from the revels. I stay still and quiet for a good long while after the footsteps cease, just to be sure. Then I collect my own box. I drop Fair Hair's lock of hair inside. Like the things in the other sin eater boxes, no folk will know the whole story of it. But it's something. A marker that I've lived and I've mattered.

There's a soft mewling as I climb down the ladder. Jane's baby in its sleep, I think. But it's not. It's a kitten. Right in the middle of the floor. Whoever opened the door must have left it. What an odd thing. The kitten has a strip of cloth tied around its neck. The cloth matches my lost shawl.

I run to the door and look out, but the road's empty. Back inside I stare at the kitten. I scoop it up and drop it in my apron pocket with the drippings jar.

I stroke the cat's fur as I slip out of the back of the house. I want to go to the Domus Conversorum to thank the Instrument Maker for his help. But I don't want to be seen. And I have an odd feeling, like I'll be seeing him again.

Instead, I go through the woad dyer's yard, since its stench makes it the last place any pursuers would want to go. I find a stout stick to help me walk on my sore ankle, and up I go along the river's marshy edge, past where the pig men dump offal and where the rakers burn rubbish, on and on until there's no more sign of folk except stone fences and pastures. I walk until my ankle can't keep on.

The kitten and I make our bed for the night in a sheepfold. It's musty and sour-smelling but warm enough. Mouse, as I've named the kitten, and I lick grease from the jar for our supper.

I'm not certain where we'll go. But anywhere there are folk, they'll need a sin eater.

AFTER

WHIPPED SYLLABUB

I COULD'VE THROWN AWAY the collar. I could've boarded a barge and made my way to a strange land. I had the choice. Instead, I chose to keep walking. I walked along wooded paths. Across fields. Through country villages. Whenever folk saw me, whenever their eyes widened at a lone beggar girl trespassing on their land, whenever their lips opened to call for a constable, I lifted my hand to the collar, and they buggered off. The collar proved right useful. I wore it every day of my walking. At night it sat in my box. I was wearing it when I found a place that felt right.

The town I've chosen is smaller than where I grew up. But there's a school for Makermen that keeps it full of folk. There was a sin eater living here when I arrived, but she didn't seem at all surprised when I opened the door to the house with the *S* hung over the door holding a skinny kitten.

She's an old body, and nothing seems to surprise her much. I go with her to Recitations and Eatings, and sometimes when she's doing poorly I go alone.

One day when autumn has begun to drive light from the mornings and evenings, I'm called to the Recitation of an old body. It's a day when the old sin eater's doing poorly. I put on my collar and go alone.

The man was a doctor, he recites. He worked for a high-born family most of his life but left their employ when the daughter of the family, by then a married woman, died in childbirth and her babe not long after. He couldn't bear to stay. But before he left, he did something. 'I partook in a grave misdeed.' He doesn't name names, but I start to put things together, because the old body doing the reciting is called Old Doctor Howe. He's Tilly's father. The lady he served was Katryna. And her stepdaughter was Bethany.

Another old body sits with Old Doctor Howe. A man with a stoop and a merry look in bulgy eyes. When Old Doctor Howe begins to weep with his rememberings, the bulgy-eyed man takes Doctor Howe's hand and holds it to his cheek, like a mother or a goodwife.

Doctor Howe tells me the rest, confirming what I guessed in the field that night, without even a prompt. 'The step-daughter was with child as well, and far along.' He slows his words. 'She made her ladies swear that when the babe was born to smother it in its swaddle.'

Old Doctor Howe gathers himself. 'We decided . . . We

agreed,' he amends, 'that we would keep her from ruin. We would bury the past, but we could not murder the baby girl. We placed her where she would be safe and never spoke of it again.'

It's the bulgy-eyed man I give the list of foods to. He has a musty-mouth smell that reminds me of the Willow Tree, but his eyes are filled with grief as he marks the foods down on a slate.

Two days later, the old sin eater and I are at Old Doctor Howe's Eating in his large home. Lots of folk come and sit. The main chamber has a big tapestry across from where they've set the coffin. It's of the heavenly plains and shows Adam, the keeper of the fields and orchards. It reminds me of Corliss's tapestry, and I recall that I never sorted out who placed the deer hearts on the women's coffins.

As I'm chewing mustard seeds, I give it a good think. Queen Bethany thought her babe was killed. She would have expected to see deer hearts on Corliss's and Tilly's coffins. Mayhap somefolk placed the hearts to continue the fiction. Mayhap they thought she would have the bastard killed if she learned of it. Or mayhap they thought she would claim it. My granddam said once a babe's out and living, a mother can't deny it. A queen with a bastard would lose her throne, and her closest advisers would lose everything with her.

I see the bulgy-eyed man in a chair at the back of the chamber. I wonder that he doesn't take a seat closer to the coffin. He must be close kin to have taken the list of foods for Doctor Howe.

Something niggles. Another old body who took a list of

foods. The Willow Tree. He collected the foods from Corliss's Recitation and the Painted Pig's. He could have added deer heart to the lists, mayhap Tilly Howe's too, then delivered the parchments to the clerk in the royal kitchen with none the wiser. Except me. Tilly said in her Recitation that he had been a tutor in Katryna's household. Mayhap he knew of Queen Bethany's pregnancy and her ladies' deception in keeping the baby alive. Or mayhap he read the secret years later in the tapestry. What I do know is that he staked his life's work on Bethany's reputation as a virgin and her continuation as queen. He must have placed hearts on the coffins to keep her from knowing the babe was alive.

The revelation sends mustard seeds shooting out my nose. The folk at the Eating mutter and sputter, but the old sin eater keeps on chewing her leek, even when I start to laugh. Nothing surprises her.

———

In the evening, the other sin eater and I sit on our stools by the hearth together, me hoping the closeness of our space will someday become a closeness of spirit. It almost works. If it doesn't yet match the sorts of company I've had before, at least I'm not alone. And, with luck, we'll have more company soon. I've drawn the sign for sanctuary on our door, the one I once scrubbed off a different door. I'm hoping folk who need safe haven will find it. And that word will spread. Mayhap even all the way to Brida and Paul.

At night as I crawl into bed, I decide I'll name the old sin eater Bessie because it feels nice. Someday, mayhap, I'll learn her real name. I curl up under an old rug that Bessie the sin eater found for me. Mouse, my cat, curls up too. My collar's sitting in my box by the bed. As I fall asleep, I am May again. Just May.

ACKNOWLEDGEMENTS

I'd like to thank my agent Stephanie Cabot, as well as Ellen Goodson Coughtrey, Rebecca Gardner, Will Roberts, and everyone at the Gernert Company. Thanks to my editor, Trish Todd, along with Kaitlin Olson and the team at Atria Books. And to Araminta Whitley of the Soho Agency and Sam Humphreys of Mantle. I am grateful to my early readers Carol Doup Muller, Jay Dunn, Nikki Reisch, Silvère Boitel, and the inimitable Boomie Aglietti. To my writing group, Soren Kisiel, Jenny Hagel, Dava Krause, Julia Price Baron, and Michelle Walson: thanks for the beer and noticings.

In writing this novel I drew inspiration from a number of books, in particular *Elizabeth's Women: The Hidden Story of the Virgin Queen* by Tracy Borman, *The Queen's Conjuror* by Benjamin Woolley, and *Rogues, Vagabonds and Sturdy Beggars* edited by Arthur F. Kinney.

This book was mostly written during my first child's second year and my second child's birth and first year. There would be no book without childcare. Thank you to everyone at the BBCDC, especially Kimberly Dalton. And to Natalie Mayne and Leah Gonsalves for bouncing on the ball. For hours. And there would be no childcare without my day jobs, so thank you to the fine people at the Neighborhood Playhouse and American Academy of Dramatic Arts, and to my (at this point) hundreds of former students for making those jobs pretty damn pleasant.

Thank you to the Salyers Hurand family for their unflagging support. My profound gratitude goes to my parents for valuing my voice and to my sisters for sharing theirs. Last and most to A, K, and G for being my folk.